PRAISE FOR TAMARA GRANTHAM

"Part *Twilight*, part *Beauty and the Beast*, readers will eat up the lush settings, mystery, and romance of *Never Call Me Vampire*. Tamara Grantham has created a high-stakes story rich with history, myth, and legend."

— ANGELA LARKIN, CO-AUTHOR OF THE BEYOND SERIES

"A masterpiece."

— LUCIA W, *TEEN READS* (FOR *THE WITCH'S TOWER*)

"A sparkling fantasy."

— *KIRKUS REVIEWS* (FOR *THE WITCH'S TOWER*)

"Grantham is prepared to make her mark in the urban fantasy scene with this one."

— *READERS' FAVORITE REVIEWS* (FOR *DREAMTHIEF*)

"Springs to life from the very first sentence."

— *IND'TALE MAGAZINE* (FOR *SILVERWITCH*)

NEVER CALL ME VAMPIRE

NEVER CALL ME VAMPIRE

TAMARA GRANTHAM

Copyright © 2020 by Tamara Grantham

For Phoenix. My firstborn.

"I want you to believe…to believe in things you cannot."
-Bram Stoker, *Dracula*

1

AMAYA

My pounding heart betrayed my anxiety. I kept my sweaty palms tucked inside my hoodie's pockets as I crossed through the domed room. The guards' eyes followed me, then went to my albino Husky, his nails tapping quietly over the marble. They didn't stop me as I exited through the former sanitarium's giant double doors.

The doors boomed shut behind, and I gave Khan a pat on his furry head.

"We made it this far," I whispered.

He peered at me with his yellow eyes, looking more wolf than domesticated house pet.

The stone archway overshadowed us. An angel with curving wings had been sculpted into granite. Its eyes, though carved of stone, were piercing and accusatory, as if it knew the secret I carried.

I rubbed the sore spot on my shoulder.

Our echoing steps made hollow thuds in the dome of the courtyard. I crossed to the grassy field behind the looming structure of Crimson Hollow. The shadow of its castle-like turrets reached out as if to catch us.

Soupy gray clouds shrouded the countryside. Below, the forest of reds and golds spread to the horizon, but I took a different path, leading to the cemetery. The air smelled of rain, and the wind picked up, battering long strands of dark hair across my face. My shorts and flipflops would've been fine if I'd been home in Miami, but not in upstate New York, where autumn came with a chill I couldn't shake.

As I approached the graveyard, a guard stood by the gate, casually hefting a rifle. The man's cropped hair and straight posture hinted at a military background, though he'd gone soft, and his navy-blue uniform stretched over his sagging middle.

He grunted as I approached. "Where are you going?" he asked, his voice hinting at a Southern accent.

I nodded toward the clearing filled with headstones. "Just inside the cemetery. I won't leave the grounds."

His eyes narrowed. "Going into the cemetery *is* leaving the grounds. Go back inside." He nodded toward the castle.

I squared my shoulders. "No."

"What?" he asked, giving me a second glance, as if he didn't expect a scrawny twenty-year-old girl to argue with him. "I said go back inside."

"My dad's buried there." I pointed.

"Sure, he is." He shifted his gun. "Everyone tries that. And your aunt's buried there, too. Also, your grandpa and your dead gerbil. Go inside. I won't ask you again—"

"The small headstone on the east plot," I blurted. "Second row from the back. Luis Joseph de la Vega. The inscription says, 'Just whisper my name in your heart and I will be there.' You can check it if you like."

He glanced over his shoulder, then turned back to me. "Amaya de la Vega, isn't it? Just arrived yesterday?"

I nodded.

"Your dad's really buried in there?"

"Yes. He died of the vampire virus on my fifteenth birthday. My mom died also. Two months ago. Same disease, but she's buried in Miami."

His eyes softened a bit. "And now you're...." He shook his head. "Well, you're here. Fine. Go inside. But..." He shook his finger in my face. "You've got five minutes, then you go straight back inside the facility. You're new, so maybe you haven't been to orientation yet, but patients are only allowed off the grounds at certain times and with heavy precautions. Including never entering the graveyard. Got it?"

"Yeah. I got it." I stepped past him, then paused, glancing at his nametag. "Um...Officer Goodman?"

He raised an eyebrow. "Yes?"

"Thanks," I said quietly. "This means a lot to me."

He nodded, and I breathed a sigh of relief as I walked through the gate. Loops of razor wire topped the fence surrounding the cemetery. I took the path leading through the gravestones.

The air turned colder. Despite my hoodie, goosebumps formed on my skin, and I rubbed my arms. Khan trailed silent as a ghost behind me.

My stomach twisted with anxiety as I approached the gravestone. It had weathered a bit. The granite was darker around the edges, and the chiseled words had faded.

Steeling my nerves, I knelt by Daddy's grave. Cold grass squished under my knees.

"I came for you..." I stopped, my voice unsteady. A chilly breeze gusted, blowing my tangled hair across my face. This wasn't going as easily as I'd hoped.

Taking a deep breath, I started again.

"I came here because—I don't know. I needed to talk to you." Talk to the dead. Right. "Please don't be mad at me. I did what I had to do. There wasn't any other way inside the facility." I rubbed the bruise on my shoulder where the needle had pricked me. "I'm going to find a cure for this, Daddy. Just like Mom. She was so close. But she never got access inside. But I have."

I ran my fingers over the granite, shocked at how cold the stone felt. Cold and dead, just like the eyes of the angel.

Khan edged closer and licked my hand resting on the gravestone.

"It's just me and Khan now, I guess." I glanced back at the fence where the form of Officer Goodman appeared as a dark silhouette against the gray sky. "I should probably go. Give Mom a kiss for me." I stood. "I've got a lot of work to do before I die."

A building on the campus of Crimson Hollow, former sanitarium, and recently renovated facility for victims of VS, also known as vampire virus, in upstate New York.

Excerpt from Man Behind the Mask: The Biography of Lucian Vidraru *by James I. Franklin. Edited by Dr. Gabriel Jackson.*

Autumn *in upstate New York. Majestic. Picturesque. The setting of a Sanitarium with a haunting past. More than a century ago, the doors of Crimson Hollow's Hospital for the Mentally Insane opened to a hopeful public. A place where light, fresh air, and exercise were thought to cure those with mental ailments. But the days of hope didn't last. Due to overpopulation, disease, and abuse, the doors closed seventy years later, leaving vacant hallways and the graves of nearly one-thousand bodies behind.*

Two decades ago, the dilapidated property was purchased by a doctor on a mission to eradicate a disease thought incurable. Viridae Sangre. Commonly known as VS, or the vampire virus. After intense renovations, the doors opened once again to a world come full circle, hopeful for a cure—and a man who would give it to them.

Lucian Vidraru. The world's oldest vampire.

The man who would become the world's most famous living human—vampire or otherwise—came from an impoverished cottage near Bran Castle in Romania. Born to a scientist father and seamstress mother, Lucian's life began as simply as any other in the year 1860. Its ending, however, may never be written.

~

LUCIAN

I DREAMED I DIED AGAIN.

A few people gathered around my coffin, looking appropriately somber, although I couldn't make out the features of a single soul. I didn't care to. No one in this life meant anything to me.

I cared more about the people waiting for me on the other side. Mamă with her wide grin, soft hands cupping my cheeks. Tată with his big mustache and newsboy cap. Barb was waiting for me, too.

Barb.

My wife of only a few years. Her life cut too short.

I could hardly remember what she looked like. How many years had it been? Sixty? Seventy, perhaps? A lifetime ago. The man who married her wasn't me anymore. My body was that of a young man's, and I couldn't claim to be the person I once was.

The dream shifted. Others waited in the shadows. Wispy forms glided on the air currents, though blood dripped from their hands. A chill went down my spine.

I woke with a pounding heart, drenched in sweat, my skin clammy.

Getting to my feet, I paced through the Gothic, cavernous room. The heavy oaken beams in the ceiling felt as if they would fall and crush me at any moment. Not like I would die if it were to happen, but one could hope.

It had been too long.

I'd been here too long, seen too many things. When would I get my turn to die?

But those were morbid thoughts.

I stepped onto the balcony, letting the crisp morning air clear my tangled web of thoughts.

"Time for your breakfast, Mr. Lucian." Nurse Teesha's voice carried through the room, the cart's wheels squeaking.

I turned to face the nurse and her cart. My stomach soured, then turned to all-out nausea.

A bag of blood hung from a metal loop. A tube extended from the bag's bottom where a syringe would be attached, one that would feed directly into my stomach.

I'd never get used to the sight of it.

"Do we have to do this?" I asked bitterly, unable to hide the disgust in my voice.

Her dark eyes narrowed. "Yes. Always. Every day. You know the drill. Now." She patted the pillow. "Time for breakfast," she repeated.

Leather gloves creaked as I fisted my hands. What would happen if I said no? If I ran away from the facility and never looked back? I could live as a vagabond, go back to Romania, haunt the graveyards like a revenant, preying on anyone who trespassed.

Flexing my fingers, I pushed the thoughts away. Maybe it

was time I started acting grateful, for a change. This was the best life I'd had in…well…ever.

I walked to the bed. My copy of *Heart of Darkness* lay open on the bedsheets. Must've fallen asleep reading it. After placing it on the nightstand, I took a deep breath, and sat on my bed.

Nurse Teesha walked to the sink and washed her hands. I did my best to keep my gaze away from the bag of blood. It looked so wholly unnatural. Blood encased in plastic. Dead blood. Cold and no longer pulsing with life.

I'd asked why they made me consume it this way, and Dr. Warren informed me that it was all about appearances and propriety. "No one wants to see you drinking blood from a cup," he'd said. "Or worse, from the mutilated artery of some poor dead animal."

But it took all I had not to gag at the sight of the bag, and I tried to imagine some way to distract myself from it.

"I heard you have a new grandbaby," I said.

Gushing water splashed the stainless-steel basin. "Sure do," the nurse answered. "Little girl. Pretty as she can be. Looks just like me if I say so myself."

"That's wonderful, Teesha. I'm so happy for you."

"Thank you, Mr. Lucian. I appreciate your thoughtfulness." She held up her stethoscope, pulled back the blanket, and lifted my shirt to reveal the tube extending from my abdomen.

Cold metal pressed to my skin as she listened to my bowel sounds.

She removed the stethoscope from her ears, turning to the table, not meeting my gaze as she rummaged through the packages of alcohol wipes.

"Do you have any grandchildren?" she asked, her tone attempting nonchalance.

I raised an eyebrow. The question was innocent enough, but she must've known she was crossing a line.

"No," I answered.

Pursing her lips, she picked up the alcohol wipe. Cold wetness chilled my skin as she cleaned the area around my tube.

"Not that I don't want them." I took a deep breath. Maybe it was time I opened to her. "I love children."

"Then…why?"

Memories pressed in. Barb on the bed. The blood pooling between her legs. I couldn't tell her everything, so I kept it simple. "That would've been awkward. Since I look like I'm eighteen, and I would have great-great-great-grandchildren who look my age." I forced a laugh. "That wouldn't have worked at all."

She patted my shoulder, as if to console me.

"Don't feel sorry for me, Teesha. I've told you before I don't remember much from those past lives."

"Past lives," she chuckled, shaking her head. "Makes it sound like you were reborn or something."

"In a sense, I was. I feel twenty, twenty-one. Barely legal drinking age in America."

She laughed as she picked up the syringe, filled it with blood from the bag, then placed the tip into the tube connecting to my stomach. I fisted the sheets in my hands, grinding my teeth.

"Mr. Lucian," she said. "I don't mean to pry, but I want to see you happy. I know how lonely you get."

I shot her a questioning glance. "Lonely?"

"Yes. Lonely. You're the kindest, most selfless person I've ever met, but you distance yourself from the other patients. Let them see who you really are."

I glanced at the book on my nightstand, not speaking.

"Do you keep yourself from people because you're afraid of losing them?" she asked.

I clenched my jaw. "Teesha, where's this coming from?"

"I've been around you long enough to see it. Why don't you go out sometime?"

I shifted, and the pillow sank behind me. "I go out all the time. To the gym. On my motorcycle…"

"But you never talk to anyone."

I ground my teeth in frustration. What had gotten into Teesha today? "All those shows I go on, and my channel, and every single interview and press appearance…I talk to people then."

"Lucian." She patted my gloved hand. "I see you locked in this room every day. There's a world of people right here in the facility—people from all over the world. We've got game night every evening in the common area. Come to it. Make friends. Meet someone."

I shook my head. She claimed to know me. She didn't. I'd kept things from her for good reason. She'd lose it if she knew the truth about me. About my lives. About what had *really* happened, and not what was in my supposed biography.

"Teesha," I said with a stern tone. "I'm not here because I'm sick."

Disappointment clouded her features.

"Please leave it alone. I'm no one's friend. I can't be."

She shook her head as she removed her gloves, placing them on the tray. Standing, she grabbed the cart and wheeled it to the door, but she stopped before leaving.

"You're my friend, Mr. Lucian." She kept her back turned to me as she spoke. "I believe I count as someone."

The door clicked behind her as she exited my room. Sighing, I picked up my book, opened it, and started reading where I'd left off.

We live, as we dream—alone.

3

From Rudolph Jesse "Scout" Gibson's journal. American philanthropist, explorer, and actor, June 29, 1917, Bucharest, Romania.

I jumped clear a mile high when that 'ol boy opened his eyes. We'd been putting my blood straight into his veins for nigh twenty minutes through the rubber hose we'd taken off the Model-T. Nobody thought nothing would happen. Not really. Not even me. Why we were doin' it was a question we didn't ask. We did it because it seemed that old corpse needed something after it'd been sitting in that museum for near a decade with not even a spot of rot. It was a cooky thing to do, most folks said. But I'd never been one for caution.

"You ever seen a real livin' vampire?" Clayton asks me after that boy sat straight up and stared us in the face.

"No, sir. I have not," I answered.

"Well, look right here. Because you have now."

Some folks asked me what sort of fellow that boy was.

He was a sad sort of boy, never a smile on his face, always looking out at the sky as if he'd left something behind when he'd laid dead in that cemetery all those years. 'How much does he remember of his past?' others ask.

I can't say. He never was one for talking, and though he got asked plenty of questions, he always gave the same answer.

"You forget the important things first." He'd say it with that accent of his, and those eyes. Never could get used to those eyes. That's what made it easier to sell him off to P.T. Barnum and Bailey's.

~

LUCIAN

I FOLDED MY FATHER'S LETTER, HIS BLOOD TURNED TO BLACK splotches that marred the ink, and I placed it back in the envelope. With my gloved hands, I was careful not to tear the hundred-year old paper, thin as tissue, and hid it in the cigar box's false bottom.

Footsteps came from outside my doorway, and I shoved the box to the back of the Victorian bookcase. A knock came at the door as I moved leather-bound books to hide it.

"Lucian." Dr. Warren's muffled voice came from outside the door. "It's me. Let me in."

My wingback chair creaked as I stood. I walked to the door and opened it. The hallway's fluorescent lights highlighted Dr. Warren's crop of white hair that matched his suit. Excessive amounts of plastic surgery stretched the skin of his face, disguising his age of seventy-something. He gave me a grandfatherly smile.

"I've brought news." He spoke with the deep, raspy voice of a smoker, although he swore he hadn't touched a cigarette in ages.

"About what?" I asked.

"Another survivor. She tested positive for the primary virus."

I knitted my brows. "You're sure?"

He held up a vial in his fingers crooked with arthritis. Blood swirled with a black tarry substance inside the glass. "Positive."

"*Oh, doamne*," I breathed the Romanian curse. I reached for the vial, but he held it out of my reach.

"We talk first."

I ground my back molars. "I'm sick of talking."

"You don't have a choice."

I furrowed my brow. I should've known this was coming, and I had to admit, he'd piqued my curiosity. Even so, I'd have to be careful. I couldn't tell him everything. "Fine. We'll talk. But not now. Later."

"Why?"

"Because I've got game night."

He raised an eyebrow. "Since when do you go to game night?"

"Since now."

He frowned. "Seems awfully convenient you've chosen now to go."

"I'm trying to be more sociable."

He chuckled, his suit creasing with the movement. "After twenty years, I know you well enough to tell when you're lying, Lucian. This is the first case of the primary virus since I revived you. Surely you realize how important this is. We need to have a conversation, and we need to have it now. This girl — the carrier — she won't last more than a month." He leaned closer, speaking quietly. "It's time you tell me what you know."

I glanced back at my bookcase, my father's letter hidden

behind the leather-bound volumes, and swallowed the fear rising into my throat. Telling him everything meant I gave him my complete trust. Was I ready for that?

"Fine," I said reluctantly. "Tonight. We talk."

He nodded, a satisfied smile creasing his mouth. "Now, that wasn't so hard was it?"

You have no idea.

4

*Transcript excerpt from Nightshift News report, air date Sunday,
September 5, 9 PM CST*

The date was December 17, 1973, when a convicted murderer died in prison, just two years after his sentencing. The man held responsible for the eventual deaths of reportedly tens of thousands of people laid silently in his own grave in a Colorado prison cemetery. That is, until something changed the fate of a sleeping corpse who held not one, but two death certificates.

Enter Dr. Victor Warren, the man who would be referred to as the father of the VS vaccine—a man who claimed he could raise the dead.

On April 4, 2000, in a quiet prison cemetery, Dr. Warren, who had spent the last seven years wading through paperwork and fighting legal battles, laid claim to his victory. The body of Romanian born Lucian Alexandru Vidraru was exhumed and, to the astonishment of the entire watching world, successfully revived via blood transfusion.

The supposed murderer who had once evoked blind hatred had come full circle. His plea for forgiveness did not fall on deaf ears. On March 11, 2006, Vidraru was acquitted from his crimes and deemed not responsible for spreading the vampire virus. His release had one qualification—he must remain under the care of Dr. Warren for the rest of his foreseeable life, which, for a man who can't die, may be an immeasurable amount of time.

~

AMAYA

KHAN SHIFTED AS HE SAT BY ME. I MOVED MY HAND OUT OF MY hoodie's pocket long enough to pat his head. He nuzzled my hand, his nose wet.

"Welcome to the coven." A girl in a yellow Hufflepuff t-shirt sat across from me. She plopped a can of tomato juice and a Duck-taped box of Checkers on the table.

I raised an eyebrow as she lifted the lid and removed the board.

"Coven?" I asked.

"Sure. We're all vampires, you know." She winked, and I couldn't help but smile.

Quiet conversations filled the area. Linoleum floors, the glare of fluorescent lights, and long tables with bench seats reminded me of the cafeteria at Miami High. Even smelled the same, the scent of grease that had sat too long in the fryer. Funny to think of home in a place so far from the familiar.

She arranged the Checker pieces. "What's your name?"

"Amaya," I answered. "Amaya de la Vega."

"Ah!" Curiosity lit her eyes. "The new girl. I'm Chloe Jackson." Her wide blue eyes contrasted her tanned skin. Her corn silk hair flowed in loose waves. "Sorry about all this." She waved to the room. "Not that I don't want more people here my age, but about the virus, you know. Nobody wishes that on anyone."

I rubbed my sore shoulder. "Yeah."

"So." She took a sip of her juice. "What's your story? Where are you from? How'd you get the virus and all that?"

"Miami," I answered.

She raised an eyebrow. "Just Miami?"

I nodded.

"You're not giving me the scoop on your whole how-you-got-the-virus thing?"

I shook my head.

"Quiet one, aren't you? What about him?" She pointed to Khan. "Who's this?"

"My dog."

"Yeah, I figured that." She chuckled. "Look." She slapped the last piece on the board. "You want to get along here, right? Feel accepted and have friends? Get well and go home?"

Not really why I'm here.

"Then you'll have to open up. Don't be shy. We're family. Everyone has the same virus, and we understand what you're going through. Keep that in mind, 'kay? Now, let's try again. I'm Chloe and I'm from Phoenix. I came here five months ago. My brother and I moved here when we contracted the virus. Everyone said it was the best place to get treatment. Turns out, this place is super creepy, especially that vampire, Lucian, you know? Guy gives me the creeps. But now we're stuck here, and there's no escaping, and I don't want to say more because you're new and I might scare you off." She took another sip, then motioned to me. "Your turn."

"Okay." I swallowed. "I'm Amaya and I'm from Miami. My dad was a cop, but he died of VS when I was younger. My mom's a...*was* a scientist. She was actually studying VS before she died of it."

"I'm sorry to hear that."

"Thanks."

"Most of us here have lost someone. Sadly, it's pretty common." She nodded at the board. "You go first."

I glanced at the black-and-red squares, my mind a million miles away from playing a game of Checkers. Images of Mom and Dad lying in their graves had invaded my mind for so long, I'd forgotten simple things, like how to jump one piece over another one.

"You move them diagonally on the black—"

"I know." I squared my shoulders and took my hands out of my hoodie's pockets. I could do this. At least, I could pretend. I reached out, touched the plastic disc, and moved it one square forward.

Letting go of my pent-up breath, the act of sliding a piece of plastic across cardboard seemed like something more, as if I'd taken a step closer to redemption. Silly thoughts to have.

Chloe slid her piece. I reached for the board when Khan barked as someone entered the room. Odd. My dog hardly ever made a sound unless something dangerous was around.

I looked over my shoulder.

The dark-clad visage of a young man entered the room. He moved on quiet feet, the whisper of a shadow come to life.

The air silenced. All eyes focused on him—Lucian Vidraru—the reason I'd come here. The reason I'd injected myself. The last piece of the puzzle my mother had started.

My heart pounded, and I found it difficult to swallow my fear.

Everything about him spoke of mystery. A dark hoodie covered his head, hiding his baldness. Hairless eyebrows rose above sunglasses masking his eyes. His angular face, olive skin tone, and strong jawline lent credence to his Romanian ancestry. His lips, though well-proportioned, were unsmiling and severe, as if he held a secret.

I remembered to breathe.

Chloe cursed under her breath. "Why's *he* here? He never comes out of his coffin."

I eyed her. "His coffin?"

She waved her hand. "His room. Whatever. He never socializes. Usually avoids the ordinary commoners like us. He's too good for us and all that." Her eyes narrowed as she tracked his movements. "Weird," she whispered to herself. She shook her head, then took a deep breath and focused on the chess board. "It's your turn."

"Oh." I turned back to the board and moved a piece. Chloe used her turn to jump mine.

"Are you paying attention?"

I wiped my sweaty palms on my cut-offs and cast a quick glance over my shoulder. Lucian stood several tables behind us, the room reflected in the dark lenses of his glasses.

"It's okay," she said.

I turned back to her. Had she noticed me staring? "Pardon me?"

"Everyone gets starstruck when they see him for the first time," she explained. "Just a word of advice, though. He's nothing like the personality you see on TV."

"Right. And by the way, I'm *not* starstruck," I said, casting a brief glance over my shoulder, my heartrate spiking at finally being so close to him. "Chloe, do you happen to know which room he's in?"

She snorted. "His room? Why? Are you planning to stalk him?"

"No." I forced a laugh. "Of course not. I'm just curious."

"Don't be," she said pointedly. "If I were you, I'd keep my distance."

A boy who resembled Chloe stopped beside our table. Her brother? He had the same skin and hair color, same eyes, though he was about sixty pounds heavier than his sister. "Did you see him come in? What's he doing here?" The boy's eyes followed Lucian as he stalked through the room.

"I was wondering the same thing," Chloe said.

"Maybe he's hungry," he said, leaning in dramatically and pulling on the collar of his shirt. "For one of us."

Chloe gave a nervous laugh. "I hope not." She tapped her fingers on the table, eyes narrowed as she stared across the room. The heavyset boy sat beside us, pulling Chloe's gaze away from the vampire.

"Sorry Amaya," Chloe said. "Forgot to introduce you. Meet my brother, Damian."

"Hello," I said.

Damian looked pointedly at me. "Lucian isn't interested in you. That's rule one of this place. Rule two. Keep your distance from him. He doesn't like us. Why he decided to come down here with the rest of the patients isn't normal. He's a freak of nature."

"Damian, that's rude," Chloe snapped.

"What?" He held up his hands. "It's the truth. He's not one of us. Amaya's cute, and she's probably seen Lucian on TV. Thinks he's a friendly, hunky vampire and all that. But she should be warned he's dangerous, and even if he weren't, he only goes for supermodels."

"Lucian's only dated one supermodel," I said flatly. "He got married in the fifties to a woman named Barbara, Barb for short, and he's dated two actresses and a fashion designer in his current life. None of those relationships lasted longer than a month."

"Ah!" Damian's eyes lit up. "So, you keep up with him?"

I chose not to answer. Turning back to the board, I reached for a piece, but Chloe grabbed my hand, stopping me. She held completely still. "Don't turn around now, but he's watching us," she whispered.

"What?"

"Just act natural."

I took a deep breath. I'd get nowhere if I couldn't talk to

him or even look at him. Why were they so scared of him, anyway? "Sorry, but I gotta go."

"Go?" Chloe's eyes widened. "Where?"

"To talk to the vampire," I said matter-of-factly.

"I warned you not to!"

"I know, and I appreciate the warning. But I'd rather judge a person for myself by getting to know them rather than believing the gossip."

Chloe pursed her lips.

"Umm-hmm," Damian said with a nod. "See what I mean? It's always the pretty ones who flock to him like he's a rock star. What'd I tell you? He's a chick magnet on steroids. Just don't fall for him is all I can say."

"I won't," I said sincerely. "Trust me. That's the last thing I'd ever do."

From Ivy Pearl Shipman's memoir, "Glitter without the Gold: A Starlet's Journey to Hollywood Glory."

It takes a lot out of me to look back on my days spent in the circus. The laughs and jabs weren't so bad when you could band together with the other performers. They called me Missy Pearl, always wearing my beads and boas with a gentleman on my arm and my Colt pistol in my boot. I got my hair bobbed for the circus, and that was before the style caught up. I never was anything more than the eye candy, introducing the acts, calling attention to the rarities on stage, until I got the gig that changed my luck and landed me in Hollywood.

I can't recall his given name. He went by Dracula during our time. Quiet boy. Never would look at you. Always wore those blue-tinted spectacles. Only took them off for his acts. And what an act it was! Drew people from all around the country. We never had enough seats, even in our big tent. Most folks ended up standing.

The act went simply enough, if one had the stomach for it. Mr. Hammond brought me out wearing a flapper's get-up with the beads and pearls. Low-cut, of course, all part of the act, they told me. Better way to show off the blood.

He strapped me to the table and left me there. Told me to count a full sixty seconds while I pretended to get free of the ropes. With the drums pounding like heartbeats, it was easy for me to get into character.

Then Dracula appeared on stage. I'll never forget that top-hat and cloak, and that red silk handkerchief wrapped around his neck. Always seemed wrapped too tightly, reminded me of the cords they wrapped around the lions' necks. If you didn't have a fright by then, all you had to do was look at those eyes. I still see those eyes when I wake at night.

When he bent over me, he always whispered he was sorry so only I could hear it, but he didn't need to. I never felt a thing. When the blood ran down my neck, always made me woozy. Never did like the sight of blood, especially my own. That was the worst part.

"Did he really drink your blood?" folks asked me. Gave me a chuckle.

Would we have sold out of every ticket if he hadn't?

~

AMAYA

I sat on the plastic cafeteria chair across from Lucian Vidraru.

The Lucian Vidraru.

He glanced up. His appearance reminded me of the flat,

angular planes hewn into modern statues—bald head hidden under his black hoodie, smoothly sloping nose, and a sharp jawline. Hairless eyebrows arched over sculpted sockets. Sunglasses concealed his eyes. He was an enigma to me. Did he possess human emotions? Or did he act as cold as he looked? Although his eyes remained hidden, I got the feeling that a predator lurked behind dark lenses.

There was a reason he'd been considered a monster for decades of his life. Fear made my fingers tremble.

I can do this.

I placed my clasped hands on the table, and his head swiveled ever so slightly, tracking my movements.

Swallowing the fear lodged in my throat, I found my voice. "You're the vampire?"

He raised an eyebrow. "Don't call me that."

His voice sounded deeper—and more severe—than on his vlog. Did he save the charming persona for the cameras?

"Vampire," I repeated. "That's what everyone calls us, isn't it? Including you. *Especially* you."

He sat so still, I wondered if he was breathing. Did he breathe? I couldn't remember if I'd read that or not. Black gloves creaked as he clasped his fingers on the table. "I prefer the term VS survivor."

I cocked my head. "Why is that?"

"Because I'm not a vampire."

"Really?" I eyed him. "But that's what everyone calls us. It's what they call *you*."

"I know."

"And you never correct them?"

"I do. They ignore me." He glanced up at the clock on the wall behind me. I must've bored him. "Who are you?" he demanded.

Well. Friendly, wasn't he? "Amaya de la Vega." Khan whined beside me. He padded silently to Lucian, sniffed his jeans, then barked.

"Who's this?" Lucian asked with a little more excitement in his voice. If I didn't interest him, at least my dog would. He patted the Husky's head, and Khan wagged his tail.

"That's Khan," I answered.

Lucian smiled, showing evenly spaced white teeth. No fangs, from what I could tell. I thought I'd read up on everything there was to know about him, so why had the little details escaped my attention? Things like fangs and breathing.

"Khan. As in The Wrath of?" he asked.

Surprise struck me. "Exactly. Most people think he's named after Genghis."

He raised an eyebrow. "What made you choose the name?"

"It was my dad's idea. He wanted to name him after his favorite movie villain. Said he wanted a name that would strike fear into people's heart." I smiled at the memory, and a bit of the tension knotting in my shoulders relaxed. "My dad was a bit melodramatic."

"Your father has good taste. The original series was the best, you know. In the sixties, when we'd never seen anything like the Enterprise, and Lieutenant Uhura, and Klingons. And tribbles. It was crazy back then." He shook his head. "I guess you wouldn't know."

I shrugged. "Everyone sees something the first time. That's how it was for me when I watched the new series."

My dog barked, furiously wagging his tail, then put his paws on Lucian's lap.

"Khan, stop." I snapped at the dog. "Sorry, I don't know why he's doing that. He's hardly ever like this with strangers."

Lucian shrugged. "Usually, animals are terrified of me. But this behavior happens every now and then with animals— usually predators." He scratched behind the dog's ears. "What kind of dog are you?"

"Husky," I answered too quickly.

Lucian's hairless eyebrows rose. "Interesting. Huskies

usually have blue or brown eyes." He gave me a sidelong glance. "Yellow eyes are more likely to belong to wolves."

I laughed nervously. "Don't tell anyone, but he's a mix. We rescued him from a shelter. They said he came from an illegal breeder in Alaska."

"I see. Your dad must be a well-educated man."

My heart clenched. "*Was*, yes."

Hairless eyebrows lifted. "He passed away?"

"Yes. He's buried in the cemetery here, actually."

"He died of VS?"

I nodded.

"Did I know him?" he asked.

"Probably not. He was only a patient for a few months. You were visiting Romania when he was here." I cleared my throat, not meeting Lucian's gaze.

"How did you know I was in Romania?" Lucian's voice turned severe, all easiness gone, replaced by a sharp edge of suspicion. "That was a top-secret trip at the time. The press reported it as a visit to Russia. How did you know about it?"

"Oh—well..." I rubbed my neck.

"How?" he demanded.

"My dad texted me at the time. Said you'd left the country. I must've thought he said you went to Romania. That's it."

"That's it?" he said incredulously, as if he didn't believe me.

"Yes." I spoke with firmness. "That's it."

"Hmm." The outline of his eyes narrowed shrewdly behind dark lenses. His calculated gaze sent shivers down my spine.

He stood abruptly. "I need to go."

My heart fell. I hadn't gotten anything from him. My throbbing shoulder seemed to pulse with the quiet ticking of the clock on the wall.

He took a step closer to me. I had to look up to take in his tall frame hidden under his black pants and hoodie of the same color. Power exuded from him. His presence was so commanding, the air escaped my lungs, and I had to force myself to take a breath. I caught myself staring at him—his full lips, the strong curve of his nose and forehead, the sharp angles of his face and jawline, and the mysterious eyes hidden behind sunglasses.

"You're her, aren't you?" he asked.

I opened my mouth to speak, but nothing came out. I turned my attention to a poster on the wall; fluffy gray-and-white kittens sat in a row on piano keys, their expressions curious. With a deep breath, I found my voice. "Excuse me?"

"The carrier of the primary virus," he clarified.

I clasped my hands in my lap. "Yeah. That's me."

"I'm sorry."

I glanced away. "Yeah."

"We're working on a cure, you know. Hopefully soon we'll make a breakthrough." His voice turned wistful. "We've been working a long time."

"Yeah. I know." My words sounded sharper than I'd intended.

He wrinkled his forehead. "You do?"

"My mom's a scientist. She studied the virus."

"Really?" He tilted his head. "Who is she?"

I swallowed. I'd envisioned this conversation going in a different direction. How had we gotten on the subject of my mom? "You wouldn't have known her. She passed away."

"I'm sorry to hear that." He placed his gloved hand atop mine, and I caught my breath at his touch. A mix of fear and excitement tingled through my body. He smelled of well-oiled leather and amber spice. My heart raced.

Get a lid on it. He's a monster. A murderer! You are not *attracted to him.*

"I understand what you're going through," he said, his words deep with sincerity.

I snatched my hand. Maybe he understood, but it wasn't something I cared to ponder. "Thanks," I mumbled.

He nodded once and started to walk away when I stopped him. "Sorry, but I was just curious, some of the other patients seem to think you're not very sociable—"

"I'm a jerk?"

"That wasn't exactly their words." I twisted my fingers. "Anyway…I-I didn't think it was true, so that's why I came to talk to you. If some of us wanted to come by later, you know, just to visit…well, the thing is, no one knows where your room is…and…"

"Two-twelve." He spoke with ice in his voice. "It's no secret, but your friends are right, I prefer to be left alone. Good night, Amaya."

Fluorescent lights shone on his dark-clad frame as he turned away. One of the bulbs pulsed with a weak electrical current, causing his shadow to fluctuate behind him.

"Goodbye for now, Lucian," I said quietly, watching until he disappeared from the room.

6

Notes from Dr. Walter Owen, lead researcher at Manzanar, California's WW2 Research Facility- January 5, 1939

The patient, heretofore designated as **THE SUBJECT**, expressed concern over the methods being implemented. The staff informed him that all precautions and sterilization techniques were being enacted. Our ultimate decision to forego anesthesia stemmed from the fact that **THE SUBJECT** was incapable of death under classical terminology, and we surmised he did not experience pain in the same manner as typical mammals. The first experiment consisted of draining **THE SUBJECT'S** blood, which resulted in a catatonic state. In any other situation, such an extreme measure would be fatal. However, in this case, when **THE SUBJECT** was once again given blood, he revived.

This led to the next tier of experiments, which consisted of removing vital organs in the succession that follows. Abnormalities are listed with an *

-Liver (wt: 1.5 kg.)

-Tongue (wt. 0.8 kg.)*
-Stomach (wt: 94 g.)
-Small bowel (wt: 1.59 g.)
-Lungs (wt. 2.27 kg.)
-Eyes (wt. 0.7 kg.)*
-Heart (wt. 310 g.)
-Brain (wt. 1345 g.)

In every case, THE SUBJECT regenerated these organs in approximately three hours. Harvesting organs for use of untested transplant technology was considered. However, the decomposition rate of harvested organs increased by nearly 300% once removed from THE SUBJECT'S body.

Upon further inspection, a post-mortem autopsy of said organs revealed the tissues had in fact converted into calcium carbonate.

**THE SUBJECT'S tongue contained 347 taste buds, as opposed to a normal human tongue containing 9,000-10,000.*

**Eyes were uncommon and presented no traditional tear ducts, instead consisting of nictitating membranes and no eyelids. The cause of the unusual coloring is unknown.*

Further testing is being recommended to determine the root of such anomalies.

∼

AMAYA

"Stay close, Khan," I whispered as he ambled beside me down the hallway. Anxiety made my heart race with quick staccato beats. I stuck my clammy hands inside my hoodie's pockets as I scanned the room numbers tacked to the doors.

202, 204, 206…

Daddy's voice scolded me as I walked.

You'll get thrown out. All our hard work for nothing.

But that was exactly the problem. I had to find it.

I had to find out Lucian's secrets.

He was the last person my mom had researched before her death. Her final words rang in my head. I imagined my last conversation with her as she gasped for air on the hospital bed.

"Find Lucian…"

"Lucian?" I questioned. "Lucian Vidraru? The vampire?"

"Yes, he has the cure, though he may not realize it. It was given to him. Ages ago. In his first life. Look for an old box. Something his father would've given him…"

"Mom." I squeezed her hand. "Save your breath."

She only shook her head.

"Get inside the facility…it's the only way."

That's when I'd noticed the tiny vial of vampire blood clutched in her hand.

I clutched the metal key hidden in my pocket. Getting it was easy enough. A trip to the front office, a chat with Security Guard Goodman, an uncomfortable conversation about menstruation and how it affected women with VS, and the key was mine.

Thanks, Dad, for insight into a criminal's mind.

I didn't imagine him thanking me.

I stopped at 212.

Khan whined as I listened at the door. Although I'd made sure Lucian was still in Dr. Warren's office, I couldn't be too careful.

Silence pressed in from the other side of the cold metal door, so I stuck the key in the lock and turned the knob.

When I opened it and stepped inside, I caught my breath.

Had I entered a Gothic castle?

Seriously, if the man claimed he wasn't a vampire, why did he live like one?

The scent of leather came from the ornate bookcases surrounding me. Old volumes comprised the shelves. I paced through the rows, past a heavy desk with the same scrollwork, to a bay window overlooking the upstate New York forest.

Stepping past the couches and coffee table to stand at the window, I caught my breath at the sight of the red and gold trees sprawling toward the sunset, such a contrast from the palms of Miami. Pressing my hand to the glass, I stood mesmerized by the swaying branches and fluttering leaves.

Khan whined, pulling me. I turned and continued my search through the room, past heavy crosses decorating the walls, past a four-poster bed made of the same dark-stained wood and Victorian details. No coffins, thankfully.

Dad's training as a detective rang in my head as I recalled a conversation he'd had with Mom.

Nothing's lost. It's always somewhere. The best thing a criminal can do when they want to hide a murder weapon is to keep it in plain sight. Blend in with ordinary things. They know we'll check under the mattresses and under the rugs. The smart ones put it inside the remote sitting right on the couch, behind the pictures in the album on the coffee table, right where we can see it. Where they know we'll check last.

"Where would I check last?" I mumbled as I wandered over the hand-scraped hardwood floors and Venetian rugs. I ended up where I began, by the door, looking at the desk.

A *Dragon-Con!* cup filled with pens, a phone, and a laptop computer sat on the desk. Behind it loomed the bookcase. A few of the volumes peeked out, as if they'd been hastily pushed.

"Where would I keep an old box?" I mumbled as I walked to the shelf and removed the books, then placed them on the desk. Shoved to the back of the case, I spotted a cigar box.

My heart leapt. Had I found it?

I glanced at the door before pulling it out. After placing it on the table, I opened the lid. It was empty except for the velvet lining. The yellowed edge of a folded paper peeked from under the lining.

A false bottom?

I lifted the velvet, revealing a folded letter of faded paper and elaborately printed cursive. Unfamiliar words jumped out at me. The name *Constatin Vidraru* scrolled across the bottom.

Lucian's father?

Khan growled at the door.

Heart racing, I closed the cigar box's lid and stepped away from the desk, searching for a hiding place.

The door swung open.

Fluorescent light streaming from the door revealed Lucian's silhouette. His sunglasses hid his eyes, though I imagined them widening as he entered, the door slamming shut behind him.

"What are you doing in my room?" he demanded.

My heart thundered in my chest. He wouldn't try to kill me, would he?

Khan barked, wagging his tail as he padded to the vampire and stuck his nose in the man's hand.

"You were helping her sneak in my room?" Despite his harsh tone, he patted Khan's head. Lucian took another step when his gaze went to the cigar box.

I was so dead.

"You were getting into my things?" He snatched the box off the table and stuffed it back inside the bookcase, arranging the books in front.

He rounded on me, his muscled chest heaving, full lips pressed into a hard line.

"What the hell?"

I swallowed. "Um. Sorry?"

"Sorry?" he demanded. Leather creaked as his hands fisted. If he had the ability to remove his glasses and shoot lighting from his eyes, he would've done it. "You'll have to do more than apologize." He crossed to the desk, pushing me out of the way as he picked up the phone and dialed.

"Goodman? Someone broke into my room. Now please." The hand unit slammed into the cradle as he hung up.

I backed toward the door, though Khan lingered by the vampire. My sweat turned cold on my clammy skin. If he came after me, could I fight him off?

"Care to explain why you're here?" Lucian asked, barely keeping an even tone.

My mind blanked. What was I supposed to say? Should I lie? Tell a bit of the truth? "It's just that you're so famous, and I wanted to see where you live…."

"You are a terrible liar."

I looked at my shoes, heart heavy. "I wanted to know more about the virus. I thought there would be something in here about it."

He pressed his knuckles to the desk's top. "You thought there would be something in *my* room? My personal space?"

"I thought you were hiding something." At least it was the truth.

"I can't believe you broke in." He scrubbed his knuckles over his face. "Why? Did you look inside the cigar box?"

I swallowed the nervous lump in my throat. "I—"

"*Doamne*," he cursed. "You did, didn't you?"

Heart thundering, I backed away from him. I glanced back at the door. Would he get violent? "I didn't see much…"

"Much?" Muscles bulged as he crossed his arms over his chest. "What did you see?"

"Nothing…" I stammered. "It was just a name." I stood straight, leveling my gaze at him, though my pounding heart betrayed me. "A name," I said, a challenge in my voice. "That's all."

Growling, he cursed in Romanian, an unfamiliar word that sounded vile coming from his mouth. "Do *not* come in this room ever again. Do you understand?"

I met his gaze. Maybe he scared the living daylights out of me, but I wouldn't let him see that. "Yeah." My tone turned defiant. "I got it."

"I'm serious. I'll have you thrown out of this facility faster than you can blink. No one comes in my room. Ever."

"I wasn't trying to steal anything."

A knock came at the door. Lucian crossed the room and flung it open to reveal the security guard on the other side.

"Goodman. Take her," he said to the guard. He stalked to my side and gripped my arm. Despite the overwhelming fear lodged in my chest, the scent of warm amber and leather caught my attention, and my heart gave an inexplicable flutter.

Lucian stood too close, the surprising warmth of his body surrounding me.

He leaned near my ear. "Never come in here again." He spoke quietly through clenched teeth before shoving me to Officer Goodman. The hefty guard's keys jangled as he took my arm.

"What were you doing in his room?" His calm expression didn't crack as he spoke.

I bit my lip, looking away from him. My emotions were such a tangled mess, I couldn't make my mouth work.

Lucian stood in the doorway and leaned against the frame. He crossed his arms in his usual defensive posture.

"You stalking him?" the guard asked.

I groaned, rolling my eyes. "Hardly," I mumbled.

Lucian sighed. "This usually happens in hotel rooms at events with crazy fans." He glanced at me. "Never had it happen here." His look unnerved me, and I forced myself to stare at the floor tiles.

"So..." Goodman said. "She's just another crazed fan, huh?"

It wasn't the truth, and I knew it. Lucian knew it, too.

"Yeah," he answered, covering for me, and not

mentioning that I'd been looking for the cure. Perhaps he felt he had as much to lose in this situation as me. If Goodman saw me as a crazed, adoring fan, Lucian kept his letter a secret, and the guard would have no need to pry further.

Goodman shot me an inquisitive glance, as if questioning Lucian's story, but Khan barked, his tail wagging as if we were with old friends, and the security guard smiled.

"You were sneaking around the graveyard, and now this?" Goodman's face lit up. "Hey, I get it. That conversation we were having downstairs. You were trying to take the key to his room, weren't you?" He poked his hands in my hoodie's pocket until he fished something out. "Look at this." He held up the stolen key. "Guess I was right." He placed the key in his pocket. "We'll have to keep an eye on you."

Lucian shifted against his doorframe and drilled his dark gaze into mine. "Keep her locked in her room. I don't want her wandering the halls."

Heat rose to my cheeks. "You can't lock me up."

"You don't think so?" He leaned forward, his warm breath smelling of mint. My scowl reflected in the dark lenses of his glasses. "Try me," Lucian shot back, enunciating each word.

The anger vibrating through me made it impossible to speak. I stuck my fisted hands in my pockets to keep them from shaking.

"Hey, no need for raised voices," Goodman said. "Let me handle this, Lucian. I'll escort her back to her room, but I'm sure there's no need to lock her inside it. We'll get this sorted out."

Lucian sneered, then jerked away from me and glanced at the security guard. "You'd better." Spinning on his heel, he entered his room and slammed the door in my face.

If he were capable of death, I would kill him, was the closest thing to a coherent thought I had.

Goodman gripped my arm as he led me down the hall, Khan trotting at our heels. I'd have to go back another time and take another look at the letter. Take a screenshot of it. I'd have to watch his schedule. Wait for him to go out. When was his next TV appearance? He'd be gone for a few days at least for that.

"If you're planning to get back inside his room, I wouldn't."

I shot him a surprised glance. "Excuse me?"

"Don't act innocent, Miss de la Vega. I know your type."

"My type?" I repeated drily.

"You heard me." He smiled, speaking with a relaxed, down-to-earth tone. "After our little encounter at the cemetery, I read up on your files. Your mother came close. Closer than anyone else, certainly closer than anyone here has gotten to finding a cure. Let's not pretend we don't know why you were in Lucian's room."

I eyed him suspiciously as he marched me down the stairwell. Who was this guy?

"Carrier of the primary virus. We both know there's only one way to get that. Dr. de la Vega left with a sample. After she died, I wondered where it ended up."

Panic sped my heart. How did this guy know so much?

When we made it to the first floor, we stopped at room 103. He didn't reach for the key as I expected. Instead, we stood facing my door.

Moaning came from down the hall. A nurse passed us. Beside her walked a patient, his hospital gown hanging off a dangerously thin frame, his hair gone completely white, though he only looked a little older than me. Goodman gave them his friendly smile.

"Ma'am," he said to the nurse.

When they disappeared, he cleared his throat.

"Let me give you a word of advice," he said quietly, all pleasantry replaced with a professional tone. "You're looking in the wrong place. If you want to find information about the cure, go to Dr. Warren's office. He keeps everything on paper in a filing cabinet. Old school. Doesn't trust computers so don't bother with them."

I eyed him. He was helping me? "Who are you?"

He gave his relaxed smile. "Just a concerned security guard. Also, just a word of advice. Don't go into Lucian's room again. He really hates that."

I narrowed my eyes at him, not answering. What was his game?

"You got it?" He squeezed my arm.

"Fine. Yeah, got it."

He unlocked the door and opened it for me. Khan wandered into the room. I stepped inside, turning to shut the door, but Goodman held it open.

"De la Vega," he said, his voice barely above a whisper. "Just for the record, this conversation never happened. Understand?" The cheerfulness drained from his voice.

"Yeah," I answered. "I understand."

"Good." His smile returned. He turned and walked, his footsteps echoing through the empty dome of the hundred-year old hallway.

7

Excerpt from Ghost Chasers, Season 2, Episode 5: The Spirits of Crimson Hollow

Frankie: [whispering] We're at Crimson Hollow, home of real-life vampire Lucian Vidraru. The admins have allowed us the rare opportunity to explore their facility, granted we stay only between the hours of 12 AM and 6 AM, and keep to the passages where their patients aren't housed.

Eli: Yeah, this is an incredible opportunity. Everyone knows the stories of abuse and... and the deaths surrounding this place. We didn't think we'd got permission. But Frankie made a few phone calls.

Frankie: You're welcome.

Eli: He has connections.

Frankie: Yeah, connections.

[Laughing]

Eli: Frankie, who did you call? For real?

Frankie: That's classified, bro. We're on the clock. You're supposed to be telling us about Mary. You did your research, right?

Eli: Dude. Do you doubt my research skills? Of course, I did. Mary Reynolds was a patient in the early 1900s. They say she hung herself in the old cafeteria, not the foyer, though we haven't been able to confirm her death. Countless people died here, so there isn't a clear number of how many. Staff claim seeing a woman in white wandering the hall outside the doorway. Others claim to hear a woman crying or moaning.

Frankie: We brought the EVP recorder, plus the spirit box, thermal imaging camera with night vision, and an EMF meter with temperature gauge. If Mary's here, we'll find her.

[BREAK]

Frankie: Mary, are you there? We heard you killed yourself in this room? Is it true?

[Faint female crying.]

Eli: Did you hear that?

Frankie: Yeah. Behind the pillar.

[EMF reader glows red.]

Frankie: Holy [bleep!] Something just scratched my neck.

Eli: Mary, was that you? Did you scratch Frankie's neck?

Frankie: Mary, can you hear us? Give us a sign, Mary. We're not here to hurt you. I'm holding out my hand. If you can hear me, touch my hand. [whispering] Do you feel that? It's cold here.

Eli: Yeah. Look at the temperature. Forty-five degrees. Forty-four. Forty-three.

[Spirit box static. Female voice whispering: "...here."]

∼

LUCIAN

"Steak?" Dr. Warren held up the to-go bag. My stomach growled at the scent of meat. Cooked, but still. It beat the liquid death they put through my bleeding tubes.

"Sure." I stepped aside, allowing him into my room. "Come in."

He followed me past my desk, past the bookshelf with my father's hidden letter. I suppressed the image of Amaya standing in that spot, dark hair and flushed cheeks. Wide eyes bright with fear. Heart-shaped lips slightly parted. I shook my head to erase the image.

Anger burned in my chest when I thought of her hands touching the cigar box, but my heart thrummed in a way I hadn't felt in a long time, an emotion too powerful and overwhelming to focus on.

I stopped at the couches and coffee table arranged in front of the dark window.

"I guess you heard about the break-in?" I asked as we sat.

"Yes, I heard. De la Vega might be a problem."

"I agree." I rubbed the knot forming in my neck.

He placed the paper bag on the marble-topped coffee table. The sack crinkled as he removed a Styrofoam container. I took it from him and popped open the lid. The scent of sizzling, seasoned meat filled my room. My stomach growled as I cut a bite with the plastic knife and ate a small piece.

Dr. Warren raised a bushy brow. "How is it?"

"Excellent. Why can't I have this every day?"

"Not good for your digestion." He smiled. "You know that." He shifted, leather creaking as he propped his arm on the back of the couch. His bleached white scrubs contrasted the dark nighttime sky coming from the balcony behind him.

I waved my knife at him. "Why are you here?"

His gaze went to the window, worry creasing the smooth

ridge of his brow. "There's been another outbreak. This time in Taiwan. I'm leaving tomorrow."

My heart fell, and I placed my fork on the table. "*Another* outbreak? Why can't we get this thing under control?"

He crossed his arms. "I share your frustration, Lucian, but VS is an extremely complex virus, and it hasn't been around long enough to be thoroughly studied."

"I've studied it my entire life. Doesn't that count?"

"It counts, Lucian. It counts a lot. We wouldn't have the vaccine without you."

I shook my head. "It's not enough. Too many people are immune to it, too many children and elderly who can't fight it off."

"I agree, but it's more than we had twenty years ago."

When I closed my eyes, all I could see were the faces that flashed on the news, all the deaths, the names and the dates, because of me. Guilt weighed on me like an anvil sitting at the pit of my stomach. They died because of me, a wrong choice I'd made. A day never passed without thoughts of their families suffering, people like Amaya, who'd lost both her parents.

Bright, worried eyes, full of innocence and desperation.

I clasped my hands, forcing the image away. Why couldn't I stop thinking of her?

"What will you do in Taiwan?" I asked.

"Same as always. See if there are any survivors. Vaccinate who I can. Give them the option to come here for treatment. Not much else can be done at this point."

"Do we have a death count?"

"Nineteen so far." He pointed to my steak. "It's getting cold."

"I know." I grabbed the knife and speared a piece of meat. When I swallowed, the anvil grew larger. How could I enjoy food at a time like this?

"Don't lose hope, Lucian." He spoke with his philosophical tone. It grated on me.

"I haven't. Not yet."

He adjusted his black-rimmed glasses, giving me a pointed, fatherly stare. "I know you blame yourself for this."

"That's an understatement," I mumbled.

He propped one leg over the other. "It was the seventies. You were seduced by a charming woman. It happens to the best of us. Plus, you were going through a dark time."

"I wish you'd stop making excuses for me."

"I'm only helping you sort out this guilt you can't seem to let go of."

Dr. Warren's reminder made memories surface, of a brunette girl with periwinkle blue eyes in my dorm room, begging me to drink her blood, the creamy white skin of her neck tempting me. Simon and Garfunkel playing a background noise. *Heaven holds a place for those who pray.*

Shuddering, I willed the memories to let go. Instead, the face of another girl emerged. Those beautiful flushed cheeks and parted lips. Those eyes.

Doamne to those lovely, dark eyes.

"You okay, Lucian?"

"Fine." I snapped, my appetite returning as I cut off a chunk of meat and stuffed it in my mouth. "When are you coming back?"

"Next Thursday. You think you can stay put until I return?"

I smirked. "I don't know what you're talking about."

He chuckled. "Of course, you don't." He sat straight. "Keep an eye on De la Vega. I'll have Simmons monitor her while I'm gone. She may very well be the key to breaking this thing."

Keep an eye on her. Right. Because I really needed someone like *her* distracting me right now.

Pushing the empty container away, my stomach felt filled and satisfied. Maybe I'd be able to sleep tonight without waking with hunger pains.

"I wish you didn't have to go."

"Agreed." He stood, and I did the same. He crossed to me and placed his hand on my shoulder, the way my father would've done. "Lucian, I don't want to worry you, but I'm afraid this outbreak in Taiwan has gained some bad press. We may need to think about damage control. You're scheduled for an interview next week."

"I understand."

"Good." Smiling, he clapped my shoulder and stepped away, unlike my father, who would've seen fit to hug me at such an opportunity. "Best of luck, Lucian." He strode out of the room, whistling, walking with an air of confidence, back and shoulders straight, not stooped with time.

The tune of Mrs. Robinson on his lips as he left my room, leaving behind an empty paper sack and plastic tray.

8

Transcript of The Madeleine Reed Show. Air Date: March 21, 11:00 AM PST

Madeleine: Welcome back to the Madeleine Reed show. Our next guest is Lucian Vidraru. The subject of much controversy, he's been nicknamed the world's oldest man, and he carries the title of a true living vampire. He's gained fame through his appearances on numerous TV documentaries, and his new book Never Departed: One Man's Journey Through Undeath, will hit bookstore shelves soon. Lucian, thank you for joining me today.

Lucian: Thank you, Madeleine. I'm happy to be here.

(Applause)

Madeleine: So, tell me: you've been called the world's oldest living human, which is a bit unbelievable. You know. Let's just say a lot of women look at you.

(Laughter.)

Madeleine: Lucian, I've got to ask the million-dollar question first. Everyone wants to know. And you know, it's something on everyone's mind, not just mine. And I'm asking for a friend, by the way. Are you single?

(Laughter)

Lucian: You're right. I get asked that a lot. You know, that's a question I refuse to answer. Personal reasons.

Madeleine: You can't blame me for trying. For my friend, of course.

Lucian: Of course. And I'm flattered, by the way. There was a time when women avoided me altogether, and I can't blame them.

Madeleine: But not now.

Lucian: Certainly not now.

Madeleine: Then I'm glad we live in modern times. Don't you agree?

(Audience applauses and murmurs agreement.)

Madeleine: Now, Lucian, what do you say to the skeptics who don't accept your history? Does it bother you when someone doesn't believe how old you are?

Lucian: No. Not at all. I've never felt I've had to prove anything. The status of my age isn't something you can believe in. You either accept it or you don't. The proof is out there. I'm lucky to have an official birth certificate in the Romanian archives, which, you know, not everyone has. So I'm lucky that way. But no, you don't have to believe anything. I've always felt you should be who you are no matter what others believe about you.

Madeleine: That's great. It's great that you're inspiring kids and teens to accept themselves. Now, I have to ask, what's with the sunglasses and gloves? Will we ever know what you're hiding?

Lucian: Google it.

(Laughter)

Lucian: Seriously.

Madeleine: Okay. I have. Everyone has because, you know, we're curious. The best image we get is a 1920's black-and-white photo from a circus. We've got it on the screen? Yes? It's like a blurry Bigfoot shot, am I right? No offense, but this is hard to make out.

Lucian: Rightly so.

Madeleine: So, you aren't removing the glasses for us?

Lucian: No.

Madeleine: What if I offered you a grand? Right here.

Lucian: No.

Madeleine: Two?

Lucian: Still no.

Madeleine: Okay, well. It's not like you need the money anyway, is it? Tell me, what could I bribe you with to remove the glasses? Blood? Are you into O negative?

(Laughter)

Lucian: A B Positive is my favorite. Sorry, Madeleine.

(Laughter and applause.)

Madeleine: Can't blame me for trying. Thank you for being with us today.

Lucian: I'm humbled to be here.

Madeleine: Lucian Vidraru everyone! Guests in our studio audience are receiving a copy of his book **Never Departed: One Man's Journey through Undeath.** *Available October 15ᵗʰ! Thank you for joining us.*

(Applause.)

~

AMAYA

"Sit here." Chloe patted the wooden seat beside her. I glanced around the room where desks were scattered over the grimy marble floor. The wall of windows allowed a little sunlight to drift through gunmetal gray clouds. The air held the scent of chalk dust.

I hugged my hoodie around me and slid into the desk. With Khan waiting in my room, loneliness turned to a chill I couldn't shake. I placed my notebook and pencil in front of me, arranging them to match the lines in the wood grain.

Patients sat in desks. I tried not to stare, but my curiosity begged me to glance at the thin girl sitting in front of me, wearing a hospital gown, her dark hair threaded with strands of white. She sat perfectly still, eyes focused forward, as if she were in a trance.

Another person sat nearby with the same haunted look.

"What's wrong with them?" I mumbled to Chloe.

"They're in the advanced stages of the virus. It makes them like that, zombies almost."

"You're sure? I've never seen anyone with those symptoms."

"It's also a side effect of the medications, so I hear." She shrugged. "I dunno, but if anyone claims being a vampire is glorious, they're dead wrong."

My stomach lurched at the sight of the others. Would I become that way soon?

"You might as well know," Chloe said. "They keep telling us they're getting a cure soon. That's why they're making us take this class. You'll get college credits. Don't be surprised when they hit you up to get your certificate."

I laughed. "That's absurd when half us of will die in five years. Or less."

"Agreed. But they keep saying we should be prepared for the real world when it happens."

Her brother Damian took a seat beside her, squeezing his beefy frame into the school desk. He rubbed his red-rimmed eyes, then stared blankly at the chalkboard.

"Feeling any better?" she asked him quietly.

He shook his head.

I leaned forward. "You okay?"

"Comes and goes." He shrugged, rubbing his eyes again, as if he couldn't focus. He laid his head on the desk.

"Did you see the nurse?" Chloe asked.

"Yeah. She gave me an injection. Told me to rest. Drink more fluids until I can't keep them down, then they'll have to start the transfusion tube. You know the drill."

Chloe's eyes went wide with worry.

My heart hurt for him, but what could I do but watch him suffer? We'd all feel the same symptoms at some point.

A balding man strutted into the room and perched on the edge of the desk in front of the chalkboard. He adjusted his suspenders, wearing a navy polo that stretched over his protruding middle.

"Dr. Simmons, R.J." He spoke in a monotone voice, his face devoid of emotion, as if he were reciting something he'd memorized. "I'm the instructor for this hour for those who've just arrived." He nodded toward me. "If you feel you need to vomit, do it outside. Second offense, you'll be banned from coming back. This is a life skills class for those not strapped to bleeding tubes. You'll be withdrawn if the disease advances. Any questions?"

No one spoke.

"Our goal is for everyone to earn their certificates by the end of the semester. Once you pass, if you're deemed non-communicative, you'll be given the opportunity to get a job working here in the facility." He cleared his throat, picking up a textbook that he slapped on the tabletop. "We've also been discussing methods of living with VS. Keep in mind, this isn't a traditional college course. You left that world behind when you came here. We won't be studying algebraic equations or Shakespeare. Your life is VS, and that's our focus. It's best to understand the symptoms and the treatments we use. I'll warn you in advance, the topics we'll be discussing will be graphic, gory, and uncomfortable, but that's your life now. That's the reality of VS."

I slouched in my seat. I wasn't sure why any of this mattered when I'd be dead in a month, when my true purpose had nothing to do with sitting in a classroom, and everything to do with the information in Dr. Warren's filing cabinets, and with the name on the letter hidden inside Lucian's cigar box.

I discreetly pulled out my phone as Mr. Simmons continued lecturing. After typing the name *Constatin Vidraru* into the search engine, a few sites popped up, and a black-and-white picture of a man with a neatly trimmed beard, wearing an old-fashioned coat and necktie.

Constatin Vidraru was a well-known scientist from Bucharest, Romania. He's known for his detailed cataloging of many species, and for his research into cryptozoology. However, he is most well-known as the father of famed living vampire, Lucian Vidraru.

Mysterious eyes hidden behind sunglasses invaded my thoughts. Hands covered by black gloves. A voice tinged with a Romanian accent. The scent of amber spice when he stood close.

Why did Lucian keep a letter from his father? Maybe it was a keepsake. But if that were the case, why be so possessive of it? Why keep it hidden in a box with a false bottom?

Something in that letter was important, and I knew it held some clue about the cure.

I scrolled through the rest of the sites, searching for more information on Constatin Vidraru.

One labeled *The Archives of Vidraru, C.* caught my attention. But when I clicked it, a single sentence popped up. *Information has been deleted from this site and is held in confidentiality of the Crimson Hollow Research Facility.*

The research facility? Behind the doors of Dr. Warren's office?

"…thirty percent are naturally immune to the disease, another twenty respond positively to inoculations, the rest come to facilities like this one," Mr. Simmons said. "Are you paying attention, Miss de la Vega?"

I nodded, hiding my phone in my pocket. "Yes, sorry."

He gave me a glare, but he continued with his lecture.

Tapping my pencil, the lead inside rattled at my nervous movements. The rest of the class went by in a blur. By the time we were dismissed, nausea irritated my stomach, and I didn't know if the feeling came from VS symptoms, stress, or another factor I refused to consider.

"We'll head out now." Chloe pointed to the door and the end of the hallway leading to a basketball court. "They give us twenty minutes for break, then lunch, for those of us still eating."

Cool autumn air brushed my face as I followed her outside to the paved courtyard, the other students gathered around stone tables or basketball goals. Voices echoed around the space, the towers of Crimson Hollow dark and looming over us, casting shadows shaped as spears. Beyond us stretched the forest, leaves of brown and gold whirling in the wind as they got tugged away from branches. I couldn't see the graveyard from here. Probably better that way.

"Want to play a game of horse?" Chloe's voice cut through my thoughts. She dribbled a basketball, its *thud-thud-thud* echoing.

"Sure." I forced my hands out of my hoodie's pockets.

"Li," she yelled at the girl on the bench, her face hidden behind a book. "You in?"

She closed her book, then stood.

"Fine." She wandered to us, her eyes bloodshot and vacant. Her thin frame bordered on anorexic.

"Where's your brother?" I asked Chloe as she took the first shot. The ball bounced off the rim.

"Sick. He went back to the room." She tossed the ball to me, and I caught it.

"Will he be okay?"

She pinched her lips, shaking her head, as if I'd asked something off-limits.

"Let me rephrase. Do you think he'll feel better soon?"

"Yeah. He needs to rest. His case is more severe than mine. Dr. Warren tells him if he loses weight and gets a healthy BMI, his symptoms will be better, but you know, he likes Sunkist and Pop-Tarts too much."

I took a shot. The ball hit the backboard but bounced off. Li caught it, her long arms and legs giving her an advantage as she sank the ball through the hoop with a swish of the net.

"Nice one!" Chloe caught the ball, planting her feet where Li had stood, then took a shot and missed. "I got an H! I suck at this. Your turn, Amaya."

I grabbed the ball from her, focusing on the goal when a looming presence caught my eye. A black-clad figure stood at the library's second-floor window, sunlight dappling his tall, imposing frame corded with muscle.

Even from here, his gaze bored into mine. My skin grew overly warm at the sight of sunglasses and hands hidden in pockets.

Unnerved, I took a shot, but it hit the rim and bounced off. Chloe caught the ball. Her eyes widened as she looked to the window. She snuck to my side and caught my arm, leaning close.

"Don't say anything, but I think Lucian's watching us," she whispered.

"You think so?" I asked.

"Yeah." She frowned at me. "What did you talk about at game night?"

"Nothing much. We talked about my dog and my parents, then he left."

She raised an eyebrow. "That's it?"

"That's it."

She pinched her lips. "I think he's into you."

"Don't be silly," I said. "You said he wasn't into girls at the facility."

"Maybe. Maybe not." She bit her lip. "He's not bad looking. He's got that dark, mysterious vibe, you know?"

I didn't answer, but yes… I knew.

Li placed her hands on her hips. "Are we playing?"

I tossed the ball to her. "You go ahead. I need to take care of something."

"You're going inside?" Chloe asked.

I glanced back at the window where Lucian stood. My stomach clenched at his presence, and my heart thudded. I only had a month to find what I needed, and I wasn't going to do that here on the basketball court. Since Lucian was in the library, the other students were out here, and Dr. Warren was gone, now would be my chance to sneak into his office.

"I've gotta let my dog out. I'll be back for lunch." Lying made me cringe, but what other choice did I have?

"Fine," Chloe said with a sigh. The dribbling ball echoed as I crossed through the courtyard, passing patients who sat without speaking, their eyes tracking me.

High ceilings rose over me as I entered the facility. Gothic arches were spaced evenly through the foyer as I crossed over the black-and-white tiles. Chilly air bristled my skin. I stuck my hands in my pockets, imagining what it would be like to keep them constantly hidden in gloves.

I breathed deeply to calm my nerves.

Lucian's presence disturbed me more than I cared to admit. I took the hallway to the right, sunlight bright on the floor, passing by a janitor who stood with a mop in hand as I walked past.

The next hallway connected the new building with the old, made apparent by sheetrock walls turned to red bricks.

I left sunlit hallways for a dim, narrow passage that ended in a room labeled *Warren, Victor Hugo, M.D. V.S.A.*

I gripped the doorknob and turned. Locked.

Of course it was. With a sigh, I turned away. Was there a chance I could steal another key from Officer Goodman? Looking through the doctor's files had been his suggestion, after all. But I got the feeling he was only willing to help me with certain things, and I couldn't push him too far or he'd have no choice but to punish me.

"Looking for something?"

Officer Goodman's voice made me jump as I stepped into the foyer. He leaned against one of the pillars, thumbs casually in his belt loops. His giant keyring jangled as he stood straight.

"Um. Bathroom?" I lied.

"Yeah. Funny thing. It's not down there."

"Oh. Sorry." I tried to sidestep him when he blocked my path.

"Might wanna come back later. I heard the janitor gets off at ten, but if you come around midnight, sometimes he leaves the door unlocked."

I gave him a searching glance. His friendly, round face, easygoing smile, and crew cut hair gave him the look of the middle-aged neighbor next door.

"Why are you helping me?" I asked quietly.

His smile faded. "Because some of us are interested in the truth," he whispered back. He pointed to the opposite hallway. "Bathroom's that way."

"Thanks," I mumbled, stepping away from him, feeling his eyes follow me.

Interested in the truth?

Was it possible my mom wasn't the only one who saw flaws in Dr. Warren's research? If so, what did Officer Goodman have to do with it?

Midnight, I repeated in my head, passing by the bathroom on my way to lunch.

9

A transcript from Emanuel Rogers, MD.Ph.D. LCSW, MFT 08.25.05
11:16 AM EST

Lucian: Fire everywhere. Smoke. I can't breathe.
Dr. Rogers: Are you afraid?
Lucian: Terrified.

~

AMAYA

My phone's alarm woke me. I stared through bleary eyes at the crack of light coming under the bathroom door. My stomach churned as I shut off the alarm and sat up. Khan, curled up by my feet, raised his head as I stood.

The hardwood floor chilled my bare feet, a shock compared to my carpet back home.

Home.

Waking to heavenly smells of French toast and coffee during Christmas break. Dad's deep voice coming from the kitchen table. Mom's quiet laughter.

A pang of loneliness gripped me so strongly, tears sprang to my eyes, and I had to push down the oversized knot in my throat.

I patted Khan's head to keep my emotions under control. With Mom and Dad gone, I'd hang on to him for as long as I could.

"It'll be okay, Buddy," I said, voice cracking as I stroked his head, golden eyes locked onto mine. "We've got each other."

With a deep breath, I stood and got my bearings. The hum of the dehumidifier played a background noise to the computer modem under the desk in the corner. The over-sweet smell of honeysuckle came from a plug-in air freshener. It masked the muskiness emanating from the building's years of disuse.

I checked the time. Ten minutes till midnight. After using the bathroom and splashing water on my face, I rubbed at the dark circles under my eyes. Standing at the sink, my reflection showed my dark irises tinted red, tell-tale signs of viridae sangre running through my blood, morphing my body. If I managed to beat this, would I go back to living a normal life again? Go back to Miami U? Become a virologist like Mom?

I combed my fingers through the long strands of my dark hair. My face had grown paler since I'd come here, not that I'd had much color to begin with, since I'd inherited Mom's skin tone. My nose was too wide, my bottom teeth crooked, and I had a mole on my neck that had caused significant amounts of teasing in elementary school.

He only goes for supermodels.

I placed my hand on the glass, covering my face's reflection, as if I didn't exist. *Dating* was a taboo subject for me, as I had no skills in the area, my life absorbed in grades and helping Mom study VS. Plus, anyone I'd been attracted to had ignored me, so I'd stopped trying a long time ago. It wouldn't be any different with Lucian.

Like I had a chance. Like I wanted a chance.

Shaking my head, I stepped away from the mirror.

"Come on, Buddy," I mumbled to him as I checked my phone. Five minutes till midnight.

After slipping a hoodie over my green camo tank top, I put on my tennis shoes, grabbed my backpack with the flashlight inside, and stepped into the hallway. Khan trotted at my side. My rubber-soled shoes tread quietly over the linoleum through the vacant hallway.

I passed through the open foyer. The black-and-white tiles turned ghostly from the moonlight seeping through the floor-to-ceiling windows that rose three stories.

Quiet footsteps came behind me.

Grabbing Khan's collar, I turned around. Nothing but pillars and an open floor surrounded me.

A whispered female voice carried through the giant, open space.

My hands grew clammy as I held the collar in a tight fist. Khan stood still, tail between his legs, sniffing intently.

"Is something there, boy?" I whispered.

A growl rumbled in his chest. Heart pounding, I swallowed my fear, my thoughts turning to the thousands of mental patients who'd died here. Some who'd killed themselves. Flashes of a photograph invaded my thoughts, a black-and-white image of woman wearing a nightdress dangling from a noose, tied to the crossbeams above me.

I sped my pace, the heavy pounding of my heart like a drum in my chest, sweat slicking my hands.

Ghosts aren't real, I told myself, but with the cold chills bristling over my skin, fear like a palpable entity brushing at the hairs on the nape of my neck, it was hard to believe.

With nothing but silence pressing in, I backed toward the hallway, leaving the foyer behind. A few lights glowed overhead, their buzzing lending to the eerie quality of the facility at midnight.

Good thing I had Khan with me.

I walked into the hallway lined in red bricks, the date *1897* stamped into one.

Focus. Dr. Warren's research. Constatin Vidraru. The missing piece to the puzzle.

The heaviness in my chest made it hard to draw breath. The hallway ended at the paneled wooden door, Dr. Warren's golden name plaque glowing with a ghostly sheen in the buzzing lights from overhead.

Fingers stiff from cold, I grabbed the knob and turned. The door opened. Unlocked, just as Officer Goodman had known it would be.

After glancing at the empty hallway behind me, I entered the office of Dr. Warren.

10

An excerpt from the journal of Constantin Vidraru. 22 April 1865.
Bran, Romania. Castle Bran

Everyone experiences life the same.
We share the same years, same minutes, same
seconds.
Time links our every breath.

~

LUCIAN

The nightmare woke me.

Four posts of my bed rose toward the ceiling, as if they watched me like standing sentinels, conjuring images from another life spent in Bran castle, in a bed like this, with gargoyles carved into the wood.

I sat up, breathing deeply, then grabbed my shirt off the bed cover and pulled it over my head. It stuck to my chest's clammy skin and I had to tug it into place.

That same dream.

Smoke. Fire. Scalding flames. Her voice screaming.

Nausea churned through my stomach, and I sat on the edge of my bed, moonlight drifting through the sheer curtains. Through the open window, the hooting of an owl came from the forest.

I scrubbed my hands over my face, breathing in the night-time air drifting from outside. Unable to shake the dream's images from my head, I stood and slipped on my sandals, leaving my sunglasses and gloves on the nightstand.

The cover of night gave me freedom.

My eyes adjusted as I walked through dark halls. Walls and doors stood out in sharp clarity, the images coming through my retinas made clearer in the night. When I stepped outside, cool air washed over me. I breathed in the scent of autumn leaves.

When I entered the forest, the sound of my shoes crunching over twigs, and of branches stirring in the wind, helped to drive away images of burning flesh. A field mouse scurried across my path. Its body heat appeared as a bright spot against a shaded canvas.

I trailed my fingers over the softness of leaves and bumpy tree bark, soaking in the moment without hands covered in leather. After weaving through the trunks, I came to the open field where granite headstones glinted with a silvery sheen in the moonlight.

Wandering paths lined in grave markers, my gaze snagged on the facility standing out against a starry sky, turrets and gray stones bringing memories of the castle where I'd grown up.

Lifetimes ago.

So long ago that the memories came like the faded images of a dream. Sometimes I had trouble believing those lives had really happened. Had I imagined Mamá, the tanginess of her cabbage rolls, the rich scent of polenta with cheese and sour cream? Maybe I'd made up the nights spent looking through

Tată's diaries of inked dragons, sphinxes, or phoenixes, his intellectual musings, his discourses on mythological creatures. His obsession with studying vampires.

Shaking my head, I pushed the memories away, choosing to focus on the present, on the headstones, the grass under my feet, the bodies lying quietly beneath me, surrounded in dirt and eternal silence. Eternal rest.

Death will hold no place for you, Lucian, Tată's words came to me. Hate ran like poison through my heart. How I wished he'd never had such dreams for me. Didn't he understand what a lonely existence he'd cursed me with? Grieving the deaths of loved ones only to experience the same again and again, until making connections became too painful, and I had no choice but to detach from humanity, to live as a ghost among mortals.

At one point, I'd foolishly thought it would get better, that the sting of death wouldn't hurt so much, but it only got worse.

A light appeared in a window. Third floor.

Cocking my head, I watched the light grow dim and bright again.

Odd.

Dr. Warren's office was on the third floor. But wasn't he in Taiwan?

Could it be the janitor?

Cleaning the doctor's office at midnight?

No. He always left at ten P.M.

Sticking my hands in my pockets, I watched the light dim and brighten, as if someone were using a flashlight.

Amaya.

Grumbling, I hiked away from the serenity of the grave-yard and to the doors leading inside.

If I had the ability to die, she would be the cause of it.

11

From the journal of Barbara Anne Johnson Vidraru, March 30, 1958

He makes me laugh. Makes me feel human. That's why I love him.

~

AMAYA

The musty scent of old paper surrounded me. I pointed my phone's light at the rows of filing cabinets caging me in. At the rear of the office, a small, spiral staircase led to another floor. How much knowledge had been hidden away here? Captured, contained, never to see the light of the scientific world?

My heart thudded with anxiousness. Mom had been researching the virus for so long but making any breakthroughs had been impossible. Her words rang in my head.

It should be cured, Amaya. Dr. Warren has a stranglehold on the CDC. He owns all the research and keeps it under lock and key. Why does this virus keep popping up in random locations all over the world? If there's one thing I've learned as a virologist, it's to follow patterns. If Ebola breaks out in West Africa, you confine it there. You keep it from spreading. But Dr. Warren hasn't done that. Why? They're hiding something. They're hiding the truth.

I'd been dreaming of this for so long, it was hard to believe I was here. Khan paced close, his nose sniffing at the dust motes. My footsteps echoed, the ceiling a dome of rock overhead, as if I were in a dungeon.

Rows of letters and numbers stood out on the metal. I stopped at the end and pulled out the drawer labeled V. I held my flashlight in one hand while I leafed through the folders with my other until I got to the folder labeled *Vidraru, C.*

I grasped the manila, but glanced up before pulling it out, making sure I was alone. An empty row of filing cabinets stretched. Still, my heart fluttered with nervousness as I sat on the floor and opened the folder.

Holding my light over the pages, I scanned through photocopied notes written in Romanian. Numbers, weights, and some scientific names—Canis Lupus and Desmodontinae, or vampire bat—I understood. A page at the back caught my attention.

Words scrawled in English were written in the margins. *The nature of the sample consists of properties inconsistent with any other creature found in nature.*

I whispered to myself. "What sample?"

I flipped to the next page. *Original viridae sangre information stored in files VC109-11.*

Placing my phone on the floor, I mulled over the information. If I could find the information on samples of the original virus, I could compare them to the virus being transmitted now. Find out why Lucian stayed alive when everyone else died.

Standing, I slid the folder into the shelf.

Khan's fur brushed my legs as I searched through the numbered cabinets.

What are you hiding here? I mumbled as I walked, then stopped at VC109 near the front of the room by Dr. Warren's heavy oak desk. A few pictures of people on a beach of powdery white sand reflected from frames on the desktop. I felt as if their eyes followed me in the light of my phone's camera.

The cabinet slid on quiet wheels as I rolled open the drawer. I took out a stack of folders, then placed them on the doctor's desk. Unease crept quietly through the dark corner of my mind, and I had to swallow the fear rising inside.

If I got caught…

No. I couldn't think that way.

Khan's wet nose sniffed my hand as I placed the manila folder on the desktop, office chair creaking as I shifted my weight, using the flashlight to scan over the pages. A clock hanging on the wall ticked too loudly. My heart pounded, and my stomach turned sour as I sorted through the pages.

I fanned through the recent records, nothing but patient names, dates, locations.

I replaced one folder and grabbed the next, moving back through the file to the last ten years of research. More names. Birth dates. Death dates. Places of origin. Outbreak locations.

Opening the bottom drawer, I pulled out an envelope marked *Travel Receipts*. After placing it on the desk, I leafed through copies of airline tickets from all over the world. *Madrid, Spain. Providence, Rhode Island. Santiago, Chile. Hanoi, Vietnam.* Were they the places Dr. Warren had traveled? I'd have to check to make sure, so I grabbed my phone and took a picture of the receipts.

I walked away from the desk to rows of filing cabinets along the back wall. After opening the drawer, I read the dates on the files. Ten years ago. I looked through them all. Still nothing.

Pointing my flashlight's beam at the last cabinet on the row, I walked to the bottom drawer and opened it.

I leafed through the files organized by dates. 1975, 1974, 1973.

I pulled out each file until I got to the last one. 1972.

The beginning.

Cold tiles chilled my legs as I sat on the floor with the manila folder opened in my lap. Flashlight in one hand, I leafed through the yellowed pages, words typed in blocky letters in purple print, until I stopped at the first page.

Primary Carrier:

Sally Louise Anderson

Female

Age at death: 21 years.

Date of Birth: 12.06.1950

Date of Death: 07.05.1972

Place of Birth: San Francisco, San Francisco County, California

Place of Death: Campus of Purdue University. West Lafayette, Indiana.

Cause of death: HOMICIDE

A newspaper clipping had been stapled to the back. WOMAN DIES AT HANDS OF LIVING VAMPIRE.

Reading the article, it described Sally Anderson, college student, who had been brutally attacked and bitten by Lucian Vidraru, which had started the spread of the vampire virus. A picture of a young woman stood out on the faded paper. Light eyes and dark, feathered hair reminded me of a young Scarlett O'Hara. Her smile didn't show her teeth.

Of course I already knew Sally's story well enough. Lucian had bitten her. Before her death, she'd gone crazy and spread the virus that eventually killed tens of thousands. He'd gotten locked up and died in prison a year later. Only…

I took out my phone from my pocket and snapped a shot of the page, then replaced the file. Another paper brushed my hand, one that had been stuffed in the bottom.

Pulling it out, I focused my flashlight beam on the page. I

had to keep from vomiting as I looked over the gruesome black-and-white autopsy photos. Dark blood contrasted light skin. A following page stapled to the back showed a drawing of a woman with locations of wounds sketched onto the neck and breasts. Seventeen bite marks were deep enough to tear through skin and sever arteries.

He hadn't just bitten her.

He'd mutilated her.

I placed a hand on my stomach. Queasiness churned through my insides. I'd chatted with him, shared a conversation about my dog. I could even admit to admiring him, but he was nothing but a cold-blooded murderer.

I shook my head, clearing my thoughts. I had to focus. After replacing the report, I shuffled through the folders until I reached one labeled *VC111*.

It read: *Modern mutations of viridae sangre.*

With a glance at the door, I turned to the paper and scanned the information. The original sample contained 200mg./ltr. antibodies per sample, as opposed to 3,500 mg./ltr in a modern sample of the virus.

I tapped my fingers on the desk. What did it mean?

The disease Lucian carried had fewer antibodies than the modern virus samples? If that were the case, then victims of the modern virus were literally being overcrowded with so many antibodies, their blood was being suffocated of vital cells and damaging organs.

But Lucian's virus had less, meaning his body could repair at an advanced rate of healing without damaging his organs.

But how had his virus mutated? What changed in 1972 when he bit Sally Anderson? Was it a natural mutation? Or had it been engineered to be more aggressive?

A scribbled note on the bottom of the page caught my attention. *Refer to upstairs vault in Archive Five for more information.*

Archive Five?

The doorknob rattled.

Heart racing, I clicked off my flashlight, plunging me and Khan into darkness. I stuffed the paper in the filing cabinet. After grabbing my backpack, I felt along the wall. Rough bricks gave way to the staircase.

I treaded on quiet feet up the winding stairs, keeping my hand pressed to the rough stone wall, Khan trailing quietly behind me until I reached the first landing.

Muted moonlight came from a stained-glass window in the tower's far wall, illuminating the form of an embellished wooden door and a bronze number 5 tacked to it.

Archive Five?

I grabbed the bronze knob, but it wouldn't turn.

Locked. I grumbled under my breath. Not surprising. Nothing came easy in this place.

Below, the door creaked open.

Heart pounding, I signaled Khan not to bark as I searched for another way out. The stairwell led up to another floor, though a chain had been strung across the threshold.

I didn't have time to second guess my decisions, so I stepped over the chain, careful not to rattle the links. Hands sweaty, I clamped the nylon fibers of Khan's leash and tiptoed up the stairs. Dust stirred, tickling my nose. Old wood creaked under my feet. In the light of the moon, we reached the tower's attic.

Moonlight glowed through a window, revealing an empty room. Framed wooden beams replaced an actual floor. Scaffolding ringed the walls and supported the ceiling. A few planks of wood were scattered atop the beams to create walkways.

A fragile stillness blanketed the area. It seemed as if the hundred-year old beams would snap at the tiniest movement.

Footsteps echoed in the room below us. Sweat slicked my skin. Nausea swirled in my stomach. If Lucian found me here, what would he do?

The image of Sally's corpse had seared into my memory. Haunting me. The dark blood. The open wounds.

Assuming it was him down there, would he do the same to me?

On the opposite end of the room sat a deep alcove hidden in shadow. Could I make it across the room without falling? Did I have a choice?

"*Come on, Buddy*," I whispered. Keeping the leash fisted in my hand, I balanced over the planks of wood. Dust stirred. Old lumber creaked under our feet. The air turned chill. A damp sheen of sweat turned cold on my overheated skin.

Footsteps echoed beneath. The stairs creaked. I glanced down. A man with a bald head stalking beneath me.

Fear settled like a stone deep in the pit of my stomach. I couldn't let him find me here. The picture of Sally Anderson left no doubt of his capabilities. He would kill me the way he'd killed her.

I hopped to another plywood board.

We made it halfway when the wood cracked. I stopped, heart pounding like a metal drum. Holding completely still, my breathing sounded too loud. Khan whined softly, his shaking body pressed to my legs. I patted his head, then shuffled another step forward.

Splintered wood exploded around me. My stomach lurched as I fell. I grabbed for a handhold. Sweaty fingers gripped a wooden beam. My left arm jerked as Khan dropped. His leash wrapped my hand and dug into my skin until my torn muscles screamed with pain.

My dog yelped. He hung suspended over the floor more than two dozen feet below. His collar choked him. His body spun as he clawed at the air. He looked up at me, pleadingly, yellow eyes wide with fear.

My hand slid on the beam.

Heart racing, I attempted to lift Khan, but the movement made splinters dig into my fingertips. My muscles burned.

Khan panted frantically, yelping a high-pitched wail.

I clenched my jaw as I tried a second time to lift him up, but only managed to slip again. Tears stung my eyes. I tasted the salty tang of sweat on my tongue.

All-consuming panic flooded my blood. I would never live with myself if I dropped him. But if I didn't, we would both fall to our deaths.

No! I couldn't lose him.

The leash slipped. His collar loosened.

"Buddy," I yelled, when strong hands gripped my arm and lifted me up.

Lucian stood over me. He pulled me up through the hole and onto the platform, then he grabbed the leash and pulled until Khan reached the floor.

Tears streamed down my face as I clutched my dog to my chest. My family. My life. Was it stupid to love an animal so much?

No. Not when he was the only family I had.

Khan's wet tongue licked the tears from my cheek. Laughing, I couldn't help but realize I was alive. He was alive. But…

Lucian stood over me. Hands hidden behind his back. Smooth head reflected in the moonlight. Facial features darkened by shadow—as they always were.

My breath came in short, gulping gasps. Hands clammy, I hugged Khan close.

"You okay?" Lucian asked, still standing over me, keeping his distance. Eyes shadowed, though the outline of his glasses was missing. Why wasn't he wearing them?

He saved me. He could've let me fall to my death. But he saved me.

"I'm fine. Shaken up."

"What are you doing up here?" he asked, his tone sharp. "I'm sure you've already realized this, but it's not safe. This tower was condemned a decade ago. I guess you see why."

"Yeah." I gulped, swallowing the lump of fear lodged in my throat.

Breathing deeply, I attempted to calm down. In the little light from the window, all I could make out was his lanky silhouette.

"You shouldn't be here." He knelt to face me, only the dark outline of his frame visible in the soft light. "You already got in trouble for breaking into my room. Do I need to call security again? Or will you tell me what you're doing?"

I let go of my pent-up breath. "I have my reasons."

I crossed my arms over my chest. Khan trotted away from me, tail wagging as he went to Lucian.

Traitor.

He patted my dog's head, and Khan's tail wagged faster.

"What reasons?" he asked, his voice deep, edged with warning.

The image of Sally Anderson's autopsy photos intruded on my thoughts. Although the world accepted him, I knew better than to trust a murderer. Even if he had just saved mine and my dog's lives, that didn't wipe away his past sins. I said nothing. But Lucian had saved us. If he wanted me dead, he would've let me fall. And I needed answers.

"I'm trying to find a cure for the virus."

"Why?" he asked.

"Because you won't."

He sat back on his heels. "That's harsh."

"It's the truth." I rose to stand over him. His eyes glinted in the moonlight. Dark eyes. In these shadows, I couldn't tell anything else about them. "My mom came here last year. Dr. De la Vega."

I flinched as he stood to face me. "Yes. She demanded things we couldn't give her. Said we were hiding our research. Keeping the truth from people. We kicked her out. Are you here for the same reasons?"

"Possibly."

He took a step closer. The scent of amber spice wafted over me. I stared into his face, chiseled features, eyes too dark to make out their color. What compelled me to stay here when I should've bolted?

Was it because he had the answers to my questions? Or was it something else?

"Sally Anderson," I said. "Why did you attack her?"

Was it my imagination? Or did he growl? "*Don't* say that name."

"Why not?"

He flexed his fists. "There's a few rules you need to figure out about this place. Number one. Never mention that person." He stepped away from me, then nodded to the stairs. "Let's go before we all fall to our deaths."

I followed him out of the room and to the stairs, my breath slowing only a little. Being in his presence made it difficult to think. Not only did fear cloud my mind, but another sensation nagged at me—a feeling that made my heart speed in an unexpected way. It bothered me more than the panic.

We reached the landing where the locked door of Archive Five stood out in the light of the stained-glass window. I still hadn't gotten a good answer about Sally. Would he answer me if I questioned him about the door? I tugged on his shirt, stopping him.

He rounded so quickly, I feared he would hit me. "What?" he demanded.

His unexpected movement made me back to the door. But I wouldn't let him see my fear, even if my heart did feel as if it would pound through my chest wall.

"The door." I nodded over my shoulder. "Why is it locked? What's in there?"

He worked his jaw back and forth, strong muscles straining with the movement. Shaking his head, he thrust his jaw. "That's another question I can't answer."

"Can't or won't?"

He pressed his hand to the door behind me, towering over me, a looming presence that sent a tingle of one-part fear and another part excitement shooting down my spine.

"Both," he snapped, anger apparent in the clipped tone of the single word. His hand fisted, but instead of striking me, he took a deep breath, as if to control his anger, then gestured to the door. "Why are you so curious about this?"

I stroked Khan's back, his fur soft and comforting, and I found the strength to let go of my fear. "Because I'm a primary carrier, Lucian, and I'd like to live."

"You don't trust Dr. Warren to save you?"

"No. I really don't."

"Why?" He took a step toward me.

I shook my head. Despite my vow not to show my fear, I took a cautious step back and bumped into the door.

"Am I scaring you?" he asked, a calculated question.

"No," I snapped, standing tall, hoping he didn't hear my voice tremble.

He reached out and touched my cheek. I held my breath. His finger was so light it could've been the brush of a butterfly's wing. My skin rippled with goose bumps. "Your heart is pounding. You're either scared…or something else."

I cleared my throat. "What do you mean?" I attempted a casual tone.

His already dark eyes seemed to grow darker, if that were possible. "The emotions that result from sexual attraction."

"I-I'm…No!"

He chuckled, a deep sound that resonated through his chest. As my eyes adjusted to the dark, I saw his roguish smile. His evenly spaced white teeth and full lips were displayed for only me to see.

"You aren't wearing your glasses," I said, finally finding my voice.

"I don't need them at night." His voice turned velvety, husky, the slightest hint of seduction laced through his words.

I cleared my throat as it squeezed shut. I almost asked to turn on the light, to see what he kept hidden, but I resisted. I'd already pushed him too far with the mention of Sally Anderson.

"Do I need to call Officer Goodman?" he asked.

I stiffened. I couldn't let poor Goodman get involved on my account, not after all he'd done for me. "No."

"Are you sure? It seems like this habit of breaking into places is getting worse."

Minty breath brushed my cheeks, and his shirt held the scent of spruce. What could I say to keep him close? "Maybe you can help me?"

He cocked his head. "Help you?"

"Help me figure out the virus. Find out why it mutated from the original virus. Help me survive."

"I'm already doing that. Dr. Warren and I have been working on it since he woke me."

Woke me. The words sounded so strange.

"But you're hiding something." I wasn't sure if I was pushing him too far, but since I only had a month to live, there was no time for minced words. "What's inside? Is it a map that points to the origins of the virus?" I pointed behind me. "Is it written in your father's letter?"

He sucked in a breath and took a step back, turning to look at the window. Moonlight illuminated his profile that resembled a Roman statue. A smooth bald scalp, flat forehead, a nose with a sloping curve that prominently protruded from his face, and a square jawline. He stood with a straight back, hiding his hands in his pockets.

"You should go," he said quietly.

"Go?"

He shook his head. "I can't talk to you."

His words stung. "Why?"

"Because you shouldn't be in here. You shouldn't be looking into things you have no business knowing about."

"Why, Lucian? What are you hiding?"

He faced me, a flash of red shimmering over his dark pupils. "Some things stay hidden for good reason." He walked to the window, standing with hands clasped behind his back, facing away from me. "Leave me alone, Amaya."

"I will soon enough." *When I'm dead*, I wanted to add, but the way he said my name already sounded so final, I thought it best not to goad further. I grabbed my backpack, made sure I had my phone tucked inside my pocket, and walked toward the stairs. Khan faithfully followed me. I pressed my hand to the wall as I descended the steps, leaving Lucian and his secrets behind.

12

YouTube Transcript from James D. Steele's channel FLUGGED, posted on August 25. 11:01 PM CST

Hello *FLUGGERS!* **Thank you for watching today's video. Before I get started, don't forget to hit that Like button and subscribe to be notified of updates, including conspiracy theories, the truth behind the government's control of vaxxing, and the latest flat earth research. Also, be sure to check out my merch. We've added some new hats with the flat earth logo which are way awesome, so check it out. Today, I'm talking about the conman who calls himself a vampire, Lucian Vidraru.**

Let me make one thing clear. Lucian Vidraru is a fraud. Plain and Simple. People have argued that if he's a fraud, why make up such a crazy-ass story?

Money. Get it? Mon-ney. The man has made a crap ton of money from his supposed life story. Don't believe his story, my friends. Do. Not. Believe. Him. I mean, look at his supposed evidence.

Did he fake his birth certificate? Hell yeah.

Did he fake the photos which are blurrier than Bigfoot's ass? You bet he did.

Did he fake the doctor's records from World War Two? Sure did.

It's called Photoshop, people.

Now let's get to the real reasons why he's a fraud.

First of all, does this man look one-hundred-and-sixty-something to you? I mean, he should basically look like a skeleton with skin. Seriously. Let's think about this logically. It's impossible for the human body to live that long. Your skin and bones and blood and organs break down. They just can't exist that long. Seriously. He's that old and hasn't even aged? I call BS.

I don't care what kind of cells you have, it's not scientifically possible for your body to survive that long without breaking down.

Second of all, if you're gonna make up a story, make sure it's believable. Mr. Vidraru, let me give you some advice. If you're gonna pretend to be a vampire, stop wasting your time with those stupid-ass sunglasses. Am I right? The man won't take them off because he's afraid he'll scare people? Give me a break. Take off the frickin' glasses, sir. You're not hiding anything from us.

Last thing, and this one's a doozy, my friends. His supposed amnesia. Yeah, you've lived two centuries, but there are gaps in your memory? If that's the case for judging what's true, then I'm the love child of Marilyn Monroe and Marvin the Martian.

Leave me a message in the comments with your thoughts. Do you think Lucian Vidraru is a fraud? Peace out. Don't forget to subscribe!

COMMENTS:

⊛ *He's a total fraud i've never believed he was a*

vampire for one minute. Give me a break. He is totally hot tho.

⊕ He's a conman. I've always known that. Good work, bro, keep up the good content!

⊕ theres 666 tattooed on his eyes and im not even lying. Seen it in a youtube video and it is real that's why he won't show his eyes. His name is Lucian and that means Lucifer. Som of you freaks may not believe me but youd better because he'll be coming after you and don't think he won't. he'll drink your blood and turn you into one of him. Not even joking. Its true and im not even lying.

⊕ I don't know why everyone pretends he's some kind of superstar. The man is a MURDERER! He killed tens of thousands of people and committed one of the worse crimes in modern history. Can't stand people who treat him like he's a friggin god and forgiven of everything. All you have to do is say sorry and you can just erase the fact that you killed all those people? Makes me so flipping enraged.

⊕ Watch here. Reverse your diabetes now!->> http://www.diablife.xo.life72899.zom.

⊕ I find the lack of research in this post deeply disturbing. Has anyone bothered to look at the evidence? The fibers in his birth certificate have been carbon dated to 160 years old, and the test has been run MULTIPLE times! The microbiological tests done on him show his cellular structure to be markedly different from any other human's. This is public record. There are hundreds of complete, intact, and clear photos of the man dating from 1917 to today, and he is unchanged in every single one. The list goes on. Look it up. Get educated. I can't believe I'm arguing this.

~

AMAYA

I took a bite of chicken patty. Was it the virus making it taste like sand?

Chloe plopped her tray across from me, spilling green beans onto the table. She sat on the bench as she picked up the soggy vegetables, then popped them into her mouth.

Her eyebrows rose as she took in my messy ponytail and my mom's old Anime t-shirt with the faded Japanese characters and a hole worn through the sleeve.

"Not feeling well today?" she asked while chewing. Her bright pink sweater with the scrolling glittery words *Smart Girl's Club* hurt my eyes.

I managed to swallow the bite of chicken. "I didn't sleep well," I admitted.

"Yeah. Pretty common symptom."

"I don't think it's the virus's fault."

She waved her fork at me. "Then why?"

I shrugged. "I don't know."

"Come clean, Amaya. Something's bothering you. What's up?"

I tapped my fingers on the table. I had no one else to talk to. What was the harm in admitting my problems to her? "Lucian," I answered, my tone bitter.

Her lips formed a thin line, as if she weren't surprised. "Umm-hmm," she said with an I-told-you-so tone. "Didn't Damian warn you?"

"Yeah. He did."

"Well, don't take it personally. Lucian's not interested in people like us."

"Yeah. I get it." I took another bite of chicken patty. *Gross.* "This food tastes awful," I said, hoping to steer the conversation in a different direction.

"Tastes fine to me, but Dr. Warren says my virus hasn't advanced. Have you been checked out recently?"

I shook my head.

"Might want to do that if food isn't tasting right." She twirled strands of hair around her finger in a nervous gesture. "You've got the primary virus, after all."

"Yeah," I frowned, placing my fork on the table. "I remember."

"Then it's probably advancing faster." Chloe frowned as she glanced at her tray. "Damian got hooked to bleeding tubes last night. He hates it. Says he wants a cheeseburger. It's so stupid. Once people get hooked up, they feel like they're starving all the time."

"I'm sorry to hear that."

Shrugging, she acted as if it didn't bother her, but I saw the pain in her eyes. She sniffed and rubbed her nose on her sleeve. "Damian thinks you're cute, you know." A hint of a smile tugged at her mouth.

"Me?" I asked, shocked.

"Don't be so surprised. You're fresh meat." She glanced away. "Um. That didn't come out the way I wanted. I guess you're not supposed to say things like that around vampires." Her gaze went to the other people in the lunchroom, quiet conversations filling the air. "I'm scared, Amaya," she said in a small voice.

"Yeah," I answered. "So am I."

I followed her gaze, looking over the several dozen people, most of them in their twenties or younger, wondering which half would make it and which would join Daddy in the graveyard.

"You want to come with me?" Chloe asked, her tone peppy again. "I promised to visit Damian after lunch. He wanted me to slip him a Sunkist."

"Is he supposed to drink that?"

"No. But he'll try anyway. You game?"

"Sure." I placed my fork aside, my stomach churning, the few bites of chicken patty threatening to come up. Nothing like a little nausea to make me completely rethink my genius plan to poke myself with a needle containing a deadly virus.

After dumping our trays and returning them to the kiosk, we wandered out the doors leading into the hallway.

I rubbed my eyes, stifling a yawn as I followed Chloe under the shadows of tall, looming pillars. I couldn't stop thinking about Lucian and Sally Anderson. What had happened in 1972? Why had Lucian, someone seemingly non-violent, bitten and mutilated an innocent college girl? He claimed he wasn't a vampire, so why had he acted like one?

Lucian had made it clear the topic was off-limits, which only made me want to know more. What were the real reasons Lucian and Dr. Warren were keeping their research under lock and key?

I'd spent a few hours last night going over Dr. Warren's travel expenses. It all checked out. Each country he'd visited had experienced an outbreak, and he'd arrived in time to treat them. But why the disease had popped up in those countries was still a mystery. Would Lucian know? Would he tell me?

Most likely not.

Which left me with researching Sally Anderson. I'd probably end up at a dead end again, but I had nothing else to go on. Plus, Lucian had a sordid history with her, and part of me wanted to know what had really happened.

Chloe stopped at a vending machine and put a few quarters in it with the clanging of metal. A bright orange soda dropped to the bottom. Chloe removed a Sunkist that she tucked under her shirt.

She pressed a finger to her lips. "No telling. 'Kay?"

I nodded, then followed her up to the second floor. We stopped at a door labeled with a sign written in magic marker that read *Quiet Please. Patient in Critical Care.*

My stomach churned at the implications of the message.

Damian had been fine when I'd met him, and now he was critical?

She opened the door and I followed her into the room. Sterile white walls, the beeping of machines accompanied by the noise from daytime TV, and the sharp scent of antiseptic reminded me of a hospital.

Damian sat propped up on pillows, his eyes vacant as he watched *The Price is Right*. His gaze went to us as we crossed to him. I sat in the only chair by the window, and Chloe sat on the foot of the bed, eyes darting before pulling the Sunkist from under her shirt and passing it to her brother.

His face lit up as he grabbed it from her.

Soda fizzed as he opened the cap. He made a face as he took a sip, then placed it on the bedside table. I tried not to stare at the tube extending from his stomach, blood running from a bag hanging on a metal hanger above him.

"Doesn't taste right?" she asked.

He shook his head. "Tastes like metal."

"Well, I tried."

He let out a lengthy sigh. "I know. Least I've got this." He pointed to the stomach tube.

She nodded to me. "I brought company."

A ghost of a smile crossed his face as he turned to me. "Hey, Amaya."

"Hey. How are..." *Wait—dumb question.* "Um, how's the show?" I nodded to the TV.

"It's okay. Someone just won Plinko. Got a thousand dollars."

"Cool."

"Yeah."

I cleared my throat, shuffling my feet over the floor.

"If you're feeling up to it, what do you think of going to Saratoga this weekend?" Chloe asked.

He shrugged. "Maybe."

I didn't hear much conviction in his voice.

"We could go to Morgenstern's and get some ice cream," she continued. "I mean, I know how much you love—*loved* it. If you're able to eat it and all. And we could go to a movie or something."

"Sure," he said with a forced smile.

Chloe glanced at me with a pleading expression, as if begging me to help her brother be himself again. But I had nothing to offer. Not yet.

Her shoulders slumped. "I guess we can't do that kind of thing anymore, can we?"

He attempted a smile. "I can eat a little ice cream, and I can still watch movies."

"Okay. Any suggestions?"

"That new heist movie. Or the alien movie that just came out. The gory one. You know which one I'm talking about?"

She rolled her eyes. "Do we have to?"

"I'm the sick one here. I get to pick." He took a deep breath as he laid back on the pillow. The last of the blood drained from the bag. A beeping monitor broke up the silence.

A nurse walked inside. She smiled as she stepped to the bag and removed it from the metal hook.

"Just need to check your bowel sounds," she said in a thick New Jersey accent. She stood over Damian and placed her stethoscope's plastic-coated tips in her ears.

"You coming for ice cream and a movie this weekend, Amaya?" Damian asked as the nurse placed her stethoscope's diaphragm on his stomach above the protruding tube.

I shrugged. "Sure, if you're up for it."

"I will be." His pained smile nearly looked genuine.

"How's your stomach? Any pain?" the nurse asked as she straightened.

He grimaced. "It hurts, but it's not too bad."

She nodded. "I'll be back with some antacids. It takes a while for your system to adjust once we start the bleeding tubes."

"Nurse, do you think I'll be able to go out this weekend?" he asked.

She raised an eyebrow. "Go out?"

"Just into town," he clarified.

"Well, that's not up to me, you know. You'll have to get Dr. Simmons to sign off on it."

"Do you think he will?"

"I suppose if you leave right after a feeding, then be back in three hours for your next one—and that's assuming you aren't running a fever or having any other symptoms."

"So, you think he'll sign off?"

"I suppose. But you're sick, Mr. Damian. Don't forget that."

"I won't." He pointed to the tube. "I kinda can't."

She squeezed his shoulder, then turned and left, the door clicking shut behind her. Damian shifted and closed his eyes, his face drained of color.

Chloe patted his leg. "You okay?"

"Just tired."

"You want us to let you rest?"

He yawned. "Okay."

She stood and picked up the full bottle of Sunkist. She looked with worry at her brother who lay breathing quietly, eyes closed.

"Love you," she whispered.

"Love you, too" he answered, eyes still closed.

We walked out of the room, shutting the door quietly behind us. Chloe remained understandably quiet as we passed by halls and stairways. Floor-length windows allowed sunlight to soak into our skin.

She tossed the bottle into a trashcan as we neared the doors leading to the basketball court. A group of teachers and nursing staff passed us on our way outside. A few kids sat on benches around the courtyard, their voices filling the air. Some stood tossing a ball to each other. I recognized a few faces, though no one bothered with a greeting. It was just as well. No use making too many attachments in a place with futures like ours.

A chilly breeze rushed past, stirring the stray strands of my ponytail. I walked with Chloe across the court, our feet crunching loose bits of cement. A grassy hill sloped away from the court, and at its bottom stood a white gazebo against the dark reds and golds of trees. A dark figure sat inside, a shadow wearing a hoodie and sunglasses.

Chloe tugged on my sleeve. "Look who it is."

My heart gave an inexplicable flutter.

"Yeah. Wonder why he's out here."

"I don't know. I thought he avoided daylight."

I gave her a sidelong glance. "Is that true?"

She shrugged. "Probably not, since he's sitting out here."

Lucian stood. His gaze fixed on us—the look of a predator. Blood drained from my face.

Chloe gave me a pointed stare, her lips drawn into a thin line. "Amaya?"

"What?"

"Why are you so pale?" she asked.

I shook my head, turning away when she grabbed my hand. "Hey! Where you going?"

"I don't want to see him."

"Why? Did he do something to you?"

"No," I snapped.

She clicked her tongue. "Spill it, Amaya."

I glanced over my shoulder. He still stood staring at us, most likely could overhear us if he really had enhanced hearing. "Not here."

Lucian stalked out of the gazebo and took the path straight to us. My heart went to my throat. I had trouble sorting out my emotions, and I had no desire to face him again, not when I didn't know what he was hiding or what he was capable of. Plus, I couldn't shake the images of Sally

Anderson—the bites opening her neck as if she'd been fileted. Still, my pride wouldn't allow me to look weak in front of him, so I stood tall and squared my shoulders, facing the full form of *the* Lucian Vidraru.

Chloe stood to face him.

"Chloe." He nodded as he passed us, and I noted that he omitted my name. "Are you doing well?"

"Um-hmm," she managed, glancing at me.

"How are your symptoms? Staying under control, I hope?"

"Yes. Fine."

Sunlight shone over his tall frame corded with muscle, his fitted black t-shirt revealing his well-formed deltoids. The wind carried the heady fragrance of amber spice, making my heart palpitate as if it would burst from my chest. I couldn't stop staring at his lips as he spoke, his words tinged with an accent that conjured images of gothic castles.

His shaded eyes met mine, and I couldn't bring myself to speak past the knot lodged in my throat. He gave a single nod and brushed past us without another word.

"*Holy freaking moly*," Chloe hissed. "He totally talked to me. He never talks to anyone."

"Yeah, he did." I playfully poked her shoulder. "Maybe he's into you."

"Not a chance." She laughed, then pressed her lips together. "But…if he were into me…what should I do about it?"

I exhaled a deep, unsteady breath. "If I were you, I'd keep my distance."

---

13

*Email to Lucian@LucianAlexandruVidraru.com from
sierralou44@xmail.com*

Dear Lucian, Is that even your name? I'm a huge fan and want to know if your name is really Lucian. Also, are you really 21? Because I read that you're 21. It's only a few years older than me. I have a handicap and I live with my mom and my dog Pepper. But then I also read that you have a birthday in April like me, so I wanted to know. You were born a long time ago and look like you're young, so how does that work? Can you tell me what it was like back then? Also, please send me your book. I love to read so it would be great to read your book. I love you so much and I love watching your vlog. You know what it's like to be not friends with everyone who thinks you're different. I'm very smart and I want to be a nurse.
  -Sierra

*Email to sierralou44@xmail.com from
Lucian@LucianAlexandruVidraru.com 04.04.19 09:11 AM EST*

Sierra,

Thank you for your message. To answer your question, you're right. I look 21. That's because I am. I was born twenty-one years ago. It's also true that I lived a long time ago. The first time I was born was in 1860. Yes, a very long time ago! The world was different, but in ways most people don't realize. For instance, we didn't have deodorant. You lived with the scent of body odor all around and got used to it. Gross, I know. But that's how it was. Also, flies. They were all over the food all the time, and we just dealt with it. We didn't know any different.

Some things that didn't change: the way people loved one another. My parents and siblings loved me very much, and though it has been many years since I've seen them, their presences stay with me. I think they know I'm here on the earth for longer than normal, and if God ever sees fit to let me pass, I'll expect them to be waiting for me.

You're right about something else. You are smart, and I think you will be a wonderful nurse. Never give up on your dreams. I'm sure your mom and your dog Pepper love you very much. Your mother gave me permission to mail you a signed copy of my book. I hope you enjoy reading it. Some of the stories are sad, but I hope you don't feel sorry for me. When you live for a long time, you have to go through some things that aren't happy, but those things help you learn, and they make you a stronger person.

I wish you all the best.

-Lucian (really my name)

~

AMAYA

Khan's tail thumped the blanket as I sat on my bed, laptop propped on my legs, and typed SALLY ANDERSON into the search engine. After pondering the virus's mutations, I'd come to realize that the clue was Sally. She'd been the first to get the newer strain of the virus. Something about her had made it mutate, and I needed to find out what. Maybe if I could find out how the virus had altered, I could discover a way to reverse the mutation.

The first few sites were social media profiles of older women. I scrolled past them to a faded picture of a young girl, close to my age, with creamy white skin and striking blue eyes that contrasted her dark hair. Like the photo in the newspaper, her soft smile gave the impression of Scarlett O'Hara.

I clicked on the first link: SALLY ANDERSON DIES AT HANDS OF LIVING VAMPIRE.

As I read it, I focused on anything that stood out. Sally and Lucian had been students at Purdue. She'd been a biology major; he was working on his fifth doctorate. Despite his academic successes, Lucian had been diagnosed with clinical depression. His mental health had put him in a compromised situation that drove him to act on his vampiristic instincts. Sally died six months after being bitten and spreading the virus. Lucian died in prison, in some of the "most detestable, horrific conditions catalogued in modern American history."

He'd been denied blood. Forced to eat common food. His vomiting and diarrhea had become so severe the janitors refused to clean it. He was then kept in constant solitary confinement and refused any food or water until he succumbed to dehydration after a week. In a deathlike, catatonic state, with no pulse, he was declared dead and buried in the prison cemetery. The horrific conditions had come to light and the prison had undergone reform.

I closed the article, my gaze going to my bedside lamp, a soft yellow light glowing over warm blankets, a cup of water, a fan humming quietly.

Hugging my arms to my chest, I shrugged away the chill burrowing under my skin, then clicked on the next article.

JUSTICE FOR SALLY ANDERSON

I scanned over it. Nothing new. Until a line caught my attention near the bottom.

Seventeen vagrants admitted to being bitten by Vidraru in the midst of the Great Depression after he lost his job working for P.T. Barnum and Bailey's. Paltry amounts of blood were taken from each victim, their bite wounds healing within days. None were found to have spread the virus, and none recorded feeling pain or discomfort of any kind because of their injuries, which they claim were given in exchange for money.

I reread the paragraph.

He'd bitten *seventeen* people during the Depression? Why didn't I know about that? It certainly wasn't something that got brought up often. Or ever.

If it were true, why hadn't the virus spread like it had after he'd bitten Sally? I read the rest of the article, but the author didn't make any more mention of it, except to say that Lucian began hunting small animals to survive, and he did so throughout the next two decades until the blood donation banks were set up.

I tapped my fingers on my knee, reading over more posts and articles, some laughable, most supposition.

Why had Sally Anderson's virus spread when others hadn't?

And why was the virus still uncontrolled? Important facts about these vagrants seem to have been completely ignored. No one had brought them in for testing or samples, to find a cure?

I went back to the search engine, combing over every entry. Only thirteen articles existed about her, which seemed unusual for someone who'd been so high profile. When I clicked on one entitled THE UNTOLD TRUTH OF SALLY ANDERSON, a page came up with an ERROR: THIS FILE HAS BEEN MOVED OR DELETED.

I got the same result with the next three sites.

I clicked my laptop closed, then patted Khan's head. "Weird," I mumbled.

Khan raised his head, ears pricked as a knock came at my door, jarring me from my thoughts. I went to it and peeked through the peephole. Chloe stood chewing a wad of gum.

I opened the door.

"Hey." A smile lit her face. "I've gotta tell you something. Can I come in?"

"Sure."

I stepped aside and she entered the room. Khan ambled to her, and she knelt and scratched his head.

"So, what's the news?" I asked after shutting the door.

She sat on the edge of my bed. "I asked him."

"Asked who?"

"Lucian, of course."

I crossed my arms. "You asked him what?"

She waved her hands. "To go out with us this weekend. He said no at first. Said he never goes out because it can get dangerous when people recognize him. Then I said it would be sort of like a double date. We'd be going with you and my brother. No pressure situation. Just a friends' thing. Then he said 'okay, he'd love to'." She gasped as she took a breath. "He said okay." She plopped onto the bed. "I feel dizzy," she added, staring blankly at the ceiling.

"Wow. I can't believe you asked him. I can't believe he agreed."

"I know! You realize this may be the first date he's taken with someone ordinary from the facility and not some famous chick from Hollywood or something?"

"It's crazy." I tried to add the right amount of conviction to my voice, while secretly wondering the real reason Lucian had agreed to go out with us.

"I'm going on a date with Lucian Vidraru," she repeated,

still staring at the ceiling. "Oh my gosh." She sat up, her eyes wide. "Amaya!"

"What's the matter?"

"What am I going to wear?"

"Um…your Princess Leia t-shirt?"

"No! He doesn't like geeky stuff like that. He's way too refined and classy. I'll wear my black dress. No. That's too fancy. How about my blue jean skirt—but what blouse? My yellow tank-top? Do you have anything? Something cute and slightly-the-teeniest-bit sexy? I mean, not that I'm trying to impress him or anything."

Of course not. I pointed to my closet. "Help yourself."

"Thanks." She jumped up, yanked the knob, and the door swung open. Smacking on her gum, she picked through my clothes.

I sat on the sofa chair by the bed, exhaustion weighing on me, still pondering who could've deleted the websites about Sally Anderson, and why, trying to understand what had driven Lucian to bite her when he'd had the blood donations available.

What if blood donations didn't satisfy him the same? What if those websites hid the truth of who else he'd bitten?

If so, did that mean he still had the urge to feed off people? Had he killed more than just Sally Anderson?

Was that what Dr. Warren and Lucian were hiding?

My mind went to Archive Five.

Queasiness soured my stomach, and I couldn't be sure I shared Chloe's optimism about going out with him.

14

Transcript from Lucian Vidraru's YouTube Channel, Surviving and Thriving, VS Warriors Unite

Hello fellow warriors! I think you'll all appreciate today's announcement. We've gotten record-breaking numbers of blood donations. In fact, we've gotten so many that we can't use them all, and we're sourcing the extras to help local hospitals. That's because of your donations.

I'm celebrating with a goblet of blood! Cheers!

I am kidding. Of course. Everyone knows me too well for that. Or maybe some of you are joining me for the first time? If you are, be sure to subscribe and press the Like button. Every penny earned from this channel goes straight into VS research.

My Ninja Warrior cup, by the way, is filled with pomegranate juice.

Till next time, warriors!

~

AMAYA

WE STOOD OUTSIDE THE FACILITY, AUTUMN AIR STIRRING THE leaves in the oak trees lining the gravel drive. Chloe smoothed her hair, which she'd straightened until it fell in silken waves over her shoulders. She wore my ivory satin blouse with the pearl buttons down the front.

"Do I look okay?" she asked.

"You look beautiful," I answered.

"Do I?" She smiled, her white teeth contrasting her tan complexion.

"Lucian won't be able to resist you."

She playfully punched my shoulder. "Stop it."

Damian walked toward us, his nurse following him. Pink tinted his cheeks, and he smiled as he approached us.

"Taxi's not here yet?" he asked.

"Not yet," Chloe answered. "But it's ten till six. You're early, big brother."

He shrugged, sticking his hands in his jeans' pockets. He wore an oversized blue plaid shirt, probably to hide his bleeding tube, and his hair was slicked with gel that had a citrus scent.

"Where's the vampire?" he asked.

"He's not a vampire," I answered.

"Whatever." He ran his hand through his blond hair. "We're all vampires, and he sucks peoples' blood, so he's especially one."

"He's a VS survivor." Chloe brushed her hair over her shoulder. "Be politically correct, Damian."

Damian's nurse handed him a small duffel bag. "Keep this with you at all times, okay? There's an emergency bleeding tube kit in there if you need it. You remember how to use it?"

"Yeah," he said with a sigh, taking it from her. "I remember."

"Good. If you start to feel faint or nauseous, you need to

come back immediately. I know you got Dr. Simmons to sign off for you, and you've already been signed out, but that's only good for the next three hours. By no means does it mean you're free of the virus, so don't act as if you are."

"I know." He slung the duffel over his shoulder.

She nodded and left us to enter the facility, taking the granite steps up to the imposing metal doors.

Dark clouds gathered overhead, and rain scented the air. I pulled my red cardigan around me, hoping to ward off the dampness. Strands of hair fell free of my ponytail, tickling my face.

"You look nice, Amaya," Damian said.

I glanced down at my flat shoes, a pair of skinny jeans with holes in the knees, and my yellow blouse—the nicest one I owned minus the one I'd loaned Chloe. I'd attempted to curl my hair, failed, and resorted to the ponytail, and my makeup consisted of lip gloss and eye shadow. My hands had been too shaky to attempt mascara.

"Thank you, Damian," I answered.

"Lucian's coming, right?" Chloe tapped her foot as she glanced at the facility's entrance. Its shadow reached toward us. Thin, finger-like spires cast a phantom stain on the gravel drive. Wind tousled the leaves from the oaks and sycamores. They rustled in the tree limbs and tumbled over the drive.

"Maybe he changed his mind," Damian said.

"Hush. He did not," Chloe snapped. "He's probably just…brushing his teeth…or something."

"Brushing his *fangs*," Damian snorted.

"He doesn't have fangs," she retorted.

Behind us, the doors creaked open. I turned, shading my eyes against a break in the clouds that allowed sunlight to shine on the dark figure stepping outside. He almost looked normal wearing a Yankees baseball cap, sunglasses, a dark blazer, and jeans. As he stepped down the steps, the wind carried the scent of amber spice.

Butterflies stirred inside me, such a powerful reaction that I had to take a deep breath. I stood straight, too aware of my messy hair, my warm cheeks most likely turned pink, and my chipped black nail polish. I clasped my hands behind my back.

"You made it." Chloe's face beamed.

"Yes." He smiled back. She ran to him, as if to hug him, but stuck out her hand instead. He shook it, gloved hands in hers, smiling at her as if she were the only person in the world.

I had to admit Chloe was a good catch. She was perpetually happy. She could cheer up anyone with her bright smile and contagious laughter. Unlike me. I hadn't felt true happiness since Mom had left me on my own. Chloe made a good partner for him. He needed some brightness in his life after everything he'd suffered.

But did I want him to be with her?

Not because I was jealous, but because I was concerned for her well-being. If he were still drinking blood and killing people the way he'd done to Sally Anderson, wouldn't it be wise to warn her? Still, my gut clenched at the thought, and I couldn't deny the feeling of jealousy gnawing.

A car engine rumbled, and a white minivan with a yellow sign on top rolled to a stop beside us. Chloe opened the van's sliding door. We climbed in behind her. She sat with Lucian in the middle row, and Damian and I crawled in behind them, buckling into the back seat.

We drove down the long driveway lined in mature oaks with sprawling, gnarled branches. Memories pressed in. The first day I'd come here. Blinking back tears. My only thought being to find the virus's cure and avenge my parents' deaths and save my life.

Lucian sat in front of me, his profile highlighted by the late afternoon sun, skin shaded in bronze. He answered "yes" or "no" as Chloe listed celebrities he'd met.

I watched his profile, a mask of calmness and genteel charm learned from ages past. What was the truth about Sally

Anderson? What was he keeping hidden in his cigar box? Was it a cure to the virus? If so, why keep it hidden?

I didn't have the answers, but maybe I'd get a chance to question him.

"You're quiet, Amaya," Damian said.

"Am I?"

"It's okay." He shrugged. "You shouldn't feel obligated to talk to me."

I raised an eyebrow. "Why do you say that?"

"I realize I may not be the most desirable male in the car." He nodded toward Lucian. "I've got stiff competition."

"Don't say that, Damian."

He smiled, though the expression didn't touch his eyes. "Don't worry about it, Amaya. I'm just glad you agreed to come. I hope this isn't too boring for you."

"I've been stuck inside the facility for almost a week. Anything beats that place."

He nodded, looking out the window as we drove out of the forest and through an open field.

"How's your treatment going?" I asked.

"Good. I feel a lot better since they started the transfusions. Yesterday I didn't think I could get out of bed. Now look at me."

"That's good. I'm glad it's helping you."

A gas station and a bed-and-breakfast appeared at the bottom of a hill, the car's engine vibrating quietly. The driver turned on the radio, a soft pop song playing. Sitting in the car, listening to music, talking to people I considered friends, all felt so completely normal, like I was just another person going out on the weekend.

"You really met Robert Downey, Jr.," Chloe echoed.

"At a Comic Con in San Diego last year. We were on a panel together."

"What about Prince William?"

"At a Star Wars premiere in London three years ago."

"Kendall Jenner."

"Twice. Neither time was memorable."

"Oh my gosh!"

Lucian gave her a friendly smile. "Why don't you tell me about yourself? What did you do before you came here?"

"Okay." Chloe blushed before rattling off a list of her accomplishments. Salutatorian of her high school class. Art major at Phoenix University. Cheerleader…

My mind wandered as she continued.

Damian pulled out his phone and launched a game. "Do you play Barbarian Siege?"

"No."

"You should. I could add you to my army."

"Cool." I tried to force some interest into my voice. I looked out the window as Damian sat glued to his phone. We passed by old barns with peeling red paint, and historic homes with gables and wrap-around porches. If I ever got a chance to live past twenty-five, I wouldn't mind settling down in a place like this, with enough room to breathe, maybe try my hand at gardening. Get a few horses. Have a family. Kids. A husband who treated me how Dad treated Mom. Eat ice cream on the porch every now and then.

Chloe's voice broke up the silence. "I also got MVP on the volleyball team the same year, which was so crazy…"

A stately home sat on a hill. Red bricks, two stories, and dramatic gables gave the impression of an estate that had seen its share of history. Snow-capped mountains rose behind it. A driveway wound through Maple trees with brilliant red leaves, over a bridge spanning a stream and ending at the home's front porch. Its rows of windows overlooked a field where horses grazed, their tails swishing. A foal trotted through the wildflowers.

"You won second in the cheerleading finals," Damian interrupted Chloe.

"First," she argued.

"Second," he said. "I remember that year. We were in New Orleans and it was sweltering hot. I had to sit in the stands with Mom and Dad for hours."

"I won first!"

The conversation devolved into an argument between the siblings, and Lucian's gaze went to the window. Although I couldn't see his eyes behind his glasses, a half-smile caught his lips in a wistful expression.

"That's nice, isn't it?" he asked so only I could hear, leaning toward me, his arm propped on the seat between us.

"Oh." Heat rose to my cheeks. Had he noticed me staring at him? "It's quaint," I answered. "Not like the beach, but still beautiful."

I couldn't stop the picture forming of what it might be like to have Lucian in a home like that with me.

Now I was really dreaming.

Damian and Chloe's argument continued, and I vaguely noted their heated conversation. Something about prize money and how much she'd earned, and how Damian had contributed nothing, when he argued he'd won two-hundred dollars playing Barbarian Siege, which Chloe said didn't count…

"It's amazing," Lucian said, voice deep and quiet. "So many sights to see in this world, yet ones like that never get old."

How many sights had he seen? I shrank in my seat, my short life spent in the Eastern states—eight I'd traveled, to be exact paled in comparison to his depth of experiences over the entire planet.

"Surely some things get boring after so long?" I questioned.

He chuckled quietly. "The facility? Yeah. That gets old. Other things?" His gaze met mine, my reflection showing in his sunglasses. "Other people—"

I had to press my hands into my lap, my heart beating as if

it might fly into my throat—"Twelve-hundred dollars?" Chloe asked in a shrill voice—and Lucian continued, speaking under her.

"No matter how many people I meet, I'll never meet them all," Lucian continued. "Sometimes I start to see patterns in personalities. She's the narcissist. He's the loner. But some people I can't figure out." He leaned toward me until the scent of amber spice made tingles run straight through me. My pulse thrummed, a pounding in my ears that drowned out Chloe's voice, the whirring tires, the hum of the engine, until the only thing I could hear were his words.

"I can't figure you out." He leaned so close, I could see the outline of his eyes—dark pools, no white—behind his glasses. "I desperately want to."

The siblings' argument continued, but I couldn't pull my gaze from Lucian's, even though I'd seen too much. Heard too much. More than I'd wanted. A glimpse at the vampire behind the man.

The van slowed as we entered town. Historic storefronts made of red brick and decorative wrought-iron railings surrounded us. Spires rose from churches, and uniform street-lamps interspersed the narrow roads. Pools of soft orange light glowed over benches and sidewalks. The quiet sense of history settled over me. It wasn't hard to hear the clopping of horse hooves and rolling carriage wheels that must've once used the same cobbled streets.

With a man sitting near me who'd lived the last century and half, in a place older than him, I felt as if I'd stepped into another lifetime.

When we finally parked in front of the ice cream shop and stepped out of the minivan, the air turned chill. The muffled quiet of evening settled around us. Faint voices and car engines came from the distance, though the sidewalk remained empty. I waited under a streetlamp as the others gathered, Chloe in conversation with her brother. A wood-carved sign with the word *Morgenstern's* hung above the door.

Lucian fell into step beside me and gave me a brief smile, which held something quietly seductive that stirred a longing deep within me—something I had trouble comprehending, like nothing I'd ever felt before. *It's just a crush,* I told myself, though the flimsy word seemed too superficial to describe my feelings.

A bell rang as we entered. The heavenly scent of warm cinnamon and cream hung in the air. Blonde-wood floors glinted in the pendant lights hanging over round tables and wire frame chairs. A few pre-teen girls sat near the back wall. Their eyes widened as they focused on Lucian.

We went to the far counter, looking over the glass display covering round tubs filled with freshly churned cream and sugar.

Their labels tempted me.

Cookies 'n cream. Peanut butter swirl. Blueberry cheesecake. Mint chocolate chip.

After placing our orders, we each took our cones from the server. I took a bite of chilled Dulce de Leche as I sat across from Damian. Chloe and Lucian also joined us, though only Chloe and I had cones.

"How's it taste?" Damian asked his sister.

"Like ice cream."

He frowned. "Hmm."

"Wanna try a bite?" She held her cone toward him.

He scrunched his face and pushed her hand away. "I'm good."

"Don't worry too much," Lucian said. "Avoiding food gets easier. Plus, you can eat some things. Meat, if it's rare. Certain juices—the red ones."

I laughed. "Because they look like blood?"

Lucian smiled. "It's all in your head anyway. That's what makes it go down easier."

"Are you teasing?"

"I wouldn't tease you, Amaya. I know better." His lips quirked—an expression entirely too unnerving. My cheeks warmed, and I glanced at the marble tabletop, suddenly interested in the striated pattern of gray and white.

"We should've planned something that didn't include food," Damian said. "Why didn't we go to a movie?"

"Still has food," Chloe said. "Popcorn. Nachos. Sodas. Hot Tamales."

"A park, then."

"Picnic lunch. Sandwiches. Chips. Watermelon."

He folded his arms over his chest. "A baseball game."

"Hot dogs. Peanuts. Beer."

Damian rolled his eyes in frustration. "Is there anything to do that doesn't involve food?"

Chloe licked her strawberry ice cream. "Pretty much, no."

Damian pulled out his phone. "There's this," he mumbled.

"That's rude, Damian." She sat up straight. "You're on a date."

He shrugged, moving his finger over the screen.

Chloe narrowed her eyes. "Put your phone away. I mean it."

Damian shook his head. "I will after I win this round."

The two continued arguing when the bell chimed, and the doors opened. Three teenage boys walked inside, laughing as they entered. They wore matching khakis and navy-blue polo shirts.

Lucian stiffened as the three strode past us to the back counter, his gaze shifting to follow their movements.

"Do you know them?" I asked Lucian.

He nodded once.

"How?"

He shook his head, gaze fixed in a predatory stare on the three boys.

The girls who had been sitting at the back wandered to us,

giggling, until one pushed another who stumbled toward Lucian.

With pink cheeks, wispy brunette hair, and a glittery purple tank top, she grinned as she held out a stack of napkins and a pen. "Hi. Are you the vampire?"

His sigh told me he wasn't fond of the nickname, but he smiled. "That's me," he answered.

"Oh!" She breathed, as if trying to keep from hyperventilating. "May we have your autograph? All three of us?" She thrust the napkins in his face. "Please?"

"Of course. What are your names?"

The girls squealed before rattling off their names, Lucian asking what their interests were before personalizing three separate napkins.

"I'll keep it forever." One girl clutched it to her chest as they walked away.

"I'm framing mine."

They giggled as they left the store.

"You made their day," I said to Lucian.

He shrugged. "Maybe."

The three boys wearing the prep school clothes walked past.

A blond boy bumped into Lucian's shoulder, then he spun around, his springy curls bouncing as he moved.

"Hey, sorry there." He spoke with mock innocence. His toothy smile showed perfect white teeth. Some girls probably found his blue eyes and body-builder frame attractive, but his mouth stretched too wide, his expression smug, reminding me of The Joker.

He laughed as he turned around, sitting by his friends near the front windows.

"Amaya," Lucian said casually, glancing at Chloe who sat arguing with her brother. "I need some fresh air. Want to join me for a walk outside?"

I studied him. "Maybe," I answered, then turned to the

siblings. Chloe had only taken a few bites of her ice cream. "You two want to come? We're talking a walk outside."

"Sure." Chloe motioned. "Let me finish this first."

"I'll pass." Damian looked at his phone.

I nodded, then followed Lucian to the door, my stomach knotting at the prospect of being alone with a vampire—the image of Sally Anderson haunting me as I stepped outside, the eyes' of the prep school boys following us.

15

Excerpt from the journal of Sally Louise Anderson. 17 July 1971

He was so charming at first. Before I knew better.

~

AMAYA

Lucian and I strolled down the quiet lane. The wind carried leaves past the decorative metal benches. I nearly pinched myself, so shocked that I was walking with *him* —the man who'd become a legend.

"I'm glad you agreed to walk with me," Lucian said.

"Did you think I wouldn't?" I asked.

"I never know what to expect from you." He eyed me. "Except I get this feeling from you sometimes, that maybe you don't like me much."

"What gave you that idea?" I asked drily.

He shrugged, hands in his pockets, walking at a casual pace, just another person taking a stroll, nothing uncommon here. I knew better. Why had I agreed to walk with him? Alone?

Despite the photos of mutilated Sally Anderson, it was hard to believe the man walking beside me was a cold-blooded murderer.

As we descended a hill, the river appeared beyond the buildings. Sounds of running water mingled with rumbling car engines and distant conversations. Red-and-white awnings added color to the darkening evening. I breathed in the cool air, a contrast to the heat and humidity I'd become accustomed to.

"What are you thinking about?" he asked me.

I shrugged, unnerved at his question. "Nothing important."

An awkward silence fell between us. Nervousness made my heart race. Despite my research, all the articles I'd read, his numerous biographies, the interviews, I realized I knew next to nothing about the real him—his interests and hobbies. His favorite bands. Did he even like music?

"Tell me about yourself, Amaya."

"What?" I asked, caught off-guard by the sudden question.

"Tell me something about you."

I couldn't stop the smile from pulling at my mouth.

"Is something funny?" he asked.

I kicked a pebble. "Not funny, exactly, but I was about to ask you the same thing."

He smiled, a genuine, boyish grin that showed his teeth—not at all the serious, dark persona plastered on his book covers and paparazzi photos. "Really?" he asked.

"Yeah."

"Okay," he said. "You go first. Ask me anything you like."

I raised an eyebrow. "Why me?"

"Because I asked first."

"Fair enough." We took the path through the buildings, bricks rising on either side, until we stepped onto the sidewalk running along the river. Dark water churned under pools of light cast from the streetlamps. Willow trees lined the shore. Long branches brushed the water's surface. Lightning shot through billowing thunderheads looming on the horizon, though we were too distant to hear the rumble of thunder.

"Do you have any favorite bands?" I asked.

"The Beatles," he answered without hesitation. "I saw them in concert in the sixties. They were amazing. I'll never forget them. If I get to pick a second, it's Simon and Garfunkel. I also love classical music, especially Beethoven and Tchaikovsky. My turn."

A group of ducks quacked from the water, the sound carrying through the open expanse.

"Go ahead," I said hesitantly. When the time came, would I have the nerve to ask what I really wanted to know?

"All right." His grin held an edge of mischievousness. "Have you ever been kissed?"

I frowned, crossing my arms. I should've expected this. "That's none of your business."

"Why not?" he asked. "I answered your question."

"Yes, but I asked something polite and non-personal."

"Music *is* personal."

"That's debatable."

"Well, have you?" he repeated.

I glanced behind us. The hairs on the back of my neck prickled at the sudden chill in the air. Did I want him to know me as a person? Part of me desperately wanted to say yes. But was that only my loneliness making me feel that way? Then again, if I wanted to know what happened to Sally—if I wanted to know why she spread the virus and died when the homeless vagrants hadn't, then I'd have to know him better. Still, he didn't need to know everything about me.

I gazed up at the sky. "I'd rather not say."

"You really won't tell me?"

I shook my head. Should I tell him what a complete loner

I'd been in high school? I'd had a few crushes, but they'd never known I'd existed, and I'd felt more comfortable that way. A loser had forced himself on me once, but I didn't count him. That narrowed it down to one.

"Fine," I said reluctantly. "I've been kissed twice. The first time was when I was fifteen. I was at a party. He was drunk and wouldn't take no for an answer. The second time… happened."

"The second time happened?" he asked, suspicion in his voice.

"Yeah." I crossed my arms, as if to shield myself from his prying questions.

"You won't tell me more than that?" he asked.

"No." We stepped aside as a jogger passed us, giving a backward glance at Lucian. She tripped and caught herself, giving a nervous laugh, then continuing down the path.

"Does that happen all the time?" I asked.

"Yes. Always." His skin scrunched around his eyes. Had he winked? "Was that your question?"

"No. Was that yours?"

"No." He jabbed me playfully in the shoulder.

"Ouch." I rubbed the tender spot.

"Did I hurt you?" His voice held a tone of sympathy.

"No. It was already sore." I didn't find it necessary to explain why.

He grabbed my hand in his, leather creaking as he inspected my fingernails. I tried to pull away, but he held my fingers in a firm grip.

"You can learn things about people from their hands, you know," he said.

My eyebrows rose. "You mean like palm reading or something?"

"No. Nothing like that." He grabbed both my hands. "Let's take yours, for example. You have a small callus on your pointer finger, right hand, probably where you hold a pen."

He rubbed my finger. "You write a lot. You're probably book smart. Take lots of notes. Keep up with your homework. Am I right so far?"

"Yeah," I answered, trying not to sound as breathless as I felt.

"Your nail polish. Chipped. You probably don't spend a lot of time on yourself. I'd guess you care more about knowledge than your appearance. How am I doing?"

I swallowed the nervous knot forming in my throat. "Pretty good."

"Your nail polish is black. Could be some kind of statement. A fashion statement, maybe, but probably not. Maybe it's a form of rebellion. Your way of standing out. But this is only your nails. You're wearing nothing else to prove that theory. So, it's something else. A tribute to someone who's passed? Could be your dad, but... Your mom, I think. Did she wear the same color?"

I managed to nod. "Yeah. We painted our nails together. I haven't worn a different color since she passed." The knot grew, making it impossible for me to swallow.

He released my hands, and my fingers grew cold.

"How'd I do?" he asked.

I shrugged, glancing away from him, unable to see his expression. "Okay, I guess. You must spend a lot of time observing people."

"A few years."

I glanced at his gloved hands. "When do I get my turn?"

He cocked his head.

"You know so much about me," I continued. "I don't know anything about you."

"Yes, you do," he answered. "You know I like the Beatles." He held up his hands. "You know I won't take these off."

"Not even for me?" I asked. "Not even if I wanted to get to know you better?"

He remained silent for a long pause. "Do you want to know me better?"

I took a deep breath. Now was my chance. "I want you to tell me about Sally Anderson."

He clenched his jaw. "Didn't I ask you not to talk about her?"

"Please, Lucian." I rested my hand on his arm. "I came to the facility to find a cure—and she's the only clue I've got."

He glanced at me touching him. "I thought you came to the facility because you had VS."

I looked away, the water running swiftly, swirls and eddies churning, hiding whatever lay beneath its surface.

"You injected yourself, didn't you?" He slipped my cardigan's sleeve down my shoulder, revealing the bruise from the injection. I pulled my arm away, but he'd already seen it. "You got the sample of the primary virus from your mom, and you did this to yourself?"

I didn't answer.

"Why, Amaya? Didn't you know what you were doing?"

"I knew exactly what I was doing," I mumbled. Should I tell him that after Mom died, I'd died too? I had nothing left. My only way to avenge her death was to find the cure. "I had to do it. There was no other way to get inside the facility." I looked at him, hoping he saw the intensity in my eyes. "Mom thought you were hiding the cure. Was she wrong?"

He didn't answer as he adjusted his cap.

"Was she?" I repeated.

"I don't have the cure, Amaya. At least, not the one you want."

"What do you mean by that?"

He shook his head.

"Lucian, tell me." I grasped his fingers. "What are you hiding?"

His gaze went to our hands, his gloved fingers against my

pale skin. His eyes hidden behind dark lenses. "I haven't told anyone in a very long time." His voice took a somber tone.

When his gaze met mine, I couldn't stop the shiver going down my spine.

"I haven't told anyone. Not since Sally," he finished.

Victims of porphyria, called vampires, were buried with stones in their mouths, their jaws broken, to prevent them from rising from the dead and drinking the blood of the living.

~

LUCIAN

I stood facing Amaya, the wind tugging strands of hair from her ponytail and brushing them across her porcelain-smooth skin.

My pounding heart, sweaty palms, and the stirring deep inside me were emotions I hadn't felt in a long time. Not in this lifetime. She held power over me, the same as Barbara. The same as Sally.

How could I push her away? She'd injected herself with the virus. She only had months to live. Weeks, maybe.

Tell me about Sally, she'd asked.

Could I do it?

"She was my first after Barbara," I said, letting out a nervous breath. Telling her came easier than I expected. "I was hurt after Barbara's death. She'd contracted VS from me. I couldn't stop blaming myself. I went to college to hide. Took every class I could. Tried to bury my feelings in books. It helped a little." I shook my head. I couldn't believe I was admitting this to her. She was so young, so innocent. Why did she need to know about my regret? But she'd asked, and I found it impossible not to answer.

"That's where you met Sally?" Amaya asked.

I nodded. "Yeah. She was…" *she was like you.* "She was charming. Beautiful. She understood me. It was easy to fall in love with her. But she hid things from me."

"Things like what?"

I took a deep breath. The sky grew darker, illuminated by lightning on the horizon, the echo of thunder silent. We reached the end of the sidewalk, the river running through the dark canopy of the forest. I placed my hand at the small of her back, stopping her from taking another step, steering her around, back into the light, the way we'd come.

"She wanted to know things," I said. "Every day she asked questions, and I answered as best as I could. She wanted to know how the virus was transmitted, how I'd gotten it, my dad's research. Every day she got more insistent. She started researching Vlad Dracula, Bran Castle, my dad's notes. Her curiosity became an obsession. Until…"

Stop, I told myself. *Don't tell her anything else.*

"Until what?"

Her question made me stop walking. How could I tell her?

Amaya grabbed my hand, her fingers firm as she stared up into my eyes, as if she didn't fear me, as if she couldn't sense the claws beneath the gloves, or the predator's eyes behind the glasses.

Thunder rumbled.

The storm drew closer.

"She asked me to drink her blood," I said.

Amaya raised an eyebrow. "*Asked* you?"

"At first. Then… she begged."

Footsteps came from the path. In the light of the street-lamps, three forms emerged. Tall and well-muscled, the blond guy wearing the prep school clothes walked in front. Blake Carmichael. My gut twisted, and I took a protective step in front of Amaya.

"I hoped we'd find you here," he called. "I haven't seen you since the funeral, Lucian. Where've you been? Wait." He held up a finger. "Let me guess. In the facility, right? Maybe going on some reality show or staying in the Ritz-Carlton or wherever people like you stay when you travel. Living like a king while Hannah lies dead in her grave. She was my only sister, you know." Blake took a step toward me. "Did you know that?"

"Sorry," I answered, keeping an even tone. "I didn't know."

"Yeah. I figured you didn't. There are a lot of things you don't know about her. She liked cheerleading. Loved French fries with ice cream. She could sing the lyrics to every song on the radio." He looked away and wiped his nose on his sleeve.

"Blake," I said calmly. "I'm so sorry for your loss. More than you'll ever realize."

He barked a mirthless laugh. "See. That's the thing. I don't believe you."

"You should. I care for everyone who dies." My words wouldn't have any effect on him, and I knew it, but I could try.

"You don't understand what we're going through," Blake continued. "You smile and laugh and live a great life while we suffer. It's time you understand what pain feels like." He pulled a knife from his pants pocket.

"We don't want any trouble." Amaya stood beside me.

"No?" He pointed the knife at me. "Because he brought it when he gave the virus to Hannah."

"Leave us alone." I hope he heard the growl in my voice.

He approached, springy blonde curls bouncing with his steps, his blade shining in the streetlamp's light.

"They say you can't die." He cocked his head, a playful grin tugging at his mouth, the promise of violence glinting in his eyes. "But what happens if you bleed out?"

His grip tightened.

Amaya stepped in front of me, shielding me with her thin body. "Leave him alone!"

I gently grasped her shoulders. "Amaya," I whispered in her ear. "It's okay. I'll handle this."

She glanced up at me, eyes wide with fear. Dark, beautiful eyes that threated to be my undoing. "Lucian, they'll hurt you."

"No." I stood straight. "He's right. They can't."

I moved Amaya aside, standing to face the three attackers.

Flexing my fists, the wild inside me demanded I fight.

Kill.

It would be so easy.

Blood pounding through arteries. Severed in his neck. Rich and flowing with life. Pulsing. I could almost taste its iron-richness on my tongue.

No.

I slowed my breathing, controlling my thoughts. Blake was suffering. He didn't understand what he was doing.

"Blake," I said, my voice carrying. "Hurting me won't take away your pain. Trust me. Healing from the loss of a loved one takes time."

"Shut up!" Blake rushed forward, knife aiming for my chest. I sidestepped, grabbed his wrist, and wrenched his arm behind his back. He cried out, dropping the knife. It landed with a clatter on the sidewalk.

I dropped Blake to the ground, then planted my elbow between his shoulderblades so he'd stay down.

The other two boys followed, running at me with clenched fists and rage in their eyes.

I dropped the first guy with a kick to the groin. The second guy jumped back, holding up his hands.

"Hey, I don't want any trouble."

"James… you moron," Blake gasped from the ground.

The second guy writhed as he held his crotch. "He kicks like a freaking… demon."

"That's because he is a demon!" Blake yelled, grabbing his knife, and pulling himself to his feet. Sweat dripped down his face, and a bruise formed on his neck.

He pointed behind me with the tip of his blade.

"Do it now!"

I spun around, watching as the two boys held Amaya between them and rammed their fists to her stomach and chest.

Rage burned through me. Coherent thoughts evaporated, replaced with the need to kill.

My vision bled red as I ripped off my gloves and glasses.

Amaya's gaze caught mine. Fear widened her eyes as I dropped my gloves to the ground. I didn't have time to ponder her reaction.

My clawed hands grabbed the guy closest to me, scraping chunks of flesh from his forearm.

My only thought was to save her.

His strangled scream ripped through the air as he fell away from Amaya.

She rounded on the remaining boy, her fist connecting with his jaw. As he screamed, I closed in, claws ripping from his chest to his navel, shredding his shirt and through layers of skin, though I managed to restrain my impulse to pierce vital organs.

Two other attackers grabbed me. The knife's blade glinted in my vision. Stabbing pain tore through my neck. I grabbed the arms strangling me, warm blood seeping around my fingers as I pulled the person off me.

Blake fell back, surrounded by his companions.

Breathing heavily, I faced the three attackers. Warm blood seeped from the stab wound in my neck.

Blake stood in front of the other two bleeding boys, holding his knife stained red by my blood. Its scent got caught on the wind, threatening to drive me to rip them apart and feast on their entrails.

I took a step toward them, my breathing ragged, their body heat highlighted yellow and red in the field of my vision.

Blake's hands shook as he pointed the blade at my neck.

"I might've opened your artery there, man," he said, almost as if he regretted it. He staggered backward, grabbing at his companions who turned and ran. Running footsteps faded in the distance as the attackers escaped.

I glanced at my gloves and shades on the ground. Shattered glass glittered on the sidewalk.

A raindrop pelted my face.

Amaya took a step to me.

"Lucian," she breathed, chest rising and falling.

Unhindered by my glasses, I saw her skin and hair as if highlighted in fire, like an angel of death come to save me from this never-ending torture called life. The spark of confusion in her dark irises stole my breath.

Clenching my fists, I looked away from her.

She would never see me the same, and my heart shattered at the thought.

A slow, steady rain started, echoing the flow of the water.

"You're bleeding." Her voice cut through the sound of my pounding heartbeat.

Her flesh touched mine.

I looked up to find her holding my hand. I jerked away, but she grabbed my clawed fingers in a firm grasp.

She didn't speak, eyes revealing no emotion, as she inspected the talon-like appendages covered in gray scales that extended up to my wrists.

"You can say it," I muttered, turning my face to meet hers.

Her eyes widened as she took in my dark red pupils and irises, the whites of my eyes turned black. "I'm not human."

She kept her hand in mine, looking from my eyes to my talons, then to the wound opening my neck.

My knees wobbled at the loss of blood.

A lightning bolt lit the entire sky in an electric glow, the roar of thunder deafening.

I found myself lying on the cold sidewalk, staring up at the dark maelstrom gathering overhead.

A voice called my name.

As I tried to answer, a dark cloud veiled my vision, wrapping me in its blissful embrace.

I knew better than to hope for death.

17

From French Philosopher Dom Augustine Calmet in a 1751 Treatise on the Apparitions of Spirits and on Vampires or Revenants.

[T]hey see, it is said, men who have been dead for several months, come back to earth, talk, walk, infest villages, ill-use both men and beasts, suck the blood of their near relations, make them ill, and finally cause their death; so that people can only save themselves from their dangerous visits and their hauntings by exhuming them, impaling them, cutting off their heads, tearing out the heart, or burning them. These revenants are called by the name of oupires or vampires, that is to say, leeches; and such particulars are related of them, so singular, so detailed, and invested with such probable circumstances and such judicial information, that one can hardly refuse to credit the belief which is held in those countries, that these revenants come out of their tombs and produce those effects which are proclaimed of them.

AMAYA

My heart lurched as I knelt over Lucian.

I couldn't deny the fear that had coursed through me when he'd removed his gloves and sunglasses. How could someone, some*thing* like him exist? How much of him was human, and how much reflected the truth in his eyes? Demon's eyes. Windows to the soul.

A monster.

A living vampire.

But how could he be a monster? He'd saved my life—and my dog's life. He defended me. He'd fought off my attackers, and he'd nearly killed them.

Dried blood clung to the tips of his claws.

He stared blankly overhead. A pool of dark red spread out beneath him.

So much blood…

I cupped his cheek turned pale and cold.

"Lucian, can you hear me?"

He lay as if he were dead.

My head spun. What could I do for him?

As if acting on instinct, I grabbed his gloves and pulled them onto his hands—*claws*—until they were covered. His shattered sunglasses would be of no use, but he'd closed his eyes anyway.

Gently, I moved his head to get a better view of his wound. The knife had gone so deep, the severed artery pulsed, leaking blood with every quiver.

Inside me, something snapped.

I had to help him. But how?

Ripping off my sweater, I pressed it to the wound, applying pressure, my hands trembling.

"*Amaya!*" Chloe's voice came from the jogging path.

I searched for the source of the sound until two silhouettes

—one with a thin, waifish frame and the other filled out and bulky—came into view.

"Over here!" I managed to find my voice.

The rain had stopped, but a dense fog descended around us.

"What happened here?" Damian demanded when he reached me.

"I—" Speaking escaped me. Panic coiled inside, and all I could do was press my sweater to the wound in Lucian's neck.

"Amaya." Chloe knelt beside me and gripped my shoulder. "What happened?"

"The boy from the prep school. He stabbed him."

Chloe gasped. "Is he—?"

"He's not dead," I snapped. "He can't die."

Damian squatted beside us. "He's gone catatonic. How much blood has he lost?"

"I don't know. A lot. His artery is severed."

"Let me see." Damian pointed to my hands.

"But I can't move my sweater." My voice quavered.

"Amaya," Damian said my name with authority. "Lucian is okay. He just needs blood. Let me see."

I swallowed the nervous knot that had formed in my throat, then moved my sweater, heavy and soaked with his blood, from the wound.

The artery still quivered, but the bleeding had stopped. Probably because it had bled out.

My stomach turned with queasiness, the iron taste of blood thick in the air. I had to stand up and distance myself from him. I walked off the path, onto the grass where the scent of rain cleansed my lungs.

"I can wake him up," Damian said. "But he needs surgery to repair the artery."

Chloe pulled her phone from her pocket. "Do it. I'll call an ambulance."

I had to take deep breaths as I stood on the bank, listening to the lapping water. Seeing Lucian laying as if he were dead, like Mom and Dad in their coffins, broke something inside me.

I wasn't prepared for this.

Under my frantically beating heart and knotted stomach, beneath the sound of Chloe's voice talking to the dispatcher, my thoughts tugged at me, gauging the way I reacted. I felt that same heaviness in my heart, those same frantic thoughts —*Was it my fault? Why did I walk outside with him? We should've stayed inside.* It was the same reaction I would've had toward someone I loved.

But I didn't love Lucian. Did I?

Damian took off his duffel bag and placed it on the ground before removing the bleeding kit. He worked methodically as he put on a pair of blue latex gloves, lifted Lucian's shirt, and swabbed the plastic tubing with an alcohol wipe.

When he pulled out the bag of blood, my nausea revolted, threatening to heave up my ice cream, and I had to turn my back. I stood under a willow tree, focusing on the yellow-green leaves, anything to distract me.

"Let me help," Chloe said. I listened to tubing being unrolled and the quiet pop as plastic attached to plastic.

"Keep pressure on the artery or he'll bleed out again," Damian said.

I fidgeted with my hands, sticky blood on my fingers, berating myself for not helping.

Wind gusted, stirring the willow branches. Tears blurred my vision. I placed my hand on the tree's trunk, hoping to stay grounded as the world spun around me.

Silence filled the area.

I chanced a look over my shoulder.

Damian sat calmly holding the bag above Lucian's body, the thin stream of red flowing from one end to the other. Chloe sat pressing her own sweater to Lucian's neck.

I wasn't sure how much time had passed when the ambulance siren blared, and three paramedics arrived.

Someone came to me and asked me my name.

I couldn't hold on to my thoughts after that. I knew we got in a car. We made it back to the facility. Chloe helped me back to my room. I heard Damian's voice.

"He'll be all right, Amaya."

I found myself sitting on my bed, Khan resting his head on my lap, looking up at me with his yellow wolf's eyes.

Patting his head, I took a deep breath.

He'll be all right, Amaya.

I lay on my bed, staring up at the ceiling, listening to the hum of the fan.

He'll be all right because he can't die.

Rolling to my side, I clutched a damp tissue in my hand, but I couldn't remember how it had gotten there. Squeezing my eyes closed, the realization that I didn't want to die hit me full force. I couldn't die. If I died, it meant everyone else was left without a cure. If Lucian couldn't die, that meant he *was* the cure. But what made him different? What made his blood different?

He had to have known. That's why he kept the note hidden in the cigar box. That's why Dr. Warren kept a locked door in his office.

Sleep overrode coherent thoughts. I closed my eyes with the hum of the fan lulling me, and the image of bloodstained gray claws, and piercing red eyes, seared into my memory.

18

Transcript from an iWitness News Report, KNYS Channel 4

This is Alicia Kensington reporting from Crimson Hollow Research Facility, where Lucian Vidraru, the world's oldest vampire, has recently returned after undergoing a successful vascular surgery to repair a stab wound to his neck.

On October eighth, witnesses claim Vidraru was brutally attacked while walking down the Saratoga trail.

Eighteen-year old Damian Jackson, also suffering from VS, described the events that night.

Voice over:

Jackson: Then I see these three guys running. Like they'd gotten in trouble or something, you know. That's when I knew they must've hurt Lucian. When I found him. Man, it was awful. Really awful. Just, the blood, you know.

Kensington: Some people are calling you a hero.

Jackson: I did what anyone else would. I don't know if that makes me a hero.

End voice over.

Vidraru declined an interview as he continues to recover, but the Crimson Hollow staff report that he is in good spirits, and he wishes to thank his fans for their well-wishes and continued support.

Mitch, back to you.

~

AMAYA

CHLOE PLOPPED HER TRAY ACROSS THE TABLE. I SAT PICKING AT boiled carrots that had turned yellow. Not even the cinnamon roll tempted me. The heaviness hadn't gone away since that night with Lucian, and my appetite hadn't come back either.

"You look worse," she said.

"Thanks," I mumbled, not meeting her gaze.

She popped a tater tot in her mouth. "Dr. Warren's coming back tomorrow. You should let him check your symptoms."

"I'm fine," I lied.

"You don't look fine," she stated, matter-of-factly.

I gave her a stern glare. "Chloe. I'm all right. Still shaken up, but I'm not sick—I mean, I'm not *that* sick. Yet."

She pressed her hands to the table. "Amaya. You have the *primary* virus. Has no one told you how bad that is?"

"Chloe," I said with equal sternness. "I know how bad it is, and believe me, as soon I start experiencing shortness of breath or heart palpitations, I'll get checked out. Until then, I'll just…" I picked at my carrots. "Try to get him out of my head," I finished quietly.

Chloe's eyes narrowed. "You like Lucian, don't you?"

"Chloe—"

"You do!" She slapped her hands on the table. "Look at me and tell me I'm lying."

I shook my head, staring at my tray. Heat reddened my cheeks.

"See? You can't do it. You can't say it. You like him." She smacked her forehead. "Why am I so blind?"

"I don't like him. At least, I don't think so." But if that were true, then why could I think of nothing except him for three days' straight? When I was capable of sleeping, why did he appear in my dreams? I rubbed my temples, a dull headache throbbing.

"Amaya, it's okay. Look. I totally understand." She ate another tater tot. "I thought I liked him, too. But after seeing him on the ground. All that blood." She made a sour face and shook her head.

I cocked my head. "You don't like him anymore?"

"I mean, he's nice and all, but he's not like us. He's different, Amaya."

"Does being different make him bad?" I asked.

"I never said bad. He's just not like us, and not only because of how he looks. He's in another league." She tapped her fingers on the table. "Don't get your heart broken."

"I won't." I frowned.

She gave me a suspicious glare.

"I won't," I repeated. I took a sip from my milk carton, the liquid bitter, but managed to take a gulp. "I need to go." I stood and grabbed my tray. Chloe didn't say anything as I walked to the trash can and dumped my uneaten food.

I walked to the opened stainless-steel doors leading to the hallway. When I made it to the hall, a nurse hurried to me. Her plump frame and dark hair were familiar, but I couldn't remember her name. Breathless, she slowed as she approached me.

"Miss Amaya?" she asked.

"Yes?"

"I'm Nurse Teesha." She straightened her stethoscope hanging around her neck. "You'll need to come with me."

"Why?" I asked.

"It's Lucian."

My stomach clenched. "Is he okay?"

She waved her hand. "He's been asking to speak to you. I keep telling him to get well first, but he's insisting. Woke up in a weird mood, too, just to warn you."

My eyebrows rose. "What does he want from me?"

"I don't know. He won't tell me. But you'd better come."

"Okay." I followed her down the hall. She walked with hurried footsteps, and I had to jog to keep up. My heart raced with worry—an annoyance that made me wonder if I had feelings for him. I swallowed the panic making my throat grow tight.

I needed information about Sally. I needed to know why she'd died, and the others hadn't. I needed to know why the information had been deleted when I went looking for it. I needed Lucian for information. *And nothing else*, I reminded myself.

We took the stairs by two until we entered the hallway and stopped at Lucian's door. She knocked once before opening it and ushering me inside, then she left the way we came.

When I stepped onto the Oriental rug, the smell of old leather came from the looming bookshelves.

My heart skipped a beat at the sight of Lucian standing with his back turned. He gazed out the open balcony windows. His shirt hugged the muscles bulging in his back. He wore all gray—a gray top and matching sweatpants, as if he were a gargoyle chipped from stone, blending in with the granite surrounding him.

He turned as I stepped behind him.

Sunglasses hid his eyes. His mouth didn't reveal any expression.

"I'm glad you came," he said.

"Okay." My pounding heart and sweaty palms made it hard to come up with any other response.

His body blocked the morning sunlight streaming inside, casting a shadow, and I couldn't suppress a shiver. Leather creaked as he flexed his gloved hands. "Did Nurse Teesha tell you what I wanted?"

"She said you didn't mention it."

"Let me show you something." He held out his hand. He expected me to take it?

"I won't hurt you," he said, voice deep and smooth. I was struck by the sound of his sincerity.

With a deep breath, I placed my hand in his gloved one. He led me to the balcony, and I gasped as I turned my gaze on the view of the amber and crimson leaves of the forest spreading out for miles around us, as if we stood on a ship in an endless ocean of Balsam and Hemlock.

"I wanted to apologize." He looked out at the view, his gaze not meeting mine. "I'm sorry you had to see me...that way." He glanced at his gloves. "It must've been hard for you to see me like I was dead. I know how hard that is, especially since you had to bury your mom and dad."

"It's okay," I answered too quickly.

His half-smile told me he wasn't buying it.

"Amaya, we both know it's not okay. Death is never okay."

Yeah. He was right. Death was never okay, so why was he hiding the virus's cure?

"I also want to apologize for you having to see me." He paused. "The real me."

"I told you already. It's okay."

"No. I wouldn't feel right unless I apologized to you. When those boys started hurting you, something inside me changed. Demanded I fight back. I can't always control my impulses. Not when the violence escalates that way. When they were hurting you." He took a deep breath, then rubbed his neck where a white scar remained of the stab wound.

"Lucian, you're not blaming yourself, are you?" I asked. "Because it wasn't your fault. Those guys attacked you."

"Yeah." His voice didn't hold any conviction.

"You're blaming yourself, aren't you?"

"Of course, I am. If you haven't noticed, I'm different, Amaya. What my father did to me all those years ago. He wasn't finding a way to live longer. He was creating a monster. Out of me, his own son."

"Lucian—"

"It's true. Don't argue with me on this. I remember his experiments in the castle. He had a lab in the dungeon. I was eleven when he asked me to help him. There were animal body parts everywhere. Cages." He shook his head, as if to erase the memory. "He collected rare species. He'd travel all over the country and bring them back. Snakes and lizards. Turtles. Birds.

"He dissected them, trying to understand their anatomy. But when he grew bored of that, he started researching mythological creatures. Dragons and such. He thought he would find the clue to longevity by doing it." Lucian's chest rose and fell. "That's when he turned to vampires. The people in Bran village were superstitious. They'd been burying the people who died of porphyria with stones in their mouths until it broke their jaws, staking them through the heart, cutting out their tongues. Father thought the porphyria victims were his answer. He started excavating them. Studying them." He shook his head, his tone dark. "What he found was how to create a monster."

"Lucian." I placed my hand on his shoulder. His bicep tensed under the fabric. "You're not a monster."

"Aren't I?" He wouldn't look at me. Maybe he'd already made up his mind. "One day he came home with a box—an old thing, rusted clasps and dark wood, cherubs and Medusa carved on it. Dragons and demons, too. Myths and legends from all over the world." Leather creaked as his hands flexed. "Father wouldn't tell me what was inside, but I'll never forget how excited he looked when he held it. He told me he'd found it. The next day, he used ether to put me under. When I woke up…" He swallowed hard, then took a deep breath. "He was dead. Blood everywhere. I'd been the only one in the room. I had blood on my…hands. Which was when I noticed I had claws instead." His Adam's apple bobbed as he swallowed. "Father had succeeded. That's how I comforted myself, knowing that, at least, he'd done what he wanted. He made me what I am. A creature born of mythology." His voice drifted, as if he were caught up in another time.

"What are you, Lucian?" I asked. "A vampire?"

"No," he answered darkly.

"Then what?" I questioned.

He shook his head. "I don't know." He took a deep breath. "Anyway. That's the other thing I needed to tell you." He stood to face me. I was taken aback by the vulnerability in his voice, the slump of his shoulders, as if he really were just another person with hopes and dreams the same as me.

"Amaya, I know you want me to give you the cure for the virus."

Surprise stunned me. "You're admitting you have the cure?"

He nodded. I shouldn't have been surprised.

"I have it. But I won't give it to you. Or to anyone, for that matter."

Words escaped me. He had the cure but *chose* to keep it hidden from the world? And here I was trying to pretend he wasn't a monster.

"You want to know why," he said.

"Yeah. That's an understatement." Anger replaced my shock. "Why, Lucian? You're dooming so many people to die. You're dooming me to die."

"I know, Amaya." His voice turned quiet. "I'll show you my answer."

He pulled off his gloves.

Sunlight revealed flaking dead scales peeling from curving fingers. Sores wept pus from cuts. Yellowed nails were cracked and blunted, as if he'd hacked at them.

I couldn't hide the half-second of revulsion that must've flashed through my eyes.

"This is why. Because I refuse to let anyone become like me."

"But…"

He replaced his gloves. "I won't do it. I loved my father, but what he did to me was wrong. I could never live with myself, knowing I'd doomed anyone to a fate like mine." He locked his jaw. "I may live a long time, but that doesn't mean my body is free of pain. I suffer every day. Not just the mental pain of remembering loved ones who've passed, who I may never see again. But the all-consuming hunger becomes unbearable. The blood transfusions do nothing to alleviate the constant gnawing in my stomach. And the sores. Have you ever had a wound that would never heal? Something that always felt as if it were cancer eating away your skin? That's the pain I experience. Every single day."

My eyes must've betrayed my pity, because he shook his head, looking away.

"Of course," he continued. "It doesn't bother me like it did when I was first awoken. I've learned to block it, but it took years. No. I won't do it. I can't give you the *cure*." He spat the word.

My heart turned to stone.

Numbness blanked my mind, leaving me a cold and empty shell as the truth sank in.

I would never get the cure.

"So, there is no cure," I mumbled.

"Oh." He paused. "There is."

I cocked my head. "There is?"

"Death," he answered.

Heaviness crushed me.

Rubbing my eyes, I tried to keep the tears from prickling.

At least you'll see your parents again, I could imagine him saying. *But I want to live!* I wished I could shout.

"Lucian, I refuse to accept your answer. I gave myself the virus to save not just me, but everyone, because I knew there *had* to be a cure. Mom knew it, too. And now you've told me there is a cure—and I'm not referring to death. There has to be more you aren't telling me."

I looked him straight in the eyes. "What's in the envelope, Lucian? What's in the locked room in Dr. Warren's office?"

He thrust his lower jaw, shaking his head. "Leave it alone, Amaya. I've told you enough."

"No," I said with heat in my voice. I refused to give up so easily. I had to convince him to help me. There had to be another way.

I took his hands, holding them gently in mine, then, without overthinking it, I released his hand to reach up and remove his sunglasses.

He didn't stop me.

He squinted and blinked, the way a newborn might do after entering the world and seeing light for the first time.

Red pupils fanned outward, then changed to black as it encompassed his eyes.

I swallowed my fear, standing with squared shoulders as I faced him.

"I'm not afraid of you, Lucian."

His eyes revealed more emotion than I thought possible. Hope and regret. And something else—a pain I couldn't understand.

He took his sunglasses out of my hands and put them back on, covering his eyes, then turned to look at the expanses of forest.

The view was beautiful, but it was one that seemed to have no end.

"Please leave me," he said, his voice distant.

"Leave?" I asked, my voice quiet.

He nodded. "Yes. And please don't speak to me again."

His words stabbed my heart. I should've seen this coming. I'd pushed him too far.

I'd played with fire, and he'd burned me.

Excerpt from the journal of Sally Louise Anderson. 17 July 1971

He'll never love anyone again because of me. I made sure of it.

~

AMAYA

"I can't believe he said that to you!" Chloe stomped around my room.

I sat in the chair with Khan sleeping at my feet. His ears pricked every time Chloe screeched, which was happening a lot. I hugged my mom's crocheted blanket around me, my flannel plaid pajamas soft on my skin, reminding me that I was exhausted, and it was past my bedtime. But Chloe wanted to talk—which translated to getting the gossip on what had happened between me and Lucian.

"I mean, he always seems so sweet in his interviews and stuff. But then, he was—*is*—a convicted murderer. Seems like everyone forgets about that." Chloe bit her nails. "Oh my gosh, that is so creepy when you think about it. We're living in a place with a *murderer*."

"He was exonerated for that, you know."

"Yeah, but who's to say he didn't kill her? I mean…that lady, the one he bit. He killed her, didn't he?"

"Sally Anderson," I clarified.

Chloe kept pacing, her sneakers plodding over the floor. "Yeah, her."

"He was acquitted," I said.

"Why?"

"Because he died in prison. He served his term."

Chloe placed her hands on her hips. "That's ridiculous."

"Maybe." I shrugged. "But there aren't other cases like his, so there aren't laws written about people who die in prison and then come back to life. Plus, the reality is that peoples' attitudes to him shifted. They hated him when he killed Sally. Now vampires are popular and swoon-worthy thanks to Hollywood, so he's got rock-star status."

Chloe tilted her head, confused. "Just because he's a vampire and people like him?"

"He doesn't think he's one, but yeah."

She threw her hands in the air. "Our world is so messed up."

"I agree." I rubbed my eyes. Every time I closed them, all I could see was the outline of Lucian standing on the balcony, sunlight glowing on his bronzed skin. The pain in his eyes.

"Did he say anything else to you?" Chloe asked.

"No," I answered with a sigh. "And since he said he never wants to speak to me again, I don't think he ever will." Which left me at a dead end.

Except for one thing.

Archive Five.

I'd have to steal the key, but I'd done it before. Assuming I could find it. Maybe I needed to have another chat with Officer Goodman.

I'd do it tonight.

Chloe's phone buzzed and she pulled it out of her pocket. She pressed her lips together as she read the screen, then sat on the edge of my bed as she typed an answer.

"Hey, if you don't mind, I gotta go," she said. "Sorry. Damian's worried about me breaking curfew. Also, he's asking for watermelon."

"Watermelon?"

"Yeah. His appetite is so screwed up. He used to hate fruit. Will you be okay?"

"I'll be fine."

"Promise?"

I smiled. "Promise. It takes more than Lucian Vidraru to get me down."

She waved her phone at me. "Text me if you want to talk."

"Sure."

"He's a jerk, Amaya. Just remember that. No one else may see it but us, but he's a total loser and not worth your time."

I only nodded. I wasn't sure I could whole-heartedly agree with Chloe's assessment. I realized Lucian was only trying to protect me and everyone else with VS. Did that make him a jerk?

Chloe patted Khan's head before stepping out of my room, and I glanced at my phone, reading the time.

10:55.

All I wanted to do was lay down and sleep for fifteen hours, but I had to keep going if I wanted to find a cure.

I tugged off my pajamas and slipped into an oversized sweater and jeans, making sure to tuck my phone in my pocket. Khan sniffed my Nikes as I pulled them on.

"Sorry, Buddy," I said. "But I'm going alone tonight. I'm not sure what I'm getting into this time, and I don't want you to get hurt again." I stroked his ears, his fur soft under my fingers.

I tensed as I glanced up at my door. Dr. Warren would be back from his trip in a matter of hours. I wouldn't get another opportunity.

Leaving Khan in my room, I stepped outside and shut my door behind me. My tennis shoes didn't make much sound as I walked down empty passageways. When I passed by the floor-length windows, lightning sparked through storm clouds, followed by a low, rumbling thunder.

I rounded the corner leading to the front office.

Quiet laughter and soft voices came from the reception area as I found Officer Goodman chatting with the janitor.

Keys jangled as he leaned against the front desk, sticking his thumbs in his belt loops as he focused on me. His usual smile lit his round face, reminding me of Dad.

"Amaya? A little late to be wandering the halls."

"Yeah, I know, but I need to talk to you."

His gaze shifted to the janitor. "Fine." He sighed. "Let's take a walk, shall we?" His light tone sounded as if he were discussing the weather, but I detected a hint of warning. He must've known what I was up to.

Dark hallways surrounded us, lit only by the lightning coming through the windows, and the occasional single bulb buzzing overhead.

Officer Goodman glanced over his shoulder, as if to make sure we were out of earshot.

"What's this about?" he asked.

"I need the key to Archive Five in Dr. Warren's off—"

He shook his head. "Not possible."

"But I've got nowhere else to look. Please!"

"Amaya." He stopped walking to stare me down. I wasn't usually frightened by his puppy dog brown eyes, but as he narrowed them at me, he managed to look menacing. "No one goes in that room."

"What do you mean no one?"

"I mean I can't let you in. Only Dr. Warren has a key." He

crossed his arms over his broad chest, his pressed uniform creasing with his movement. "What do you think you'll find in there?"

"The cure."

He raised an eyebrow.

"Lucian admitted he has it. He won't give it to me because he doesn't want people to become like him. But he doesn't understand what he's doing. Playing God. He has no right to keep the cure from us."

"What makes you think it's in the room in Dr. Warren's office?"

"Because I've done some research," I explained. "Something about the virus changed when Lucian bit Sally Anderson. If I can find out what made it mutate, maybe we can find a way to reverse it. There's a file in Archive Five that may explain how the mutation works. If I can get the file, I can find the answer."

"Hmm." He rubbed the scruff on his chin. "Maybe."

"Can you at least help me get inside?" I asked.

"Why would I do that, Amaya? I'm supposed to be keeping you out. I'm the security guard."

I crossed my arms. "We both know you're more than that."

He cocked his head. "That's a dangerous thing to admit."

"Why?" I challenged.

"Because you're a patient here. You're supposed to be in your room right now, not wandering the hallways. You need to leave the business of finding the cure to the professionals."

"The professionals?" I scrutinized him, the apparent security guard who knew too much, who'd helped me sneak into Dr. Warren's office.

He grabbed my arm in a firm grip, not enough to hurt, but just enough to warn me that I was crossing a line. "Look, it's true that something isn't right in this place. There are certain people in high levels of government who share your mother's concerns. Dr. Warren controls the VS vaccine, and with that, he controls the virus. In the wrong hands, a virus like VS could be catastrophic."

"So, are you with the government?"

His eyes narrowed.

"I'll take that as a yes."

A line of worry creased his brow. "I'm here to make sure the virus stays controlled. That's it. Dr. Warren was able to gain an unusual amount of control over it. Most of the legal work was done before he revived Lucian, so no one thought twice about signing over the research to him. As you can tell, he keeps the studies to himself. But I'm not here to find a cure. My job is to protect the world from VS. That being said, I won't stop you if you happen to stumble on a treatment, but I can't help you, either."

I wasn't getting anywhere with this. Time to try a new tactic. "What if I happened to find something in Archive Five that benefitted you?"

"Like what?"

"Like why the virus appears all over the world without explanation?"

He pinched his lips. "You think you could find that?"

"I think there's a good chance I could."

With a nervous breath, he ran his hand through his coarse brown hair. "All right." He unhooked the keys from his belt loop, then removed a slender metal rod with several teeth protruding from the end. "Don't tell anyone—I mean *anyone*—that I gave you this. Understood?"

"Got it." I nodded to the metal device. "What is that?"

"An old universal key. I don't know if it'll work on the door, but this place is old, and not all the locks have been updated. It's worth a try." He placed it in my hand, the metal cold and heavier than it looked. "I'm trusting you, de la Vega. I expect you to be in and out as fast as you can, then return that to me."

"I understand."

"I hope you do. This is my job on the line. And I don't mean security guard."

And it's my life on the line, and everyone else who has VS, I thought as I backed away from him.

When I made it to the hallway leading to Dr. Warren's office, I sprinted through the dark hall and up the stairs. The dim passage surrounded me until I reached Dr. Warren's door. Breathing heavily, I wedged the metal rod into the lock, prying at it with shaky hands. Sweat coated my forehead in a thin sheen. My fingers froze, and I had to slow down, take deep breaths, and maneuver the rod until I heard a click.

Unoiled hinges squealed as I stepped into the dark room. The blocky shape of a desk and bookshelves took up the center of the space. As I stepped inside, wooden floorboards squeaked under my feet.

Pulling my phone from my pocket, I pressed the flashlight icon to turn on the light. Thunder rumbled outside—a long, drawn-out sound that didn't fade until I reached the spiral staircase leading into the tower. My phone's light shone over the rough stone walls. I kept one hand pressed to the wall, the gray granite reminding me of the scales covering Lucian's hands.

A shiver went down my spine as I thought of him.

Lucian.

Scaled claws. Blood-red eyes. A velvet-smooth voice meant to put me at ease. The scent of dark amber. Butterflies dancing through my stomach as I stood in his presence.

I reached the landing.

The stained-glass window highlighted the coating of varnish gleaming from the door. Lightning flashed, illuminating the red glass squares in the window, making the door appear to glow crimson.

Silenced pressed in.

Don't go in there, Amaya, Lucian's words whispered in my head. *No one is allowed in Archive Five.*

With a deep breath, I stepped to the door. I fumbled with the key until I managed to pull it out of my pocket. After sticking it in the lock, I wiggled the mechanism. The bronze doorknob rattled as I twisted the rod.

Thunder shook the floor.

Come on, I muttered, turning it one way then the other. My sweaty hands slipped. I dropped the key. Its loud thump startled me. I wiped my palms on my pants before picking up the metal dowel and starting again.

Jamming the rod into the lock, I twisted with more force. A click echoed.

I grabbed the doorknob and turned.

The door swung open.

20

Excerpt from The Philosophical Dictionary *by Voltaire; Published*
1764

These vampires were corpses, who went out of
their graves at night to suck the blood of the
living, either at their throats or stomachs.

~

AMAYA

BOOKSHELVES SURROUNDED ME. A HEAVY DESK AND WING-
backed chair took up the center of the space. I clicked my
phone's light, illuminating the rows of leather-bound volumes.
Motes drifted past as I crossed to the shelves. Dust covered the
worn books, their bindings frayed, pages turned yellow.

I read the spine of one the books.

Classic History of Vampires.

My heart sped. I paced down the shelves, reading each title.

Vampire Mythology.

Gods and Demons.

The Vampire in Europe.

Dracul

Strigoi: A History of the Dead

"You're not a vampire, huh Lucian? Then why are you researching them?" I reached for the book titled *Dracul.* Carefully, I leafed through the brittle pages, smelling of old print, and read a passage:

Dracul, translated as dragon, is the origin of the name Dracula.

Dragon.

Interesting.

I flipped to the next pages, long passages on the history of Vlad Dracula.

There is no evidence supporting the theory that Vlad Dracula visited Bran Castle, much less lived there. However, the legend was perpetuated with the release of Bram Stoker's Dracula. *Despite overwhelming evidence of the truth, the legend of Vlad Dracula roaming the halls of Bran Castle persists.*

I replaced the book and paced down the row until I arrived at a narrow door set into an alcove. When I opened it, the scent of rotting food wafted, forcing me to hold my breath. My phone's light illuminated the shape of a single bed and a table. Rust peeled from the metal bedframe, and chicken bones with bits of rotten meat littered the table.

Shock held me rooted to the spot.

Shaking my head to recover, I wandered inside, but stumbled over something that made a soft thump as it tumbled away.

Stopping, I shone the light on a book. I picked up a paperback novel of *Jane Eyre.* The image on the cover was that of a woman wearing a black dress, her hair coifed and curled in front with the look of a model from decades past. I opened it, revealing yellow, brittle pages that held a musty scent, and I read the copyright date. *January 1971.*

I flipped through it when something fell out, hitting the ground with a quiet thud. Kneeling, I picked up a passport.

Holding my light in one hand, I focused on the picture of a middle-aged woman. Her sallow skin and sunken eyes gave her the look of a drug user. Grays streaked her frizzy blonde hair. Glaring red lipstick highlighted her pinched lips, as if she were using the makeup to hide something.

Constance Lynette Barrington

Age: 54

Height: 5'6"

Weight: 115 lbs.

Place of residence: Manhattan, New York, USA

Hmm…

Who was she? Was she living here? If so, why? And if she lived here, how did I not know of her?

I took a picture of the passport photo and the woman's information, then flipped to the next pages. Most of them were stamped.

Bangladesh, South Asia. Mumbai, India. Toronto, Canada. Prague, Czech Republic.

She was certainly well-traveled. I tapped the passport on my chin, considering the possibilities of who the woman could be.

What if she was someone searching for the cure like me? What if she'd traveled the world looking for it and ended up here, hiding in an attic? But if that were so, then where was she?

Fuzzy mold grew on the chicken bones. It seemed whoever had been here hadn't lived in this room for some time.

Maybe she'd been killed…

No. I couldn't go there. Lucian wouldn't kill anyone. At least, not again. Right?

I didn't like where my thoughts were taking me, so I placed the passport back where I'd found it inside the book, then I replaced the paperback on the floor.

As I stood, the thought nagged me that perhaps the woman was a victim of Lucian's appetite. Maybe he kept victims in this room until he was ready to feed on them.

Heart pounding, I did my best to shove the thought from my mind, but it only niggled into my thoughts even worse, until I couldn't focus on anything else.

At least I hadn't found a body.

Not that Lucian would need to hide them here when he had a whole cemetery at his disposal.

Rubbing the chills prickling my arms, the need to be out of this room loomed over me like a black shroud. I left the small space and shut the door behind me. Wandering through the shelves, I was struck by the enormity of research. Rows and rows of tomes on vampires and mythical creatures stretched into the darkness. I stopped at a shelf labeled *Viruses*.

Placing my phone on the ground, the light shone in a narrow area, illuminating the golden lettering on the spines while leaving the rest of the room in darkness. One read: *Virology and Mythology--Making the Connections.*

I pulled it out and flipped it open. Pages of illustrations and captions caught my attention. Most was supposition. Wild theories on myths and science, how some civilizations blamed creatures of myth on illnesses. They'd taken steps to eradicate the diseased victims. It usually resulted in burning or torturing.

The illustrations of people burning in pits, and demons dancing around them, soured my stomach, so I replaced the book on the shelf.

As I picked up my light, a wisp of air whispered behind me. I spun around. Empty rows loomed behind me. The cold in the room grew more intense. I rubbed my hands over my arms for warmth.

Across from me, a shelf labeled *Lab Journals* caught my attention.

I pulled out several slim tomes and flipped them open.

Handwritten notes took up the pages. After glancing around the room, I scanned through the entries until got to one labeled *Virus Mutation- January 21, 1972.*

Virus was extracted successfully from donor. Refer to letter from C. Vidraru for source and location.

I flipped through the rest of the entries, but nothing of substance stood out.

Letter from C. Vidraru.

What were the chances that very letter was housed in a box with a false bottom in the room of Lucian Vidraru?

Now I'd come full circle.

If I wanted to find the source of a virus, I needed that letter. I shelved the journal, grabbed my light, and paced down the pathway through the books.

"I'll find it," I muttered to myself. "I've only got to convince Lucian to help me." I bit back a sigh of frustration, and I counted the things I'd found.

A woman named Constance Barrington.

A clue leading to Lucian's journal.

And a cure waiting to be found.

21

Vampire Hunting Kit for Use in Protection Against Modern Vampires

With the onset of the Vampire Virus, modern vampire hunting kits are being introduced to protect yourself in case of vampire attack. Act fast! These kits are selling out quickly. Included are a wooden cross, a wooden stake with mallet, a hand mirror, and NEW! are three wooden bullets etched with the symbol of the cross, and two syringes filled with holy water. Comes in a wood-stained box. $210.00. All sales are final. Do not ingest. Handle with care. By purchasing this item, the buyer agrees to be exclusively responsible for its use and the seller's responsibility ENDS.

~

LUCIAN

Dr. Warren sat in his usual chair in my room. He held a steaming mug in one hand, newspaper in the other. He acted casually, as if he'd always been there sipping his coffee, as if he were a constant fixture in my life.

I sat on the couch across from him, morning sunlight streaming from gaps in the clouds through the tall glass windows. The brightness didn't bother me, but if I wasn't wearing my tinted glasses, my retinas would've been burning by now.

"No survivors from Taiwan?" I asked.

He took a sip of his coffee. "No."

"Why?"

He shrugged. "The virus was in advanced stages when I got there. Most were elderly and young kids. Didn't have a chance in the first place, although I did find two people in their twenties. Another was eighteen."

Hope sparked in my chest. "What happened to them?"

He placed his newspaper on his lap. Wrinkles creased the taut skin of his freshly tanned face. "They refused treatment. News about your accident with the prep-school students made headlines, so they thought it was too dangerous to come. I couldn't convince them you were harmless."

I flexed my gloved hands. "That's a shame."

Dr. Warren shrugged. "It's not a surprise. We've always struggled against stereotypes."

"I suppose. What do we do, then? Do we send the vaccine to Taiwan?"

"We're shipping enough in the next four months to vaccinate their entire population, but as you know, not everyone will accept it. A quarter of the population is immune to the vaccine."

Heaviness weighed on me. "How many dead?" I asked, dreading the answer.

"Forty-seven by the time I left. Two-hundred more infected."

I glanced out the window. The sun had already risen. The pinks and purples streaking the sky had faded, replaced with dreary, low-hanging clouds. "Isn't there anything else we can do?"

"Like what?" he asked.

"Improving the vaccine?" I suggested.

"We've been working on that for fifteen years. The virus evolves too quickly for us to keep up with, and the symptoms are different for every patient. It's a complicated problem without a clear solution. Have patience. We'll get there eventually. Look at how long cancer's been around, and we still don't have a cure for it." He spoke in a monotone voice, as if he'd memorized the phrases. His newspaper crinkled as he pulled it up. The headline snagged my attention. LIVING VAMPIRE RETURNS TO FACILITY AMIDST SCANDAL.

Now it was a scandal, huh?

Frustrated, I ran a hand over my bald head. Why couldn't I stop this virus from spreading? Why did every death feel as if a nail were piercing my heart?

The walls decorated with heavy crosses and dark mahogany bookshelves felt as though they caged me in, so I stood and paced to the window, balling my fists. Sometimes I felt as though chains covered my hands, and not merely leather.

I pressed my hand to the glass. Fog covered the forest, and I could only make out the silhouettes of trees, and none of the colors. I'd come to the facility to help with the research, but I was a prisoner here, too. I could never live anywhere else. Sure, I could travel with the proper paperwork, but I'd never call anywhere else home.

I was still a murderer. I always would be.

Sally's face flashed into my memory. With a wave of revulsion, I pushed the image away.

"Are you upset about the headlines?" Dr. Warren asked.

"Among other things," I answered with a frown, not turning to meet his gaze.

"It'll blow over," he said in a casual way, a smile on his lips. "Always does. But I am curious." Holding his coffee, he stood and walked to me, looking through the window. "What were you doing in Saratoga?" His question held a hint of accusation.

I stuck my hands in my pockets. I'd have to choose my words carefully. "Went on a date."

His eyebrows rose. "A date?"

"Yes. Chloe—eh…can't remember her last name. She invited me. I agreed."

"You went on a date?" His eyes narrowed. Why?"

"Because I'm trying to be more sociable," I answered casually. "She asked me to go out and I said yes."

"More sociable?" He cocked his head. "Where did this come from?"

"I don't know." I stuck my hands in my pockets. "Sometimes I like to pretend I'm not permanently lonely."

"I see," he muttered, suspicion in his voice.

I rubbed my neck where a tension knot was forming.

"Strange that you went on a date with a fellow student." Dr. Warren sipped his coffee. "I thought you'd agreed not to do that."

"It was a double date," I explained. "Don't read too much into it."

"Double date with whom?" His tone reminded me of an overprotective parent.

I shrugged, hoping he didn't detect anything out of the ordinary. "Her brother and his date. Amaya."

"De la Vega?"

I nodded.

"Primary virus holder. She's doing remarkably well for someone with that strain of the disease. Have you found out how she contracted it?"

"Yes. She took a vial from her mother."

He pinched his lips. "She injected herself?"

I nodded. "She wants to find a cure. Thought we had it and wanted us to give it to her."

"You didn't give it to her, did you?"

I frowned. "Of course not."

"That was a bold move on her part. She must've known she couldn't have gotten into the facility any other way."

"But she must've also known she'd die by doing it," I said.

"Can you blame her?" he asked. "She was desperate. Both her parents died of the virus."

I eyed him. "You knew that?"

"I knew it when she came here, of course. Miss de la Vega hasn't escaped my notice." He sipped his coffee. "I found her on my security cameras last night. She broke into the tower in my office."

My heart raced. She'd been snooping again? What was wrong with her? Why couldn't she understand we were doing everything we could? "Did she find anything?"

"Nothing that will be of consequence." He let out a breathy sigh. "It's a shame she'll die so quickly. Someone as smart as her would've made a good researcher."

"Yeah. A shame." I would add her nail to the thousands of others piercing my heart. But the thought of losing Amaya hurt with a pain worse than the nameless others, which was proof I was growing too attached.

I stepped away from the window, my gaze snagging on the black dome of my motorcycle helmet sitting on the table. I hadn't been out for a ride since I'd been released from the hospital. Maybe it was time to get away again, to feel the wind on my skin, leave the confines of the facility, and to sort out my emotions.

"Rain's coming," Dr. Warren said as I picked up my helmet.

I couldn't help but laugh. Of all things, bad weather was the last thing I had to fear. "That's okay. I need some time to think."

He nodded, coffee mug cradled like a newborn baby in his hand as he faced the window. "We could cure her, you know."

I swallowed the sudden thickness in my throat. "No."

"You're sure?" His eyebrows arched.

"Yes," I answered firmly. "You know as well as I that it's not a cure. It's a curse."

Dr. Warren didn't meet my gaze. Gray light seeped through dark clouds, highlighting his white scrubs in a dim pallor. "Every virus presents differently, which means every cure will present differently as well. We could give it a try."

I shook my head. How could he consider this? "No." I forced the word through clenched teeth. "I won't do that to her."

"You're sure?" he questioned. "You can't be convinced to try? She'll die otherwise."

A hole opened in the pit of my stomach. *Death.* Everyone feared it but me, and I was the only one who'd never experience it. "It's for the best. I won't doom her to this existence."

"Lucian—"

"No," I repeated, my voice stern. "I won't allow it. I refuse. We're not meant to play God, Dr. Warren. My father tried, and he failed."

He nodded, lips pinched. He wasn't happy with my answer, but it was the only one he'd get.

With my helmet tucked under one arm, I grabbed my leather jacket from the side closet. I gave one last glance at my bookshelf where I kept Father's letter.

No. I wouldn't let him taunt me, though I had to admit, after all these years, my father's words still had power over me.

But this delusion had to end now. We'd find a cure with our own research. We didn't need Father's hand involved in this.

I wouldn't subject anyone else to the cure.

Two failed attempts were enough.

22

Craiova, Romania: From the police report of the grave of Andrei Kovo

The deceased **ANDREI KOVO** date of death October 29, 2015. Body was found exhumed and in an unusually grotesque state. When questioned, the people of Craiova village claimed to have gotten violently ill after the death of KOVO. Some claim to have seen visions of him in their dreams. The deceased was deemed a vampire. The villagers dug up the body. They reportedly found proof when the deceased was found with blood on his lips, and hair and nails that had continued to grow after death. They cut out the heart and cooked it to make a potion. The affected townspeople then drank the potion to rid themselves of the supposed vampire's curse. The townspeople claimed that the visions ceased and considered the anti-vampire ritual a success.

AMAYA

MY EYES BLURRED AS I STARED AT MY COMPUTER SCREEN. I clicked another link. Finding anything out about Constance Lynette Barrington from Manhattan was a pain. Every link I found had the wrong age, wrong profile picture, or wrong ethnicity.

Another page loaded, revealing the profile of a teenage girl with braces and a *GO TIGERS!* flag decorating the frame.

Seriously.

Where was this woman?

Did she even exist?

I rubbed my temples where a headache pulsed. Khan lay by my feet. He'd been asleep since midnight, and it was almost one in the morning.

Frustrated, I had nothing to show for my research, which left me with one conclusion.

Either Constance Lynette Barrington didn't exist, or she'd been erased from online records.

"Where are you?" I mumbled, clicking another link. A website called FindAnyoneOnline.com.

An ad popped up.

Download ID now! Upload PhotoChoose NameGet passport or Driver's License ID!

Hmm. How totally legit and legal. Was it possible Constance had used just such a site to create the passport?

I clicked the link. The garish yellow page, Comic Sans font, and misaligned paragraphs gave me the feeling this wasn't the most professional webpage in the world.

A button labeled *Upload Profile Image* took up the center of the screen. When I clicked it, the caption asked me to upload my photo, then GET YOURS LEGALISED PASSPORT NOW!

Scanning the site gave me an idea.

I clicked back to my web browser. If Constance were using

a fake name, how would I find out? I typed *photo identifier* into the browser. Several sites popped up. One was an app that claimed to use social media tagging recognition to identify anyone's picture posted on the internet. I picked up my phone, downloaded the app, and uploaded the image of Constance's passport photo.

Khan woke as I waited for the results to load, ears pricked as he studied the door. A low growl rumbled in his throat.

"Something wrong?" I asked quietly, leaning forward to pat his head. He stayed so intent on watching the door, he didn't move as I touched him.

"Khan." I spoke firmly. With a final growl, he laid his head on his paws, his tail thumping the bed sheets.

I stood and crossed my room, the floor cold under my bare feet. Standing at the door, I hugged my arms to my chest, a sudden chill causing my skin to bristle with goosebumps. Silence came from outside. No voices or footsteps. Nothing.

I grabbed my doorknob, the metal ice cold.

Wild thoughts crowded my imagination. Would I find anyone outside? Anything?

Ghosts…

No. My inner scientist told me to cut it out.

After turning the knob, I opened the door a crack and peeked outside. An empty hallway spanned in either direction, lit only by a dimly buzzing bulb glowing so far away, shadows crowded outside.

My phone pinged from my bed, startling me.

I closed my door, locked it, and did my best to ignore my heart beating too fast. The facility was so old, Khan had probably heard the clanking water heater, or the wind, for all I knew.

As I sat on my bed, I grabbed my phone and scrolled through the results. Twenty-one images found.

I clicked the first one.

A woman in Dulles International Airport had been tagged

in a photo. No name was assigned to the picture. She stood behind a posed family. Her face was slightly blurred as she must've been walking behind them when the picture was taken, though her red lipstick was unmistakable.

I clicked the next one.

A woman in an airport again. This one at India International. As with the first, no name.

The next showed a woman in a lobby where a chandelier gleamed. Her wide-brimmed black hat shadowed her eyes. She didn't look at the camera, half her body hidden behind two men wearing tuxedos.

I clicked the next few with no name assigned to her photo until I reached one near the bottom.

The faded picture showed the woman smiling, her hair lighter and teased to frame her face, her expression happy as she held a margarita. She wore a red bathing suit as she sat on a lounge chair on the beach.

Adelle Gibson

No date. No location. Just a name and a picture. After searching the rest of the photos, the one on the beach was the only one with a name.

Something seemed so familiar about the photo. As I studied it, the white sand and turquoise blue water caught my attention. I'd seen this beach in another photo—the one sitting on Dr. Warren's desk. But was it only a coincidence that the beach looked so similar? The same colored sand, the same hue of the water.

I copied the name *Adelle Gibson* into the search engine. I sorted through the entries, until one caught my eye. It was a rental contract for an expensive downtown Manhattan apartment. *The Residences at Waterline Square.* Adelle Gibson was listed as a current resident. Her picture, taken during a meet-and-greet for the residents, matched the images of Constance Barrington.

Something thudded against my door.

Khan's hackles rose. His lips curled as he snarled.

Steeling my nerves, I rose from my bed.

Some stupid kid was pranking me. Had to be.

"You'd best leave me alone, jerk." I approached and grabbed the knob, then I yanked the door open, once again revealing an empty hallway. Swallowing my fear, I stepped out of my room. The overwhelming scent of gasoline burned my eyes. When I took a step, my toe caught on something.

Glancing down, I found a paperback book, *Jane Eyre* printed on the cover beneath a picture of a woman wearing a black dress and an outdated hairstyle.

Heart racing, I knelt and picked up the book. Sharp fumes made me hold my breath. Soggy pages dripped with honey-colored liquid. A piece of notebook paper stuck out of the pages. I unfolded it and read the single handwritten word.

BURN.

The hiss of a match echoed. A flame burst to life from the dark hallway, illuminating a woman wearing a white dress. The crazed look in her eyes made me stumble backward. A wicked smile lit her face before she smashed something on the floor. Glass shattered, and the pungent scent of kerosene carried through the open corridor.

Blue flames licked at the exposed fuel, trailing over the floor and up the walls, moving so fast, I wondered if she'd doused the whole facility. Heat singed my face as a fireball erupted.

The blast knocked me inside my room. I fell to the floor, hitting my head so hard, stars danced in my vision, just as the flames consumed my ceiling.

23

Interview between Lucian Vidraru and Steve Redden for Our World Magazine

Steve: Tell me about your earliest memories.
Lucian: That's a funny question. People tend to remember emotions more than anything else. Fear or pain. I'm no different. My first memory is of pain. I was very young when my parents lived in a cottage. It was a cold day. Rainy and windy. I remember sitting by the fire to get warm. I wore a wool shift, full of holes, too big as it had belonged to my older brothers. I remember shivering, wanting to be warm when I backed into the coals. My shift caught fire. Burned half my body by the time I got it off.
I laid in bed for three months trying to recover.
Steve: It seems you remember that pretty well.
Lucian: Well, what can I say? It's hard to forget. Pain is a memory that stays.

~

LUCIAN

Wind rushed past my face as I rode down the dark road. If I had wings, this was what flying would feel like. I soaked in the nighttime air that smelled of spruce and a hint of rain. My bike's headlight illuminated the curves and dips of the highway. I was tempted to turn it off and let the dark of night envelop me, let the heat of the insects and rodents appear as bright dots in the forest, but I had to keep other motorists in mind. Wouldn't want them to hit a vampire riding his motorcycle.

I growled under my breath.

How did such a name ever get started?

Even Amaya called me that. But did she have any reason not to? Of course, she didn't, because I'd never given her proof of the opposite. And I never would.

Amaya.

The girl haunted my thoughts. I couldn't shake the vision of her dark, pleading eyes. When she'd asked for the cure, for a moment, I'd almost given it to her. But to do such a thing would've been selfish. How could I doom her to a life like mine knowing what she'd have to endure?

No.

I wouldn't do it.

Dr. Warren was sure to find something soon. Some of his research was promising, and with the right treatment, Amaya could expect to live months longer than originally predicted.

But was it enough?

Even with a year to live, could I so easily let her go?

I would. I'd let go of everyone else.

Gripping the handlebars tighter, I raced around a curve, leaving the forest behind me to enter an open field. I didn't love her. Not yet. But I knew if I didn't keep a lid on my emotions, it would happen.

I'd tried talking myself out of it—tried remembering

Sally's face and the horror I'd brought to her. But I'd lived long enough to know something as unpredictable and powerful as love couldn't be controlled.

My only choice was to keep my distance from Amaya.

I'd already told her I never wanted to speak to her again. The hurt in her eyes had shown me just what my words had done to her. She was so young, chances were, she really believed I wanted nothing more to do with her.

The familiar pang of heartbreak tugged at me, threatening to weigh me down. I wouldn't let it. Not this time. It was better for us to be apart. Better to let Dr. Warren continue with the research. Better to keep my distance from her before she persuaded me to cure her.

Those same dark eyes loomed in my memory again. Pleading and intense.

I ground my teeth as I rode to the top of a hill. A traditional two-story house stood under the moonlight, the pale glow illuminating the red bricks and white-capped water running in a nearby stream. Horses stood by a barn. I stopped my bike near the drive and cut off the engine. As I removed my helmet, the sound of running water replaced the roar of my bike's engine.

I stood unmoving.

A gentle wind that smelled of fresh hay wafted, tugging at the tree branches. Not many leaves remained on skeletal limbs. Winter would come soon. I already felt the chill in the air, the taste of ice that would soon bury the fiery colors brought by autumn.

Life kept going. One cycle after another.

I stood apart, watching from a distance. Life in a house like that, in a place where I could wake every morning and feel at peace, where I could be a part of life and not an observer—no. Why was I letting my thoughts go there?

After strapping on my helmet, I grabbed my bike, kicked

up the stand, and revved the engine. The roar replaced the velvet calm of night.

I turned around and headed back to the facility, where I belonged.

Maybe I wouldn't go out riding anymore. I didn't need the unexpected emotions.

As I rode down a hill, a buck stood in the forest. It raised its head, ears pricked, antlers curving with twelve points.

Its body heat glowed against the thick bramble of hedges and tree trunks. Pulsing blood warmed the air around it. The wind carried the scent of wild meat.

I gripped my handlebars until my fingers cramped, suppressing the urge to rip through its neck and sever its life vein. To let its blood flow over my hands.

No.

I wasn't that person anymore.

The deer darted away as I passed, rustling tree limbs and splashing through puddles until the glow of its body heat disappeared.

Sweat beaded on my neck. I slowed my bike as I took deep breaths. My pounding heart revealed my heightened anticipation.

Focus, Lucian.

Now I allowed Amaya into my thoughts—the soothing calmness of her voice, the brightness of her smile, the lavender scent of her skin, and the dark depths of her intelligent eyes. My racing heart slowed. My breathing evened out.

Maybe it was wrong of me to use her that way, to let her become such a part of me that I relied on her to keep me human. But I wasn't hurting her. At least there was that.

The sharp scent of smoke filled the air, carried on the wind from the south. I traveled along the road, tires crunching loose asphalt until I crested a hilltop.

Smoke thickened on the horizon, heat appearing as a yellow cloud blocking out the stars.

It couldn't be the facility. No way. Had to be a farmer burning his field. Or a brush fire. But I couldn't ignore the sinking in the pit of my stomach.

I pressed my accelerator until my speedometer passed ninety. Fear prickled the back of my neck, tingling with an unspoken warning.

When I rounded a curve, the brightness of flames licking at the facility's west tower burned my retinas. I shielded my naked eyes against the glare.

My heart dropped to the pit of my stomach.

Amaya.

My first thought was to save her.

Why such a thing crossed my mind, I didn't question.

My speedometer passed one hundred, but time felt so slow, I couldn't breathe. When I turned onto the drive, my bike swerved, and I barely managed to stay upright. Gravel spewed behind my tires, creating a rut that cut deep into the road.

I regained my balance and punched the accelerator until I reached the end of the drive.

Shouts mingled with the crackling flames and pungency of charred wood. Firetrucks crowded the front lawn. Jets of water arced toward the facility.

I clutched the brake so fast I nearly flew off my seat. Tires skidded with a shriek. I killed the engine as I leapt off. The facility loomed over me, a hulking, hellish nightmare glowing with hellfire. Crackling orange flames consumed the windows and licked at the stone towers of the west wing.

Amaya.

Please God, let her be alive.

Such a stupid thing to ask when she was doomed to die so soon, but the thought of losing her gripped me with fear, an emotion I hadn't anticipated—one that conjured memories of seeing Barb bleeding out on the bed.

Terror drove me forward as I sprinted over the lawn, the grass wet from spray of the pumper trucks.

The red glare of lights tinted the bricks crimson.

People wrapped in blankets and wearing pajamas gathered on the lawn. Their wide eyes fixated on the burning building. I pushed through them, recognizing some. Nurse Teesha rushed to me. Tears streamed down her face. Her haunted expression held the look of a startled animal, and clumps of hair stuck up in every direction. She grabbed my shoulders and hugged me to her.

"Lucian, thank the Lord." Sniffling, she pulled away, wiping her face with a damp tissue. "Were you inside?"

"No. I was out on my bike. What happened?"

"Fire alarm went off twenty minutes ago." She waved behind her. "They're not telling us anything. Don't know how it started. Not sure how many are still inside."

I glanced at the crowd, at the faces of each person, my heart heavy and pounding, sweat beading on my clammy skin as I didn't find who I searched for.

"Have you seen Amaya?" I asked, though I feared the answer.

"Miss De la Vega?"

"Yeah."

She craned her neck, scanning the crowd. Bodies jostled and shouting echoed from the firefighters near the facility.

Nurse Teesha shook her head. "I haven't seen her."

I squeezed her arm. "Stay here."

"Lucian, wait—"

I marched toward Dr. Warren and Officer Goodman who stood talking in hushed voices.

Dr. Warren's gaze met mine. Relief replaced his fear. He grabbed my gloved hands between his.

"Lucian, I was so worried. Where were you?"

"Out on my bike when I saw the smoke." I looked pointedly at the two men. "What happened?"

"We aren't sure," Officer Goodman answered. "But we've got a head count of one-hundred forty-two people out here.

Three are missing. Yo Chen, Sarah Murphy, and Amaya De la Vega. Firefighters are inside looking for them now. They were all housed in the west wing where they suspect the fire started."

My heart squeezed painfully tight. I unzipped my jacket and ripped it off, dropping it on the ground. These people were my family, my responsibility. My life.

I pushed past Dr. Warren toward the firefighters. They gathered around the entrance. Several men sat on the ground with their coats off, faces darkened with soot, breathing heavily through an oxygen mask.

Frantic voices shouted, mingling with the roar of fire and the thick pungency of smoke.

Lights flashed strobe-like over the towers. When I made it to the steps leading to the entrance, I passed two firefighters covered in soot. Trails of sweat streaked their faces.

"Hey." One of the men grabbed my arm. "Where are you going?"

I nodded to the open doors. "In there."

"No way, man," the second firefighter answered. "It's too dangerous."

I growled under my breath. "Not for me, it isn't."

The two men traded glances.

"Vidraru?" The first man asked, wiping sweat off his brow.

"Yeah. That's me."

"You can't die?" the second man asked.

"Exactly." I pointed to the entrance. "Where are they?"

"You can't be serious," the first man said.

"I'm dead serious." Maybe not the best choice of words in such a situation. "Where are they?" I repeated.

"West wing," the first man said, eyes mirroring exhaustion. "Two on the second floor. One is trapped on the bottom floor."

Amaya's room was on the first floor.

Shouts came from inside. A group of firefighters exited, one holding a pale-faced girl wearing a white tank top and blue shorts covered in powdery ash. She stared in shock, her eyes wide as they carried her to a waiting ambulance.

"We found Yo!" they yelled. "Two left inside."

Sarah and Amaya. I raced past the firefighters carrying Yo and into the burning building. Heat radiated. Flames crackled, and only then did my terror of being burned alive rear its evil head.

With shaky hands and labored breaths, I did my best to push the fear aside and ran for the stairs—to the second floor, to Sarah—a split decision I hoped didn't haunt me. But choosing between the death of two people—no matter how much I might've cared for one, couldn't be dictated by emotion.

It didn't matter. I'd save them both.

I sped past walls and corridors, through thick billowing smoke, though my eyesight allowed me to see the heat of the flames as I dodged them. On the second floor, I ran down a hallway, my feet thudding the tiles, my labored breath choked and hoarse from the smoke.

"Sarah!"

Heart pounding, I sprinted to the next hallway, adrenaline fueling my movements the same as during a hunt, giving me added speed and endurance. I raced around a corner when the image of a girl's body lying motionless in the hallway stood out in bright oranges and reds in the darkness.

I knelt beside her. "Sarah?"

I ripped off my gloves before taking her hands in mine. Pressing my fingertips to her wrists, I felt for a pulse.

Fluttering movement beat with a strong, rhythmic pattern.

"Hang in there." I picked her up, then moved down the hallway, smoke billowing from either side as it spewed from open doorways, though I steered us away from the flames.

A firefighter neared me, his loud, mechanical breathing

announcing his presence.

"I found her," I called.

Sarah's body remained limp and unmoving as I passed her to the man. He took her and rushed her down the hallway, back the way he'd come, leaving me alone.

I maneuvered through the hall until I reached the stairs. I took them by two until I reached the bottom and raced down the corridor.

The smoke rose toward the ceiling, leaving charred wood and piles of ash behind. Emergency lights glared through broken windows. Glass crunched under the soles of my shoes.

The blare of alarms echoed in the distance. I turned down the hall leading to Amaya's room. The outline of her door stood out in the glare of red emergency lights.

Frantic barking came from ahead.

"Khan!" I called.

Boards creaked, followed with an earsplitting crash as a wall collapsed in my path, spewing ash and charred wood into the air, knocking me backward.

I landed on my side. Sharp splinters cut my face.

Sitting up, I rubbed at the stinging pain in my neck, my hand brushing over a piece of wood lodged in my flesh. I grabbed it and pulled it out. Warm liquid seeped from the open wound.

Great. Now was no time to lose blood.

Getting to my feet, I reached for a wooden beam when flames burst to life.

"Amaya!" I yelled, praying she could hear me.

Nothing but the roaring flames answered. Not even Khan made a sound.

Searing heat exploded from the ruined wood and insulation. I held my arm across my face and gritted my teeth as I walked into the wall of flames.

Are you afraid?

Terrified.

24

Notes from the field journal of Constatin Vidraru. January 9, 1873.
Tinos, Greece

Here we arrived at the highest mount in Tinos—
the place called a windy revenge, where
Hercules killed Vorias, the god of the north winds.
Vorias' revenge was to blow a perennial—and exceed-
ingly strong—northern wind over the island. Today
we experienced the fury of this very wind on our
quest to the mountain's peak, where I have great
confidence in finding the treasure that will alter the
course of human life expectancy.

~

AMAYA

I WOKE ON THE GROUND, WET GRASS STICKING TO MY ARMS
and backs of my legs. As I opened my eyes, I had to narrow
them against the flood lights looming over me. Lucian's face
entered my field of vision.

He didn't wear his glasses, and his shirt was little more than clumps of ash sticking to his exposed chest.

"Amaya," he breathed. His voice cut through the noise of chaotic shouts.

He picked me up and held me to him, the warmth of his body enveloping me.

His show of affection shocked me, but with the warm strength of his essence surrounding me, I didn't push him away.

Fragmented memories of the past half hour came as bursts of images:

The book of *Jane Eyre* heavy with gasoline. My fingers soaked with the liquid.

The woman in white. The crazed look in her eyes as she lit the match.

Fire.

Consuming my room, flames searing hot as they neared me. Khan whining at my side as I'd passed out.

The next thing I'd remembered was waking to the sound of the collapsing wall.

Rubbing my head, my hands smelled of gasoline. Blisters covered the skin of my arms, and even small movements sent fire running through my nerve endings. A dense fog crowded my thoughts. I only wanted to close my eyes and sleep. With Lucian holding me, my lucid thoughts turned to him, the strength of his arms, the way his face softened when he looked at me.

"Lucian," I mumbled.

"Amaya, I thought I'd lost…" His voice trailed off, and I glanced up at his lidless eyes rimmed in minuscule gray scales, devoid of tears, though it wasn't hard to imagine them there. The shiver of fear I might've experienced at such a sight was absent. I soaked in the moment, the strength of his arms, the heavy beating of his heart against my breast.

"You saved me?"

"I couldn't leave you in there, could I? Couldn't leave him either." He nodded behind him when a furry mass of white fur shuffled to us. Khan's wet tongue licked my cheek. Tears stung my eyes as I hugged my dog to my chest.

"Silly beast," I mumbled. I stroked his head. Khan whined as he sat beside us. I hastily wiped the tears from my face when Lucian reached out, running the pad of his ungloved thumb across my cheek to wipe a stray tear, his scales surprisingly smooth, making warm tingles replace the chill from my damp clothes.

"You said you never wanted to speak to me again," I said.

A ghost of a smile creased his perfectly formed lips. "Things change when you have to watch someone almost die."

Terror ran like cold water through my veins. I'd thought after Mom and Dad died, going to join them wouldn't be so bad. But now, the idea of going to my own death frightened me more than I thought possible.

I placed my hand on Lucian's chest, feeling the pulsing rhythm of his beating heart beneath my fingers, never wanting to move. He brushed a strand of damp hair from my forehead, the tips of his claws lingering.

"Amaya, I have to apologize."

"For what?"

"I'm sorry I kept the cure from you," he answered, his voice velvety soft. "I realize it's not my decision to make."

"What?" I gasped, breathless. "What are you saying? You'll give me the cure?"

"Well…" his voice trailed. "I can't give it to you. Not yet. I don't have it here. To find the cure, we'll have to go back to my original home. Romania."

"Romania," I repeated the word, one that sounded foreign as I spoke it. "But…you're not joking, right? You really will give me the cure?"

"Yes," he said resolutely. "I'll give it to you."

"What changed your mind?"

His eyes, red pupils and indiscernible irises that flooded to black pools, flashed with fear. "It's selfish. I decided I don't want to watch you die—and that's the only reason. I wish it were something more noble, that I wanted to save humankind from a deadly virus, that I wanted to bring hope to a world full of despair. But I'm not doing it for that. I'm doing it for you. Because I can't stand to be without you." His Adam's apple bobbed as he swallowed. "Amaya, before we do this, I want you to know that even if we inject you with the anti-virus, we're not sure what will happen. You could become like me— or you could become… something else."

"Something else?" I tilted my head. "What do you mean?"

"I can't explain everything now, but this isn't the first time I've tried this."

The image of Sally Anderson flashed in my memory. "You tried with Sally, didn't you?"

He nodded.

From the facility, shouts echoed. Sitting up, I focused on the glare of lights, the billowing smoke.

My heart stopped as the fog cleared from my brain. I grabbed Lucian's bare shoulders, his skin shockingly smooth and warm.

"Did Chloe and Damian make it out?"

"Yes," he answered, his calm voice silencing my fears. "Everyone made it out. You were the last one."

I sagged in his arms, relief flooding through me.

Emergency workers approached. One of them told Lucian to put me in an ambulance. Everything happened in a blur. By the time I got checked out and cleared, rays of pink tinted the sky.

Only wet, roiling, black clouds remained of the flames.

Lucian stood beside me as we faced the facility. A warm breeze stirred the grass. I hugged a blanket around me. Others sat in cars, though most had relocated to the hospital or hotels.

Lucian placed his arm around me, and I couldn't deny how right it felt to have him there beside me.

Hope swelled in my chest.

For the first time since I'd stood over Daddy's grave, I had a path to freedom—to life.

Whatever the future held, I was ready.

25

Notes from the field journal of Constatin Vidraru. January 10, 1873. Tinos, Greece

When we entered the cave, we were grateful for walls that blocked wind, until we started along the trail. The human skeletons were most disturbing of all. What could have lived in this ungodly place? My studies on creatures of myth had been done while reading inked words on pages. I wasn't prepared for the physical manifestations of such unearthly and vile creatures—if such things existed. One thought drove me: to find what I sought I had no choice but to move forward.

Even if those incarnations would be the death of me.

~

AMAYA

SUNLIGHT STREAMED THROUGH THE WINDOW, WARMING ME AND Khan. Outside, most of the leaves had fallen from the trees, blanketing the ground. Their once-vibrant colors turned to lifeless shades of brown.

It had been a week since the fire, and I'd spent most of it in the hospital. I'd returned to Crimson Hollow amidst the sounds of hammers and the beeping of backhoes. I patted Khan's head, peering around my new temporary space—a large room in the outer building that had been spared from the fire, a place once used for the more severe mental cases. High ceilings with crown molding rose overhead. Periwinkle blue paint decorated the walls, though it was cracked and peeling in places. Tables and furniture covered with cloth sat along the edges of the room. The air held a musty odor, the smell of disuse mingled with Pine-Sol.

Chloe and Damian entered. As I sat up, bandages tugged at the scabs on my arms, and my smile must've looked more like a grimace.

Chloe rushed to me. "Amaya!"

When she hugged me, I did my best not to wince as her bony arms pressed against my burns. Her customary smile lit her face as she pulled away, and I couldn't deny how good it felt to see her.

"You're lucky to be alive," she said.

I gave Khan another pat. "Yeah."

Damian shuffled to us, hands hidden in the pockets of his oversized jeans. "How are you feeling?"

"Okay." I shrugged. "Second degree burns on my arms. They said I didn't inhale as much smoke as I could've, so I got lucky there."

"Oh my gosh, Amaya," Chloe said, her eyes lit with excitement. "I heard the news. Are you seriously going to Romania with Lucian?"

"I don't really have a choice. He's helping me get the cure. Hopefully, I can convince him to give it to everyone else, too."

Chloe bounced on her toes. "That's *so* freaking insane. You'll be in every tabloid. You'll be famous!"

I bit my lower lip. "I'm not sure I'd go that far."

"You will." She grabbed my hands, and I couldn't hold back a quiet "ouch."

"Oops." She let go, pressing her hands to her sides. "Sorry, got a little excited there."

Damian frowned at his sister. "She's injured, you know."

"I know. But I'm so happy for her. She's going to Romania with a vampire. It sounds so completely romantic." She placed her hands on her hips. "I'm jealous, you know. You'd better send me lots of pics. I hear the capital is amazing."

"I'll do my best, but you realize it's not a sightseeing tour. I'll be a little busy with trying to find the cure and all."

"Fine." She sighed.

Voices came from the hallway outside. Damian glanced over his shoulder, and I noticed the sweat beading on his brow before he pinned me with a fearful gaze. "Amaya," he said quietly. "How are you? We all saw what happened."

I cocked my head. "What do you mean?"

"Lucian," he answered. "When he carried you out…" He pinched his lips, not speaking.

"When he carried me out?" I prodded.

"He was on fire," Chloe finished for her brother. "Well, basically. His shirt was in flames before—you know." She made a *poof* sound and wiggled her fingers.

I rubbed my eyes. "I don't know what happened. After I passed out in my room, the next thing I remember was waking up outside."

"That dude's for real crazy," Damian said. "We heard the rumors. Heard he could live forever and all that. But I never really believed it. Even being here and seeing him all the time, I thought maybe it was a hoax. Photoshop or something. But…" He shook his head and looked out the window. "For real crazy," he repeated, his voice a whisper. His eyes grew wide and haunted, as if he'd seen a ghost.

A ghost.

The woman in white invaded my memories.

I hadn't told anyone about her. What would I say anyway? I'd seen a ghost and she'd set the place on fire? I didn't even believe it. How could anyone else? But I *had* seen something. Maybe I could tell Lucian. He was a vampire, after all. He of all people should believe in the paranormal.

But was he *really* a vampire? Or was he a person with a condition that made him unusual? I couldn't keep calling him by the name. He hated it, and I had to agree, it wasn't the most apt description. If he weren't a vampire, could he be something else?

A dragon, perhaps?

I ran my fingers through my hair. Ghosts, vampires, and dragons, what on earth would I believe in next?

No. He was nothing more than a person afflicted with a virus—albeit a super-strange one.

"You look worried," Chloe said.

"I'm not worried." I picked at my bandages. "Exactly," I added.

"Are you thinking about the trip to Romania?"

"Sort of." I gave Khan a pat on his head. "Lucian said he wanted to meet with me before we board Dr. Warren's private jet. I'm not sure what we'll talk about. I'm also not sure what we're supposed to find in Romania."

Romania. The name sounded so foreign. Was I ready to leave?

"Amaya," Damian said, seriousness in his voice. "Whatever he says, be careful. A person like him—someone super-human—you can't trust them. Not when they can do things we can't. He doesn't fear death. He embraces it. He could hurt you. It may be unintentional, but it could happen. He's dangerous."

"Thank you, Damian," I said solemnly. "I'll be careful."

He pressed his lips, as if doubting I understood his warning. Did it matter if Lucian was dangerous? When the source of finding the cure was so close, I had to take risks.

"We'll miss you, Amaya," Chloe said.

"I'll miss you, too. I'd take you two with me if I could."

"But you'll come back soon," Chloe said.

"And you'll come back alive," Damian added.

"Yes to both." I smiled, and a pang of loneliness tugged at me at the thought of being without my friends.

Friends, I repeated the word in my head. I wasn't expecting to find any when I came here, but I couldn't deny that I was glad I had.

Nurse Teesha entered the room.

"You ready?" she asked as she neared me.

I took a deep breath, nervousness forming a tight ball in the pit of my stomach, and I stood. "Yeah. I'm ready."

I grabbed my donated suitcase. Most of the clothes and toiletries inside were bargain buys from the discount store, as I'd lost everything in the fire. The wheels ran smoothly as I tugged it alongside me with Khan trotting at my heels. The wide hallways with sunlight streaming inside felt unusually empty. This area of the facility hadn't been used in decades, and it showed. Paint peeled from the walls, and though the floors had been thoroughly mopped, the linoleum was discolored and scuffed. What had this place been like a hundred years ago? With mental patients wandering these same hallways, the sound of quiet voices, and people playing card games in the common areas? Maybe not so different from today.

My thoughts went back to the woman in white. The insanity in her eyes. The book I'd found in the attic. *Jane Eyre*.

We stepped outside the building and bypassed a pathway partitioned with yellow caution tape, then entered the main facility and took an out-of-the way route to reach Lucian's room. When we started up the stairway, I stared in surprise at how undamaged the area was.

"Did Lucian's room get damaged in the fire?" I asked.

"No. This area was saved, thank goodness," Nurse Teesha said.

The wheels on my suitcase clattered up the steps until we made it to the top. Khan stayed close behind. We stopped at Lucian's door, and Teesha knocked before turning the doorknob.

"It's us, Mr. Lucian," she called.

A rush of nerves flitted through my stomach as we entered.

Lucian sat propped on the edge of his desk, wearing his gloves and glasses, and a black suit—the same one he wore in the magazine photos.

My stomach gave a nervous pinch, and I steadied my breathing as I approached him.

"Hello, Amaya." He stood over me, seeming taller. His voice held an edge of formality, as if he were my employer, and not the person who'd risked his life to save me, the one who'd held me in his arms as if I meant the world to him.

I'd obviously read too much into that situation. Of course, I couldn't be too hard on myself. It wasn't like I'd been in my right mind.

"Hello, Lucian," I answered, my tone equally as formal.

Nurse Teesha gave a brief smile. "I'll leave you to it," she said, then exited, closing the door behind her with a quiet click.

I clasped my hands behind my back. "What did you want to talk about?"

He motioned for me to sit in the chair by his desk. I decided now was no time to argue, so I crossed to the leather, wingback chair, and sat. He crossed his arms.

"I want you to reconsider going to Romania," he said.

"What?" I sat up straight. "Why?"

He tapped his finger on his arm. "We're traveling to Bran —where I once lived. You should know I'm not popular there. In fact, there are people who'd love to see me dead. It won't be safe for me, and especially not for you."

"I don't care," I argued. "I'm going anyway."

He gave a long-suffering sigh. "I figured you'd say that."

"You can't die anyway," I said. "And I'm dead if we don't get the cure."

"True, but I don't feel comfortable taking you to a place like that. I won't always be able to protect you."

I narrowed my eyes at him. "You don't need to protect me, Lucian."

"I think I do."

I crossed my arms. "This isn't the eighteenth century. Women are a little more independent now. I'll be fine. I can look after myself—have been since both my parents died."

He clenched his jaw. "I'm aware of what year it is. You can't blame me for wanting to protect you. This won't be an easy trip. We'll have to enter the dungeons of Bran Castle, and I'm not sure if there's anything left of my father's research to begin with. It's not a safe place. Romania isn't like America. Here, most people think of me as a champion of VS. There—I'm a myth come to life. A vampire." He spoke the word with venom in his voice. "You haven't seen the things I have. Haven't seen what humans are capable of doing to each other." He shook his head as if trying to erase the memories.

"Lucian, I understand," I said softly, hoping he heard my sincerity. "I know I haven't had as much life experience as you. I haven't seen the evil you've seen. But I need to have this chance. Please don't take this away from me. I have to find the cure—to make my parents' deaths mean something. Please, Lucian. Let me try."

He looked away from me, to the wall of windows looming behind us. The view revealed blackened, skeletal towers already fitted with scaffolding. Construction workers with bright orange vests and hardhats gathered around. The clang of hammers and mechanical hum of saws came through the glass in muffled sounds. Repairs already being made after only a week. Proof that hope survived after the fire.

"You've looked and looked," I said. "I'm a new voice, a fresh perspective." He half-turned, considering. "We'll do this. We'll find the cure together, and we'll bring it to the rest of the world."

He didn't answer, and I shifted my gaze away from the window to him, who still held the look of a man haunted by his past.

26

Excerpt from the journal of Constatin Vidraru. April 22, 1873. Bran Castle, Romania

The bond of science runs stronger than blood.

~

AMAYA

"Load it in the back," Dr. Warren shouted as we stood on the tarmac facing his private jet. I gripped Khan's leash, the roar of plane engines echoing, a stiff breeze gusting dark strands of hair across my face. Lucian stood beside me as we waited to board, our luggage being wheeled on carts up to the small plane.

We stood with several others from the facility, Officer Goodman among them, who hadn't offered me anything but a smile since we'd traveled to the airport. I wasn't sure what to think of his silence. He adjusted the taser holstered to his belt as he focused on Dr. Warren. The elderly doctor wiped the sweat from his brow, his cheeks red as he directed the workers.

"Careful with that," he shouted as they pushed a long trunk into the cargo hold.

"He's particular about his luggage," I questioned Lucian.

Lucian adjusted his sunglasses. "He's got most of his research in there, plus samples of the virus. You can't blame him."

I held my hand to shield my eyes from the sun. "How much longer?"

"Not long. We'll board soon. That's the last one." He pointed to the long trunk being carefully maneuvered into the open hold.

As soon as the back hatch was closed, Dr. Warren motioned us forward. "That took longer than expected. We'll have to hurry if we want to keep our schedule."

We followed him along with the others to the mobile staircase leading up to the open hatch.

Khan shuffled alongside me, and I tightened my grip on his leash, my palms sweaty. I glanced back at the airport, a looming building of metal and glass reflecting the afternoon sun. Unease coiled like a tight ball inside me. I'd make it home, wouldn't I?

Maybe it would help if I knew where home was to begin with. It wasn't at the facility, and it wasn't back in Miami.

Lucian's warning stayed with me as I grabbed the metal railing and climbed to the open cockpit. Following behind Dr. Warren, I dodged a flight attendant as I entered the fuselage. Goodman came aboard behind us, I noticed as I glanced back.

Plush white seats were arranged around deep-stained lacquered tables, and soft glowing lights shone artfully over each one. The air held the scent of clean leather. Insulated walls blocked the noise from outside, and I felt as if I should remove my shoes as I stepped onto the patterned white carpet.

I almost pinched myself to make sure this was real.

"This is crazy," I said to myself.

Lucian trailed behind me. "Never been on a plane like this?"

"I've never been anywhere like this."

I kept Khan close as I sat by a window, sinking into the plush cushion. Lucian sat across from me, opening a book as he settled in. Khan stayed close, pressing his body to my legs.

Dr. Warren's voice carried from the front of the plane. "…Bucharest first. Yes, I know it's closer, but we're expected at a dinner with the press and dignitaries, so we head to the city then the castle the next day…"

A dinner? Was I supposed to go this dinner?

The rest of the passengers from the facility loaded, a half dozen nurses and personnel. I tapped my fingers on the armrest, anxiety making it hard for me to sit still for the next eleven hours.

I pulled out my phone and launched an eBook, but the knot in my stomach wouldn't let me concentrate, so I closed it and placed it in my lap.

It took half an hour before we were airborne. Dr. Warren had finally settled in after double checking the luggage arrangements. He sat across from an attractive nurse—one from the facility—and chatted quietly with her as they sipped champagne.

A flight attendant came by and asked for our drink orders. I took a Coke. Lucian asked for tomato juice.

As afternoon turned to evening, with the hum of the jet engine creating a quiet background noise, I tapped my fingers on my phone's screen, questions nagging me. Did Lucian know of the ghost I'd seen? Did he know of the book she'd had and the note inside it? Since the fire, I hadn't gotten a chance to research Constance Lynette Barrington aka Adelle Gibson. But the image of the woman in the red bathing suit on the beach wouldn't stop popping into my memory. Why did she have a pseudonym? Why was her passport photo in the book of *Jane Eyre*? And why was a picture of the same beach on Dr. Warren's desk?

Lucian hadn't said much since we'd boarded, and now was a perfect opportunity to question him. But why was it so hard to talk to him now? Maybe I wasn't prepared for the answers. It didn't matter. If I wanted to know the truth, I'd have to ask.

"Lucian," I said hesitantly.

"Yes?" He didn't look up from his paperback. *Fahrenheit 451*. Weird subject for a person terrified of fire.

"I need to ask you something."

"Sure. What is it?" He spoke casually, staying hidden behind his book.

I hesitated. "It's…it's about Constance Barrington."

His eyes shot up. "How do you know about her?"

"Well—I might've found her passport."

He placed his book in his lap. "Archive Five. Didn't I tell you not to go there?"

I shifted in my seat. "Yes."

"You shouldn't have," he said darkly.

"Can you blame me? I was trying to find the cure to the virus, which you were hiding from me. I thought it might've been in Archive Five."

He rubbed his forehead. "What do you want to know about her?"

"For one, who is she?"

He shook his head, glancing out the window, over the tops of puffy thunderheads that would soon grow into a storm. "She was Dr. Warren's wife."

I scrunched my brows. "He was married?"

"For a short time, yes. I never knew her. It was during the eighties when I was…you know. Dead."

"What happened to her?"

He shrugged. "It didn't work out. I heard they got divorced. They were only married a few years when things went south. She died of a drug overdose a few years later.

Don't bring up the subject with Dr. Warren. He doesn't like talking about her."

"Good to know." I glanced at the doctor. His profile stood out against the gathering clouds as he smiled at the nurse. Smooth, tanned skin stretched over his face, masking his age, though he held his champagne glass with crooked fingers marred with liver spots.

"Lucian, there's something else I wanted to ask you about. Do you realize there's a squatter living in Archive Five?"

He arched an eyebrow. "A squatter? Are you sure?"

"Positive. There's a room up there with a bed and some rotting food. I found Constance Barrington's passport inside."

"Well…" he rubbed his forehead. "That doesn't surprise me. Dr. Warren keeps all his ex-wife's keepsakes up there. He stored them there after she died. As far as the squatter goes, we've had two patients go missing. One we found a mile down the road trying to walk home. But the other one…young seventeen-year old kid. Jayden Black. He wasn't responding well to the treatments. One day he disappeared. We looked everywhere, then called the police. Searched the grounds. We tried to notify his parents only to find his family had all died of the virus. The weird thing is, all his belongings were still in his room. Then the kitchen reported food missing, but we never found him."

"You think he's still living in the facility?"

"Maybe."

"That doesn't disturb you?"

Lucian shrugged. "There's not a lot I can do about it."

"Fine," I said with a sigh. "There's one more thing. Before the fire started…" I swallowed the nervous stone lodged in my throat. "I think I might've seen a ghost."

His lips quirked. "A ghost?"

"You must've heard the rumors about the place," I said. "It's famously haunted."

He nodded. "But I've never seen anything."

"All right, then. Never mind." I chewed my bottom lip as I glanced at my dog sleeping by my feet. Why had I wanted to bring it up to him? Now he must've thought I'd lost it.

"I've heard the rumors, too," he said. "What exactly did you see?"

"A woman," I said with a sigh. Maybe it didn't matter if he believed me. "I was up late. Doing some research." I omitted the part about the type of research. "I heard something bang on my door. Went out to look but didn't see anything. Then it happened again. I went out a second time when I saw her. Wearing a white dress. And there was a book by my door. A copy of *Jane Eyre*. It was soaked in gasoline." My memories of that night came in bursts, like flashes of a dream. "I found a note inside the book."

He leaned forward, his lips pressed to a line. "What did it say?"

"It was one word. *Burn*."

He remained quiet. I wasn't sure what to think of his silence.

"She did it, Lucian. She set the place on fire. She held a match and lit a kerosene lamp, then smashed it on the floor. It only took seconds to engulf the place."

His face pensive, jaw clenched in concentration, he tapped his fingers on his armrest. "That doesn't make any sense."

"I know. But that's what I saw."

He shook his head. "I've heard the rumors. The woman in white who committed suicide when the place was a mental facility." He let out an exasperated sigh. "Sometimes I hate Crimson Hollow."

"Yeah."

"I don't believe in ghosts," he said, his voice held a pleading tone, as if by saying it, he would make it true. "For the same reason I don't believe in vampires. They can't be real, because if they are, then what does that make me?"

"I understand. But have you considered that you could be

something other than a—what you think you are?" I'd almost used the word vampire but thought better of it.

"Like what?"

I hesitated before answering. "Do you realize the name Dracula comes from Dracul, which means dragon?"

He shook his head. "Don't go there. My father was obsessed with cryptozoology. Thought the creatures held the key to longevity. It was never sound science, despite his claims."

"But he found something. Otherwise, how do you explain what you are?"

He didn't answer. His gloved hand went to his blazer's front breast pocket. Paper crinkled when he touched it. Was he carrying his father's letter?

"You know something, don't you?" I asked.

Pursing his lips, he waited before replying. "I'm not a vampire, Amaya."

I sighed. "And you don't believe in ghosts."

"No."

"Then how do you explain the fire starting? And the book with the note inside? Maybe there's something significant about it. Jane Eyre. What was it about again?" I'd read it in Sophomore English, but only fragments of the story came back to me. "Wasn't there a fire and a ghost in that story, too?"

Lucian worked his jaw back and forth, as if pondering what I'd said. "Yes. But perhaps it's only a coincidence. I don't have any answers, Amaya. I'm sorry." He picked up his paperback and opened it to put an end to our conversation. The next hours passed in silence, until the nurse came over and asked Lucian if he was ready for his bleeding tube transfusion.

He gave a nod and left with her to a separate compartment.

When night came, I settled into an uneasy sleep, my dreams plagued by nightmares of the woman in white.

27

An interview with Dr. Victor Warren. April 28, for Fame Magazine

No one has more faith in Lucian than I. He's strong-willed and capable. He understands what it's like to pass through trials and come out a better person. Some people ask why I revived him. Was it for the fame? The inevitable funding?
Of course not. It was for him. He's like a son to me.

~

AMAYA

The jolting plane woke me. Tires skidded as I opened my eyes. Khan whined and propped his paws on my knees. I patted his head, lingering nightmares sticking to me like tendrils of cobweb.

Lucian sat across from me. His face held a pensive expression, lips drawn, hands fisted in his lap. "Welcome to Bucharest," Lucian said in a quiet, somber tone, one that could've easily been saying *welcome to hell*.

"You didn't want to come back here, did you." It wasn't a question.

His eyes didn't meet mine. "What gave it away?"

Gray morning light illuminated the flat plane of Lucian's forehead, the bridge of his straight nose, and the hard set of his angular jaw. What was he thinking about? Were memories of his childhood surfacing?

I pressed my hands to my stomach as the butterflies stirred to life. Lucian had promised to help me find the cure, but he'd said nothing beyond that. He certainly hadn't professed his love for me. He had no reason to, anyway.

Sure, he'd saved me from the fire, but I hadn't been the only person he'd rescued. I took a deep breath to control the sudden onslaught of nervousness. I couldn't expect anything from him. He had his demons to deal with, and I had mine.

When the plane rolled to a stop, I stood, my muscles stiff. My stomach roiled with acid, my head pounded, and my heartbeat came in erratic bursts. Was the virus progressing?

If so, there wasn't much I could do about it. Nothing but the cure would do me any good.

While we waited for the flight attendants to open the hatch, Dr. Warren and the nurse approached me and Lucian.

The nurse, a blonde with a waifish frame, smiled as she stood by me. She wore white scrubs. Her hair was artfully pulled into a ponytail with well-placed wispy curls fanning her cheeks, unlike my own sloppy hair which was pulled into a bun to hide my tangles.

"I'm Bianca Rhodes," she said with a smile, her eyes wide and lined with dark eyeliner. "How are you feeling, dear? You look pale."

"I'm okay. A headache. It's the jet lag, I'm sure."

She squeezed my arm. "We'll get you medicated once we're settled in at the hotel."

"Medicated? I'm not sure I need it."

"Trying to be brave, huh?" She smacked on her gum

before winking. "We'll talk later, okay?" She gave my arm another squeeze before sliding next to Dr. Warren.

When we left the plane, cool autumn air smelling of rain surrounded us. Khan instantly relieved himself on the tarmac. Dr. Warren laughed as we stood around my dog defecating on the pavement.

"He managed to hold it for eleven hours. That dog's a keeper." He clapped Lucian on the shoulder, then turned away, whistling as he led Nurse Bianca toward the looming glass and art deco façade of the airport.

Lucian and I trailed along behind the others.

"Khan didn't hold it," I mumbled to Lucian. "He went on the bathroom floor. I had to clean it. Don't tell."

Lucian's mouth quirked to a smile. "It's our secret."

We followed the sidewalk to the terminal, wind gusting around us, a soupy gray sky gathering overhead. Workers driving carts whipped past us, and the rumble of airplane engines mingled with distant thunder.

Familiar nervousness twisted inside me.

"I've never been to another country," I admitted to Lucian —the man who'd practically traveled the world. "How much of a culture shock am I in for?"

He shrugged. "The Romanians in the city are friendly. We shouldn't have any trouble except for the press, but I have that problem everywhere. If they happen to find us, don't answer their questions. Most of them are from tabloids. It's better to ignore them. If you give them any time, they'll twist your words—do anything for a story. It's best to stay quiet."

"Got it. What about when we're not in the city?"

He gave me a sidelong glance. "I already warned you about that, so it shouldn't come as a shock. Superstitions hold on in secluded places."

I bit my lip, my thoughts turning to stories of bodies with stones in their mouths and stakes driven through their chest cavities—and that's what they'd done to the corpses. What would they do to living vampires?

We neared the sliding glass doors and Lucian grabbed my hand. Soft leather warmed my cold skin.

I looked up at him, my shocked expression revealed in the dark tint of his sunglasses.

"You looked worried," he said, as if that explained his sudden display of affection.

"Oh," I breathed. My cheeks grew hot and ears burned as we entered the airport. I tightened one hand around Khan's leash and the other I held to Lucian with a firm grasp, as if the two were my lifelines. In a way, they were.

As we walked past benches and tall stone pillars, a gaggle of reporters with cameras swarmed around us, lightbulbs flashing, blinding me.

"How did they know we'd be here?" I asked.

"Word travels faster than us, apparently."

Dr. Warren stepped in front of us, fielding questions like a professional. His voice echoed off the vaulted ceiling.

A tall female reporter sidestepped the doctor and blocked our path. She wore a pantsuit that fitted her willow-thin frame. Arching, penciled eyebrows accentuated her accusatory eyes.

"Lucian Vidraru? Ioana Marius for *Gossip Magazine*. We hear you're traveling to Bran Castle. What are you doing there?"

Lucian didn't answer as he pushed past her. The woman's eyes narrowed. As she glanced at our entwined hands, a slight grin made her eyes sparkle.

"Who's this? A new girlfriend?"

"No questions, please," Lucian said, but the woman grabbed my arm, stopping us.

"You're a fellow patient, I'll assume?"

My throat grew dry.

"I—"

Officer Goodman shoved his way forward. "Move along," he said to the reporter in a commanding voice, one I hadn't heard often.

She pressed against me as the crowd surrounded us, thrusting the microphone in my face. "Are you dating Lucian? What's your name? Can you tell us how you met? Are you carrying VS?"

I kept my hand in Lucian's as we rushed through the terminal. Flashing bulbs blinded me, but I stayed focused straight ahead, on the signs overhead with unfamiliar words, and below them, in English, the words EXIT—BUCHAREST MAIN BLVD DOWNTOWN.

We left the airport to enter a world of taxis and crowds of people. The sharp Romanian accents carried from the masses. We made it to a waiting limo—one that had a boxy shape and a flying eagle hood ornament, reminding me of a Rolls Royce from the thirties. Officer Goodman pushed through the waiting gaggle of photographers and reporters as we loaded into the car.

"Get in quickly," he said in a businesslike tone as he waved to our group. I tugged Khan into the limo with me, then the others followed. Tinted windows blocked out the sunlight. When everyone loaded, Officer Goodman pulled the door shut, blocking out the shouts and flashing camera lights.

"Well." Lucian tugged on his shirt collar. "We got through that smoothly enough."

"Smoothly?" I wrinkled my nose. "It was awful."

"That was nothing. You should see what happens when I go to L.A."

"Ugh. I'd rather not." I patted Khan's head. As we sped down the road, passing buildings crowded together, my chest grew tight at the thought of being boxed in. What would it be like to live a life like Lucian's, with every detail under the magnifying glass of the press?

Had I become part of that?

I could only imagine what the headlines would read now that he'd held my hand in public. I cast him a sidelong glance.

Had he done it on purpose?

The car sped onto a highway. The sprawling metropolis of Bucharest spread out before us. Communist block buildings contrasted modern structures.

We took an exit and drove down narrow streets, past sprawling limestone buildings decorated with ornate architecture. Iron-black statues of men on horses dominated city squares, and bubbling fountains interspersed the city hustle.

The others in the car spoke quietly. My gaze remained fixed out the window, at this new world we'd come to, full of exotic customs and languages. What would it have been like to grow up in a place such as this more than a century and a half ago?

Lucian's gaze also went to the window. Though I couldn't see his eyes, the tense lines surrounding his pinched lips told me he must be deep in thought.

"Has it changed much?" I asked him, my voice almost drowned out by the din of the purring car's engine.

"Yes," he said quietly.

"How so?" I asked.

"The lights, for one thing." He pointed at the streetlamps. "I remember how excited I was as a child when the first gas lights were installed. They were like magic. There was a horsecar tram we'd take occasionally. I went with my father once. I remember the sound of the horses' hooves on cobblestones, a sound that echoed through the city no matter where you went." A smile curved his mouth. "The smell was different too, but I'll not go into detail about that." He took a deep breath. "Some of these buildings existed." He pointed straight ahead. "The National Bank of Romania. Built in the seventies."

"The seventies?"

He chuckled. "Eighteen-seventies."

"*Eighteen*-seventies. Right." A grin tugged at the corners of my mouth. "You're the only person I'll have a conversation with like this, you know."

"Yes, I know," he said smugly, though smiled as he said it.

I turned back to the window. "What else is different?"

"The obvious things. Cars, more buildings, more people. You'd be surprised at how much doesn't change, though."

"What do you mean?"

"People. They're all trying to live a full life, laugh every now and then, be happy whenever they can. Family meant a lot then, and that doesn't change. Most people would do anything for family." He swallowed, glancing down at his gloved hands clasped in his lap.

You're no different, I wanted to say. He still wanted a family, even though there was little chance he'd have one.

A shadow loomed over the car as we passed by a colossal building resembling a Roman colosseum, with arching pillars connecting over hundreds of windows.

"The capital," Dr. Warren said. "Beautiful place, isn't it?"

"It's lovely," Nurse Bianca answered.

"It's also the heaviest building in the world," the doctor added. "Did you know that? Weighs so much it's sinking a few millimeters a year."

"My goodness." She laughed, a delicate, fluty sound.

"There's a nuclear bunker beneath it, too," he said.

"In case of the vampire apocalypse." Lucian winked.

"Pretty sure that's already happened," I said. "I don't think the bunker helped much."

Officer Goodman shifted his weight. "No, but that's why we're headed for Bran Castle. Preventing the spread of the vampire apocalypse. Some might call us superheroes."

"Not everyone will call us that," Lucian said. His tone turned somber, and the car went quiet.

By the time we reached a hotel—an impressive work of architecture that mimicked the Roman design of the capital—

my thoughts had turned to our task. Finding a cure. Nothing mattered but that.

Before then, I wouldn't mind taking a long shower, eating an actual meal, and sleeping in a real bed. Evening descended when we got settled into a massive four-bedroom suite—one larger than the apartment I'd grown up in. Everything about the place felt surreal, as if I'd walked into someone else's life, someone who hadn't grown up living in cheap apartments and eating canned spaghetti.

"You look starstruck," Lucian said as he stepped beside me. We stood on the balcony overlooking an ocean of city lights. The sun sank, turning the sky a shade of rose red. A lazy wind blew strands of hair across my face, tickling my cheeks.

"This is completely alien to me, Lucian. I've never been anywhere like this." I rested my fingers on the ivy-shaped ornament decorating the balcony railing, the metal warmed by the sun that had already disappeared. How long would it take before it grew cold?

"I know," he answered. "Does it bother you?"

I bit my lip before answering. "It's so different. I feel like I don't belong here. I mean, look at me." I tugged on my Fruity Pebbles t-shirt and stretchy yoga pants. My five-dollar flip-flops didn't feel worthy of walking over the million-dollar marble floors.

"Amaya," he said gently. "Believe me, I understand where you're coming from. I grew up in a hovel. Lived as a circus bum, then a vagrant. Ended up in prison. The entire population of the world hated me at one point. No one cared when I died. I was laid to rest in a prison cemetery with no one there to mourn me. How do you think I felt after Dr. Warren woke me and took me to a place like this? When people started fawning over me and calling me a hero and a superstar? I couldn't believe it. I still don't. If you want to know the truth, sometimes I still feel like that boy who lived in a hovel with his parents, hoping my father earned enough for bread so we could eat that night and not go to bed starving."

"I thought your father was a scientist. Didn't he earn enough to feed you?"

"Not at first." He shook his head. "It wasn't until he started making breakthroughs in animal biology that he earned anything from the palace university. By then, I was half grown. Places like this—" he ran his hand over the railing — "are really just as foreign to me as they are to you."

I eyed him. When he wore his sunglasses, I could never be sure if he told the truth. Was he only saying those things to make me feel better? "You mean that?"

"Every bit of it." He reached up and slowly tucked strands of hair behind my ear, his gloved hands lingering on my cheek. I wished I could've felt his touch without the leather barrier—wished I could've peered into his unmasked eyes and seen the depth of his emotions. But he rarely let his guard down, even around me. No matter how much he claimed to understand me, we'd always be worlds apart.

"What are you thinking?" he asked softly.

I shook my head. "I don't know who you are."

"What do you mean?"

"This." I lifted his hand, holding it between mine. "And this." I tapped the rim of his glasses. "You never let me see the real you."

"Do you *want* to see the real me?" he asked, a challenge in his voice, words that hinted at a deeper meaning.

Did I?

How close was I willing to let Lucian get to me? Was I prepared for the outcome? I was already falling for him. I couldn't stop thinking of him—he lingered in my mind as if he were already a part of me, a piece of my subconscious that had interwoven itself into my being.

I grasped his hands, and peered into his face, to my own reflection mirrored in dark lenses.

"Yes." My voice was soft yet laced with an intensity that surprised even me. "I want to see you. I want to know you. I want…" I trailed off, my heart beating so hard I feared it would crack my ribcage. Describing the emotions coursing through me would be impossible, so I settled for something simpler. "I want you, Lucian."

He didn't speak. The wind gusted around us, drowning out the sounds of car engines and drifting voices, until all that remained was us. Two people together, as if we were the only souls in the world.

"Let me see you," I repeated, my words so soft only he could hear. I reached up and cradled the stems of his sunglasses, then I removed them.

Red pupils faded to black, so dark I feared they would drink me in. But the shock I'd felt the first time I'd seen him was gone, and though some might've found the color of his eyes disturbing, to me, they were exquisite.

I placed the glasses on a garden table, then reached for his gloves.

"Wait." His grip tightened on my hands. "Amaya, before you do this…" He trailed off as he took a deep breath. "You should know I was burned pretty badly. My flesh isn't… are you sure about this?"

Concern fired through me. "Are you all right?"

"Not sure, really. It's never taken this long for me to heal. I thought you should be prepared."

I nodded, grasping his gloves and pulling them off. Bandages covered his wrists and several fingers. The unbandaged flesh had blackened. Scales sloughed, revealing deep wounds that ran fissure-like over his hands.

"Don't I repulse you?" he asked, raising a hairless eyebrow, his eyes revealing the seriousness of his question.

I threaded my fingers through his, looking up into his ancient eyes. With my free hand, I cupped his cheek.

"Never," I answered honestly. "When I look at you, I see a

person of honor. Someone who cares deeply for others. Who wants to help. Who shows compassion. Who knows what it's like to suffer, and tries to make sure no one else has to. That's what I see, Lucian. I see you. The real you."

His Adam's apple bobbed as he swallowed. "Thank you, Amaya. That means more to me than you'll ever realize."

I only nodded, words escaping me at the intensity I heard in his voice, the passion I saw—*actually saw*—in his eyes.

Heat welled deep in my stomach, an emotion that threatened to overwhelm me if I let it. He stood close, the scent of dark amber washing over me. The rough pad of his thumb caressed my cheek. He drew me to him, brushing his lips over mine. My breath stuttered. Stars danced in my vision. His warmth enveloped me as he kissed me, lips soft and pliable, drinking me in.

I pressed my hand to his chest, the beating of his heart a steady thump beneath my fingers.

When he drew away, he left me breathless.

After such an experience, how would I ever be the same again?

"Three," he said quietly.

I raised an eyebrow. "Three?"

"That's three people you've kissed."

I groaned. "Don't remind me. Trust me, yours is the only one I'll remember."

He smiled, and I couldn't ignore the mischievousness dancing in the dark depths of his pupils.

He hugged me to him and kissed my forehead. We stared out over the city, his arm hugged protectively around me, and I rested my head on his chest. I couldn't ever remember feeling so content, as if this was where I belonged.

With him.

The sun disappeared, leaving the sky dark. The stars remained invisible against the glare of city lights.

2 8

Bran Castle. Bran, Romania.

"And in those days shall men seek death, and shall not find it; and shall desire to die, and death shall flee from them."

-Revelations 9:6

~

AMAYA

When Lucian and I reentered the suite, Dr. Warren held his phone to his ear. He stomped through the main room, a classy place with white carpet, soft lights, modern furniture, and the scent of cloves hanging in the air.

"Have you seen my luggage?" Dr. Warren asked.

Lucian arched an eyebrow. "Luggage?"

"Yes." The doctor moved the phone away. Anger lit his normally calm eyes. "It's gone missing. *Missing!* Can you believe it? We were on my private jet, for God's sake. Where the hell is it?" He pressed the phone to his ear once again. "Yes, damn it," he yelled. "At the Epoque Hotel. Room service? No! Take it straight here—straight to room 403." He shook his head, giving us a withering look. "Sorry," he mouthed.

Lucian nodded in return.

"An hour?" Dr. Warren asked. "You've got to be kidding." He cursed. "Yes. I'll meet you in the lobby. Whatever you do, don't drop anything. Understood?"

He pressed a button to end the call.

"They found it?" Lucian asked.

"I can't understand how luggage on my private jet could even go missing. I'm sorry about this." The doctor went to him and rested his hand on Lucian's shoulder. "I don't think I'll make it in time for dinner."

"Don't worry about it. Amaya and I will be fine."

"Good." He clapped Lucian's shoulder, then stalked away. "Let's hope they get that luggage here soon, or I swear they'll have hell to pay."

He marched out of the room and slammed the door behind him.

"That was tense," I said.

Lucian shrugged. "He doesn't like inefficiency. Drives him crazy." He looked at the door, jaw clenched, and voice turning pensive. "It's not unexpected—especially when it comes to his research."

Research, yes. But why did he care so much? Besides the vaccine, which he'd introduced shortly after waking Lucian, his *research* hadn't resulted in any breakthroughs. Maybe I'd get a chance to question Lucian about it.

"He mentioned dinner?" I asked.

"Yes." He turned to me, his worry turning to a slight smile. "We'll have to change. It's a black-tie sort of thing. Some of the Romanian dignitaries caught wind I was coming. They arranged a special dinner."

I eyed him. "Am I supposed to be there?"

"Of course! You're my plus one."

I blanched. "Are you serious? Lucian, all my clothes were burned. I have nothing but dollar-store bargains to wear. Why didn't you warn me?"

"Because." He walked to me, taking my hands in his, that sly grin tugging at the corners of his perfect lips. "I wanted it to be a surprise. I got a dress for you. I hope you don't mind."

I raised an eyebrow. "A dress?"

He nodded, a hint of a smile on his lips. "I hope it's okay. I had the valet hang it in your closet."

"A *dress*?" I repeated.

"Yes. You've worn a dress before, haven't you?"

"I—" My words stuttered. "But—"

He placed a finger over my lips, quieting me. "Don't argue. Just try it on and see what you think. If you hate it, you can wear your Fruity Pebbles shirt and flipflops."

I couldn't hold back a smile. "Is that a promise?"

"Cross my heart." He squeezed my hands. "I've got to take care of some business downstairs, so I'll meet you in the restaurant in half an hour."

"Fine," I managed to mumble as I left him to enter my suite. When I stepped inside, Khan lay curled on the bed. He pricked his ears as I entered but remained on the comforter. I gave him a pat on the head, his tail thumping, as I prepared to face my closet.

Thick carpet cushioned my footfalls as I crossed to the sliding pocket doors. I opened them, not sure what to expect.

I pulled out a delicate rose gold-gown with crystals covering the bodice. The mermaid skirt swished as I moved to stand in front of the mirror. The silky fabric brushed my skin.

As I held the dress to me and stood to look at my reflection in the floor-length mirror, I had to force myself to catch my breath.

"*Holy flip*," I gasped.

The gown was something from a fairytale. It must've cost a ton. I had trouble wrapping my mind around not only the dress, but everything: this place. Romania. The person I traveled with. Lucian Vidraru.

Lucian Vidraru.

The entire journey.

From losing Dad and Mom. Giving myself the virus. Preparing myself to die if this didn't work out. At the time, not caring.

But now, I cared if I lived.

My life mattered because I'd found someone who I cared for more than I cared for myself. Someone I would be willing to share the rest of my life with.

The thought should have frightened me. Instead, I felt hope spring to life, as if for the first time, I could live, and maybe enjoy it in the process.

But only if we found the cure.

I tried not to let that deep well of discouragement open a hole in my heart. I couldn't let it happen. Not now. When I could look forward to dinner with Lucian, I would push aside my doubts and fears. I would enjoy the moment.

I undressed and pulled on the gown. The bodice hugged my frame until it fell into a swooping skirt that flowed around my legs. The fabric swished as I walked, and as I looked at my reflection in the mirror, I had to laugh.

Such a gorgeous gown didn't belong on a girl with crazy messed-up hair and a pale, unmade face.

Didn't Lucian realize I wasn't that girl? The one who wore expensive gowns and went to events for the rich and famous?

I pressed fisted hands to my stomach.

I would never be that sort of person. But neither was he. And that was okay.

A shoe box had been placed in my closet. After opening it and unwrapping the tissue, I pulled out a pair of rose-gold stilettos matched to the gown.

"For real?" I muttered as I strapped them to my feet. To my shock, they fit perfectly.

In the bathroom, I pulled the hair tie from my tangled strands, then brushed it until it shone and fell in soft waves down my back. Nothing but tons of hair product and a straightening iron would completely tame it, but I would make do. I managed to apply a little makeup—some lip gloss, powder, and even mascara.

I scrunched my nose as I looked at my reflection, doing my best not to pick apart every feature that didn't look perfect —*stupid mole*—second-guessing why Lucian would have any interest in me.

No. No self-doubts tonight.

With a deep breath, I left the suite and wandered the hotel. I managed to get the hang of walking in the shoes by the time I made it to the bottom floor. A waterfall feature made a quiet trickling as I wandered past potted ferns.

When I neared the hotel restaurant, I fidgeted with the beads on my gown. Cool air came from the air-conditioning, and goose bumps formed on the exposed skin of my arms and neck. The sweetheart neckline didn't plunge low enough to be revealing, but I still felt a fragile vulnerability following me like a stalking shadow.

The naked skin on my neck made me too aware of the photos I'd seen of Sally Anderson—her flesh split open to reveal muscles and tendons.

Lucian had done that.

But I no longer really believed that. What was the real story?

Would he tell me now?

"Amaya."

I turned at the sound of his voice. I thought I'd already caught my breath more than any human possible, but I couldn't help but remind myself—once again—to breathe as I faced Lucian, a tall figure, broad shoulders, wearing a perfectly fitted tux.

He crossed to me, his shoes echoing on marble tiles, and smiled as he gently grasped my ice-cold fingers. Supple black gloves sheathed his hands. He held my palm to his lips and pressed a lingering kiss to my flesh.

Shivers that had nothing to do with the cold danced over my skin.

"My goodness, Amaya." He held me at arm's length, his face roving the length of my gown. "You are enchanting."

Stupid mouth. Why couldn't I make a word come out?

"Are you okay?" he asked with a deep, sultry chuckle.

"Me?" My hand went to my neck in a panicky gesture. I wasn't expecting the onslaught of nervousness—and of another feeling—an altogether magical one that sent my heart racing and heat rushing through me.

"Should we go inside?" he asked.

"I…um. Yes."

He placed an arm around my shoulder. "You look nervous."

"Do I?"

He laughed quietly. "You've got nothing to worry about. You're smart and you're strong. You convinced me to help you get the cure, and I doubt there's another person on the planet capable of such a thing. Eating dinner in a restaurant can't be nearly as hard as that. Right?"

"You're right." With a deep exhale, I released my pent-up anxiety. "I can do this."

"Good." He squeezed my shoulder.

We entered through the open doors to an expansive space. Gold leaf gleamed from pillars supporting the overhead glass-dome that allowed moonlight to seep inside. Flickering candles sat at the center of each round table covered with white tablecloths. Quiet voices created an echoing murmur.

Pearls and diamonds sparkled from the women wearing elegant gowns.

A server with a dark suit carrying a white cloth over his arm approached us.

"Mr. Vidraru," he said, words crisp with only a slight accent. "The dignitaries are assembled in the garden. Shall I take you there now?"

"Yes, please." He spoke with a smooth, controlled voice, as if he'd done this sort of thing a million times. Maybe he had.

The server led us around tables and through a doorway at the back. We entered a courtyard. Fireflies winked around wrought-iron tables. Cool nighttime air washed over us as we walked among people who chatted at the tables. The press stood on the outer edges behind a fenced area. Bulbs shot in bright bursts, blinding us.

All eyes went to Lucian as we crossed to a podium on a raised platform at the center of the garden. Dark roses bloomed around it, their scent mingling with the aroma of spiced foods. A balding man in a tux stood at the podium. Smiling, he held the microphone and announced something in Romanian. I understood "Lucian Vidraru." Clapping ensued, and Lucian waved to the crowd.

He went to the man at the podium and said a few words in Romanian. I crossed my arms and bit my lip as Lucian gestured to me. Was I supposed to say something?

Lucian gave a polite smile—the one he used for magazine photos.

The flashing lights popped on and off, until the man at the podium said something, and security guards appeared, escorting the reporters away from the area.

When the man left the podium, the area quieted, and Lucian pushed his way through the bodies to stand by me. He gently grasped my elbow and followed two security guards back through the crowd until we reached a secluded table away from the others. Ivy vines grew along trellises, blocking us from the other restaurant goers.

"What was that about?" I asked.

"Formalities," he answered with a long exhale. "Everywhere I travel, I have to attend some official event or another. But it's over with now, so I suggest we eat while we get the chance. I asked for a private table." He pulled out a chair for me.

I had to swallow a nervous knot in my throat. "That's for me?"

"Yes." He laughed. "Who else?" He motioned to it. "Will you join me for dinner, Amaya?"

"Um, yeah." I sat on the plush cushion, and he scooted me forward. Flames flickered from the candles on the table's center. A menu had been placed in front. I grabbed it while Lucian sat across from me.

The din of voices quieted in this area, and I felt secretly grateful to be away from the crowd. I held the menu with unsteady hands. Unfamiliar words jumped out at me. I raised an eyebrow at Lucian. "It's in Romanian."

"I can translate it for you."

Smoothing a hand over my dress, I placed the laminated cardstock on the table. Nausea swelled in the pit of my stomach. "I'm not sure you need to. Not sure I can eat anything."

"You're not feeling well?"

I shrugged. "I'm okay. A little nauseous."

"Try the soup," he suggested. "Ciorbu."

I tilted my head. "What's in it?"

"Chicken. Sour cream and garlic." He waved his hand. "You'll like it."

I fidgeted with the napkin as I placed it in my lap. "Maybe. What are you eating?"

He cocked his head. "Eating?"

"Right, sorry." I rubbed my head. Even with excessive

amounts of painkillers, the throbbing wouldn't stop. "I forget you don't eat. And you're always hungry."

"Yes. All the time. The bleeding transfusions help, but sometimes…" He glanced away, clasping his hands on his menu.

"Sometimes what?" I asked.

He breathed deeply before answering. "Vampire, you know."

"Vampire. Right. But you said you're not one."

"True." He straightened his fork on the table.

"You have cravings?" I asked.

Surprise lit his face.

I leaned forward, speaking quietly. "Do you have cravings for blood?"

He laughed, but it was a forced sound.

"Lucian?" I pushed.

"Amaya." He mimicked my tone.

"Can you please answer me honestly? Do you have blood cravings? Is that why you…did what you did to Sally Anderson?"

His hairless eyebrows shot up above the rim of his sunglasses. "Do we have to talk about this now?"

I glanced around us. The trellises blocked out the people around us. The hum of voices grew too indistinct to hear. "When else will we talk about it?"

He tapped his fingers on the table. "You really want to go there? I might ruin your dinner."

"I think it's ruined anyway thanks to the vampire virus."

He nodded. "True."

The waiter came and served glasses of water and a loaf of round crusty bread. Steam rose from the yeasty top. I cut a small piece and placed it on my plate but pressed my hands in my lap.

My stomach's roiling queasiness kept me from eating it.

"Your virus is progressing," Lucian said, his voice edged with a serious tone.

"I know," I said quietly. "All the more reason to tell me about Sally." I looked him in the eyes. "While you still can." *Before I die*, I could've added, but thought better of it.

"Yeah. Sally." He glanced away, jaw clenched, secrets held behind dark sunglasses. "I'd be lying if I said I didn't love her. She was my girlfriend after Barb passed." He shook his head, letting out a shaky breath. "You'd think after all this time you'd stop loving someone, but it doesn't work that way." He sipped his water. "I met Sally in Microbiology. She was charming. Very young. Especially compared to me." He laughed quietly. "She was full of life. Funny. But she kept things from me."

"What kind of things?"

"She had reasons for forming a relationship with me—ones that had nothing to do with love or friendship. I was nothing to her but a means to an end. I guess it takes a few decades of looking back to see it in the right light." He gave me a concerned stare. "You really want to know about this? I thought people hated hearing about exes."

"Yes, Lucian," I said pointedly. "I would like to know."

"Well, you'd be the first."

"That's okay."

The waiter came back and asked for our orders. I took the soup. Lucian ordered a steak—extremely rare.

When he left, Lucian still wouldn't look me in the face. "Sally came to visit me in my dorm one day. Summer. Sweltering hot. Said she'd been studying about my condition. She was always obsessed with learning about virology. Reminded me of my dad.

"She thought she could help me, even when I told her I had it under control. 'Stop repressing your true nature,' she'd say. 'Let me help you.'

"It didn't take long before she started asking me to drink

her blood. She'd cut herself on purpose to make me smell it. 'See? You do want it. You know you need this.'"

He removed his glasses and rubbed his eyes, his hands shaking, as if he were reliving the past.

"She became relentless. Came up with all these random facts about animal biology and the food chain. Human nature and how it coincided with representations of mythical creatures. How my biology was similar to birds of prey and I needed to feed it to become whole. Bullshit."

I'd never heard him swear before, and it caught me off guard.

He clenched his steak knife, sunglasses sitting on the table.

"She hated when I told her no. Sent her into a frenzy. That's when she started getting violent. 'Just bite me and I'll leave you alone, Lucian,' she'd yell.

"I finally gave in. Bit her once. She left after that. I never saw her again until they called me in to identify her corpse."

"Wait. What? You… you didn't kill her?"

"I gave her the virus. So yeah, in that way I killed her."

"But you… you didn't tear her neck open?"

"Why on earth would I?" he asked darkly, replacing his sunglasses.

"Then how did she get cut up like that? Like she'd been mauled by a predator."

He shrugged. "I never found out. They put me in handcuffs, gave me a sham trial then locked me up. I don't know. I don't care to know."

"You don't care to know how Sally died?" I placed my hands on the table. "Lucian, don't you see? Someone killed her. And you went to prison for it."

"Yes. And that happened more than forty years ago. It was probably some random thug, and he's most likely dead. Does it matter anymore, Amaya? I'm free. I'm living a decent life. They pardoned me for her death."

"But you were accused of something you didn't do."

Sally's opened neck flashed in my memory, arteries and tendons splayed as they'd been bitten. "Whoever did it wanted you to go to prison. They set you up."

The waiter arrived with our food. Steam rose from the soup's broth, smelling of roasted garlic and cream. I stirred it slowly as Lucian cut his steak.

"Now you know why I don't like to talk about her," Lucian said.

"It sounds like she manipulated you."

He nodded.

I took a small sip, the broth creamy and well-seasoned, though it turned to ash in my throat as I swallowed it. I did my best not to gag.

"Why?" I asked, placing my spoon aside.

"I don't know. Maybe she was crazy. Anyone wanting to get infected with the virus must be."

"Does that make me crazy?" I asked tentatively.

"No. You didn't want the virus. You wanted the cure. There's a difference. Sally—she wanted to be a vampire. She wanted to infect others."

"You know that?"

"Yes." He tapped his steak knife on his plate. "After I bit her, I remember the way she smiled. I don't often think of people as evil. But that look in her eyes…like she'd gotten what she wanted. Like I'd played right into her hands. She didn't say anything. Just smiled, then left me alone. Never came back. A week later I heard the news reports about the spread of the virus. It was then that I realized what she'd wanted all along. Genocide."

"But why would anyone want that?"

"I don't know." He shrugged. "Because she was crazy? Evil? I've stopped trying to figure it out."

"But you were blamed for what she started!"

"You don't have to remind me."

"I don't understand. What reason did she have? There's

got to be more to it than she's evil or crazy." The autopsy photo nagged at me, as if there were some vital piece of information I were missing. "She couldn't have been working alone. Someone killed her. They wanted it to look like it was you who did it. Why?"

He only sighed as he shook his head, as if he didn't care to know. But I did. "Did you have any enemies at the time?"

"At the time? Let me think. The entire population of the planet. So, yeah. I guess you could say I had enemies."

I frowned. "You know what I mean."

He took a bite of his steak, then waved his fork at me. "Amaya, let me assure you that I've been down this road more times than you can count. Thinking of who killed Sally, who she was working with, and why the hell they did it is something that I could obsess over. So I don't. I don't talk about her. I don't think about her. Because when I do, she has power over me, and I won't allow her any more control over my life than she already had."

I glanced away, biting my lip. Maybe we'd never have an answer to the mystery. Maybe that was okay. "I understand," I said with a nod.

"Good. Now. How about we talk about something else?"

I stirred my soup. "Like what?"

"Like us."

I raised my eyebrows. "Us?" The word sounded so strange, but it felt natural as I repeated it.

He took off his glasses, looking at me with those dark, penetrating eyes—ones that could lead to my undoing. "Amaya." He said my name with emotion in his voice, and heat rose to my cheeks. "I'm falling for you."

My pulse began a rapid staccato. My mouth grew so dry, I didn't know how to answer. Powerful feelings I'd suppressed for far too long flared to life. Could I admit the same thing to him?

"I-I'm." I took a deep breath to steady my pounding

heart. It didn't work, so I pushed ahead anyway. "I'm falling for you, too."

There. I said it.

A grin lit his face—that bright, charming expression laced with a hint of seductiveness. My stomach twisted into even more knots than I had thought possible. He rested his chin on his hands. "You mean it? Wasn't it only a few days ago that you swore never to talk to me again?"

"*You* said that." I grabbed my spoon and pointed it at him. "But I'm under the impression you didn't mean it."

He raised an eyebrow, his smile gone, replaced with an intensity in his eyes that held me spellbound. Reaching his hand across the table, he gently took away my spoon, as if it were my last defense, the last chink in my arsenal of barriers I'd created to keep from forming attachments. He looked down at my fingers and traced their outline with his gloved thumb. "I didn't want to hurt you. You know what kind of life I live."

My stomach flipped as reality reinserted itself. I pulled my hand back to my own side of the table. "I know."

"Are you okay with it?" he asked, his gaze lifting to bore into me until I felt as though he pierced my soul. "You'll be in the tabloids soon. They'll be asking you for interviews. Every piece of information about your life will become common knowledge—and half of it will be false. Are you prepared for it?"

My mind spun, remembering all the times I'd seen him in public or on TV. The cameras and shouted questions. The articles I'd read on his life, some of them so unbelievable, I'd been sure they had to be made up. Could I live like that?

He sighed, pulling me from the mire of thoughts and emotions trying to drown me. "You're not, are you?"

I couldn't meet his gaze. "Maybe I just need time to adjust."

His brow creased, and I knew I hadn't given the answer he

wanted, but he didn't press the issue. We continued the rest of the meal talking about Romanian superstitions, the legends of Vlad Dracula and how he'd never set foot in Bran castle, laughing at the ridiculousness of it. Talking to him came naturally, and I found myself genuinely smiling.

By the time we walked back up to the suite, I realized I hadn't worried about the virus, about Mom and Dad, about my life that I would be losing soon unless I got the cure. Not once, all evening.

Lucian clasped my hand, and we walked down the hallway, our footfalls quiet. Musicians played downstairs, a violin and piano, their haunting melody carrying from below to where we stood on the balcony.

"I had fun tonight," I said as I squeezed Lucian's hand.

His brilliant smile caught me off guard. "Me too. To be honest, I haven't felt like this in forever. Not in this lifetime, for sure." He reached for my cheek and tucked a strand of hair behind my ear, his fingers trailing. "You're so beautiful. I never knew one person could bring so much joy to my life. I haven't felt this happy in a very long time."

"You haven't?" I asked. Afraid of the skips of my heartbeat, I downplayed it "Surely you're exaggerating."

"Not at all."

"But you have everything," I argued.

"Do I?"

"You're famous, everyone loves you, you're rich—"

"Those things don't bring happiness. Not true happiness. Before I met you, I was isolated. Unhappy. I thought living such a long life was a curse. I wanted to die."

"You did?" I questioned, concern in my voice.

"Absolutely. I was jealous of people who could be free of life. Free of pain and loneliness. Then I met you and everything changed."

"I'm nothing special, Lucian. Just an ordinary person."

"No," he said firmly. "I've met enough people to know

that's not true. You're unique. And you've made my life a better place. I would do anything for you, Amaya."

"Anything?" I gave him a sly smile. "That's a dangerous thing to admit. What if I asked for a billion dollars?"

"You wouldn't." He returned the smile. "I know you too well." He tilted my chin to his face.

He pressed a kiss to my lips. The world faded until only we existed.

More than ever I wanted the cure, so I could experience a thousand more moments like this one.

29

From THE SCOOP! ONLINE CELEBRITY GOSSIP MAGAZINE

OUT AND ABOUT: VAMPIRE LUCIAN VIDRARU SPENDS TIME IN ROMANTIC BUCHAREST LUXURY HOTEL WITH MYSTERY DATE

During a rare trip outside the walls of the Crimson Hollow Research Facility, vampire Lucian Vidraru is spotted in his home country of Bucharest, Romania with a young woman who THE SCOOP! identified as Amaya de la Vega of Miami, Florida, who spent time with him during a dinner for dignitaries at the Epoque Hotel. The mystery woman is neither wealthy nor famous, a diversion from Vidraru's usual dates, and some speculate how long the relationship will last. Is she a long-term commitment? Or merely a fling? Time will tell, although THE SCOOP! is betting on the latter.

AMAYA

I LAY IN BED STARING UP AT MY CEILING. MY HEART HADN'T stopped pounding since Lucian kissed me, and I didn't know if the butterflies would ever stop flitting through my stomach. Khan slept beside me, his head resting on his big paws. I stroked his neck, and his eyes twitched but didn't open.

"What am I supposed to do now?" I whispered to him. How could I be falling for Lucian Vidraru? That had never been part of my plan for finding the cure. But now that I truly realized what I'd been searching for all along—not a cure, but a life.

I took a deep breath, hoping to dispel my nervousness. Now, more than ever, I wanted to live. I wanted to live so I could experience my dreams of becoming like Mom—of finding a path to the cure. I wanted to do it so no one else would have to go through the heartache I had felt, and I wanted to live so Lucian could have a chance of experiencing a life worth living with me.

Looking back, I still didn't know what other choice I had, or what I would've done differently. There wasn't another way to get inside the facility except by infecting myself with the virus. I'd done what I'd had to do.

But if we didn't find the cure in time…

No.

I wouldn't go there.

We would find it. Still, a nagging feeling pulled at me. Too many unanswered questions remained about Sally Anderson. About the ghost I'd seen in the facility. About Dr. Warren and his bizarre behavior.

I closed my eyes and pulled the sheets over me. The air conditioning hummed.

Something about coming to Romania bugged me. The pieces of the puzzle were scattered, the picture indiscernible, too many unknowns plaguing me.

Dr. Warren's research surfaced in my memory—his obsessiveness about the missing luggage and his research.

Research that hadn't resulted in any breakthroughs in over a decade.

What was he trying so hard to hide?

The sheets soft on my skin and the lulling hum of the air conditioner begged me to stay in bed. But the more I pondered Dr. Warren and his research, the more compelled I felt to find out the truth.

I'd seen the doctor loading his suitcases in the extra bedroom. He'd left them alone to sleep in the larger suite.

Opening my eyes, I stared up at the ceiling. Moonlight drifted through the parted curtains, lending a milky blue sheen to the wainscoting and the digital clock, which read 3:02.

I could go straight to the room, check through the suitcases, and be back in a matter of minutes. No one would be awake right now.

But why was I bothering? Didn't I trust the doctor? Lucian did. He thought of the man like a father, yet besides waking Lucian and giving him a place to live, what had he done to deserve such status?

With a groan, I sat up and put on my slippers. My Wonder Woman pajamas would be less than inconspicuous, but I wasn't planning on meeting anyone on my way out.

After closing the door behind me, I crossed through the living area.

The door to the extra bedroom loomed in the dim light, a ghostly white door against the eggshell blue wallpaper. I went to it and turned the knob, giving one last glance behind me before entering.

The glow from a computer monitor illuminated the small space, and the modem created a quiet hum. Papers were stacked and stapled neatly beside the keyboard.

I leafed through them. Receipts for plane tickets to Romania. Others were receipts for travel and food. Dr. Warren had written on each one in neat printed letters and numbers. I scanned the one sitting on top.

V/S. SLA. MCO to ICT.

V/S would likely refer to the viridae sangre virus. But what were the other letters for?

I rubbed my forehead, wishing I could think through the fog in my brain, the headache that only got worse, and the sourness swirling through my stomach.

Frustrated, I straightened the papers and stepped away from the table.

What was he hiding? *Was* he hiding anything in the first place?

The long suitcase he'd been so particular about sat on the floor along the back wall. I went to it and knelt. The container was lined in an outer metal shell that felt cold when I touched it. It didn't escape my notice that the case was the length of a coffin. Weird thing to be traveling with in the company of a supposed vampire. After popping one latch and then the other, I lifted the lid open. It snapped up with a pressurized hiss.

Blue lights glowed from the edges, reminding me of the sterile hue in my mom's lab. Tubes, like those used in IVs, ran the length of the inner lid. I ran my hand over the bottom lined in plastic casing, the fluorescent bulbs warming my fingers.

Footsteps echoed behind me.

I closed the lid and spun around. Heart pounding, I searched the room.

"Is someone there?" I asked, my voice shaky.

Standing, I forced my breathing to stay even as I faced the empty room.

"Hello?"

The blank computer screen lit the room in a dim glow, illuminating the desk, two chairs, and a stack of boxes.

Had I imagined the footsteps?

I crossed to the door, searching behind the boxes and under the desk. All empty. No one here. With one last glance at the small space, I opened the door and stepped outside, half-expecting to see Dr. Warren blocking my path, but the suite remained empty. I walked on quiet feet until I entered my own room and shut the door behind me.

Before going back to bed, I went to the bathroom and stood at the sink. Cold water chilled my hands before I splashed my face, letting the sting of the liquid root me into reality.

A wisp of a woman's silhouette in a white dress ghosted in the mirror.

Terror skittered down my spine as I spun around.

My pulse pounded loudly in my ears, drowning out any other sounds.

"*Nothing's there,*" I whispered, as if by saying it, it would become true.

As I walked back to my bed, the air turned freezing. I rubbed at the chill bumps covering my arms.

"Nothing's there. Nothing's there," I repeated as I crawled under my bed covers. I patted the bed, but I found it cold without Khan. Where had he gone?

"Khan?" My voice came out as a startled hiss. "Buddy?"

Whining came from under my bed. The dog slunk out, still whining as he jumped onto the mattress with me.

I patted his back. He shivered as I stroked his fur.

"What's the matter?" I asked gently.

He only nuzzled me, shaking so badly he made the mattress springs creak.

"Poor pup. What's got you so worked up?"

I knew what had spooked him because it was the same thing spooking me. Admitting that I was being stalked by a ghost, even an ocean away from the facility, was a difficult thing to admit. My mom's scientist voice intruded on my thoughts, telling me to keep it in check. *Ghosts don't exist.*

I hugged my dog close to me and squeezed my eyes shut. Ghost or not, I had seen something, and so had my dog. *Ghosts don't exist,* Mom's voice repeated in my head.

30

Transcript from *The Journey Channel's* Destination Explorer *with host Ben Ryder. Original air date June 29, 2017.*

RYDER: We begin our journey at Bran Castle, rumored home of Vlad Dracula, the man you can thank for impaling wooden stakes through hearts. Nestled in the Transylvanian mountains rises the blood red towers of the Gothic castle, a place steeped in myth and legend. No surprise Bram Stoker chose this place as the setting for his novel, Dracula. But who was the real Dracula, and will we find our answers here?

GLENN: If you want to know the truth, head down to the crypts.

RYDER: The crypts?

GLENN: Yeah. Look there.

RYDER: What's in the crypts?

[Footsteps echoing down stairwell. Torch flames sputtering.]

GLENN: Look in the tombs.

[Men screaming]

RYDER: *Holy [bleep]*

~

LUCIAN

The taxi bumped over the uneven road. I pressed a gloved hand to my suit's pocket, the weight of my father's letter dragging me down as if it were a wooden stake and not mere parchment.

Amaya shifted beside me and laid her head on my shoulder. Beneath her long lashes, dark circles shadowed her eyes. I smoothed my hand over her soft cheek, and a slight smile ghosted over her parted lips.

"You look exhausted," I said.

She only nodded, not speaking. It must've been the virus sapping her energy. She hadn't been the same since this morning. She'd hardly spoken a few words at breakfast, her eyes round and haunted as she'd stared around the hotel, as if she were expecting to see something.

Her spooked attitude hadn't lifted since we'd gotten in the taxi and started down the road to Bran castle. A caravan of taxis followed behind ours, enough for Dr. Warren's team and luggage. I'd been lucky to maneuver it so that Amaya and I shared the taxi. I would treasure my time with her, no matter how little it was.

"Is something bothering you?" I asked quietly, my words nearly drowned out by the Volvo's tires rolling over the winding mountain switchbacks.

She grasped my hand and held it in her lap. "Nothing now," she said with a strained smile.

"Nothing?" I rubbed my thumb over her palm. "You can tell me. Are you afraid we won't find the cure?"

She opened her eyes at that—lovely, dark eyes that spoke of intelligence beyond her twenty years.

"Yes," she said, though her gaze darted away, and I questioned her sincerity.

"Is that all?"

She shook her head. "You wouldn't believe me if I told you."

"Why is that?" I asked.

"Because I told you before," she answered. "Nothing's changed since then."

"Ah," I said, realization dawning. "Is this about the ghost?"

Her face paled as she nodded. Although I had trouble accepting anything supernatural was at work, something had clearly upset her.

"What exactly did you see?" I asked.

"Only a reflection in my mirror last night. A woman wearing a white dress. I don't understand it. I think I might be going crazy." She rubbed her eyes. "Could the virus be causing it?"

Her words disturbed me more than I wanted to admit. "The virus does have random symptoms that vary from person to person. I've never heard of anyone experiencing hallucinations, but I suppose it's a possibility."

"So, I'm going crazy then?"

"Amaya," I said sternly. "You're *not* going crazy. There are other explanations."

Her brown eyes widened. "Like I'm really seeing a ghost?"

"No." I locked my jaw. "But you're seeing something."

We passed through a tunnel, the light disappearing, revealing our reflections in tinted glass.

"I thought the facility was haunted," she said, shifting so she sat straight. "But that doesn't explain what I'm seeing now."

"Yeah." I didn't know what to tell her. What did she expect me to say?

"So," Amaya said, attempting a casual tone. "What are we supposed to do when we get to the castle?"

She was changing the subject. I let her turn away from the supposed ghost. "We'll have to get into the dungeons under the castle in order to enter the crypts. They keep them locked, only let certain people inside. This may be a short trip."

Her eyes narrowed. "Do you think we'll get in?"

"We'll see." I smoothed a stray strand of hair behind her ear that had fallen over her pale cheek. "Once they know who I am, it shouldn't be too difficult. Sometimes being famous comes in handy."

Her gaze went to the window as we drove over steep, rocky cliffs and past towering spruce trees. "Can you explain something to me?"

"Sure," I answered. "What is it?"

"What happened in Romania when you came here last time?"

I stiffened. I should've expected the question.

"Were you looking for the cure?" she asked.

I hesitated before answering. "Actually, I was looking for the opposite."

She narrowed her eyes. "What do you mean?"

"I wanted to die."

She tilted her head. "You were looking for a way to kill yourself?"

I took her hand, squeezing it gently. "You have to understand, I wasn't the same person then. I had nothing to live for. The thought of continuing forever without any release drove me crazy. I knew if there was a way for me to die, it would be in my father's research."

"But you didn't find it?"

"Obviously." I smiled, hoping to dispel the tension. "Those had been dark days, ones I hoped were behind me. But the truth was, the fear of life continuing forever still haunted me. Dr. Warren had woken me to a better life than the one I'd had before, but what if I were to die again and awake to something worse? Death would never release me."

I closed my eyes, hoping the pain of the past would disappear quickly. Amaya rested her head on my shoulder. Her hair held the scent of lavender, and I breathed it in, letting her presence calm me.

My world had been a darker place without her. I hadn't felt this way about anyone in so long—and certainly not in this life. The thought of losing her terrified me. She was a beacon in a world of confusion. If I had her, I would be happy. I would never wish to die again.

Of course, I'd never told her such things. If I did, what would she say? Did she feel the same about me? Or would I scare her away?

She was too young to know how terrifying the world could be. But I could protect her. I could give her an amazing life if she gave me half a chance.

Couldn't I?

I rubbed my forehead as confusion plagued me.

What kind of life did I live? One surrounded by press and cameras, one that never allowed for privacy.

Wouldn't it be better if I left her alone?

But I could never do that. Maybe it was a selfish thought, but I needed her.

On the horizon rose the somber towers of Bran castle. My stomach squirmed with unease. A rush of memories swallowed me.

Riding on the carriage, my father at my side and my brothers and mother behind us. I remembered how optimistic he'd looked as we neared the castle—that glint in his wide, hopeful eyes, the way his smile lit his face, his big mustache and sideburns, his patched hat.

This had been his salvation.

If only he'd known it would be his death.

Ancient towers rose above the mountains. Crimson roof

tiles contrasted the dark greens and grays of the forest. Years of chimney smoke had blackened the stones.

Amaya sat up straight to get a better view. "That's it?"

"Yes," I answered, my voice dark. "Welcome to Bran castle."

31

A dungeon below Bran Castle. Bran, Romania.

~

AMAYA

Our footsteps echoed over cobblestones as we hiked up to the castle. I held Khan's leash, my fingers stiff with cold in the mountain air. Thick granite walls punctuated with small windows rose above us. The red terra cotta tiles looked the color of dried blood.

Lucian grasped my free hand, and his warmth surrounded me.

"It reminds me of a fairy tale," I said.

"A Grimm fairy tale, perhaps." Lucian spoke with an edge of warning in his voice. "They were a bit darker than how we think of the stories now. Bloodier. More violent and gruesome."

"Maybe so," I said, a gust of wind nearly drowning out my words. "But it's still enchanting."

Dr. Warren and Officer Goodman followed behind us. We

passed crowds of tourists who gathered along the branching pathways. Some of them turned to look at us, mouths gaping as they focused on Lucian.

I glanced up at him. What was he thinking?

"What was the castle like when you were young?" I asked.

"Surprisingly, not so different, except for the tourists. The caretakers have done a good job restoring the place. It was built in the middle ages, you know. They built it to last through the ages as a fortress, and that's exactly what the place has done." As his eyes roved the towers, it seemed as if he spoke of a familiar person and not merely a structure of mortar and stones. "It can't die," he said quietly. "Like me."

We stepped under the shade of a portcullis to a ticket booth. The elderly woman sitting inside stood as we approached. Her eyes widened as she took in the man in the sunglasses and hat, wearing the dark duster that contrasted his skin.

"*Domnule Vidraru?*"

"*Salut,*" he said casually, resting his gloved hands on the booth's counter. He said something in Romanian, perhaps asking to purchase tickets. The woman waved her hands, speaking with passion.

Lucian turned to me. "She says she won't sell us tickets since this is my home. We can enter for free."

"That's nice." I smiled at her.

She gave me a nod, then said something else to Lucian.

"She says they've kept my father's vaults locked," he explained. "No one's been inside in decades." Lucian took a stack of tickets from her, and the woman said something else to him, her eyes darting.

"She's giving us a warning," Lucian explained.

"What kind of warning?" I asked.

He nodded at her, then turned to me. "Not surprising." He placed the tickets in his pocket. "The locals know I'm here."

I gave him a questioning glance. "Will they do anything about it?"

"I don't know." He clenched his jaw, his face pensive.

Dr. Warren and Officer Goodman caught up to us. Lucian explained what he told me, and Officer Goodman stood straight, his hand going casually to his belt.

"Not to worry. That's why I'm here. Security detail." He pointed over his shoulder at three Romanian men. "We've got them, too, should we need them."

"Who are they?" Lucian asked suspiciously.

"Extra security," Officer Goodman answered.

"Fine," Lucian said brusquely. "Let's make this quick, shall we? This isn't a sightseeing tour."

We left the ticket booth area and entered the courtyard, where our footsteps echoed up through the towering walls that looked at least six feet thick. The shell encasing the castle—reminding me of the barrier that had surrounded Lucian's heart for most of his life.

Khan trotted at my heels, sniffing at the people passing us by, and I tightened my grip on his leash. We entered through a narrow doorway. The scent of wood polish came from the gleaming floors. As we followed behind our group, the quiet murmur of voices bounced around the stark white walls.

We left the tour group to follow Lucian. He moved through the hallways and rooms without hesitating, as if it had only been yesterday since he was last here. Red and gold rugs matched the comfortable leather furniture. Fireplaces rose from imposing white walls.

Heavily carved Victorian armoires and mirrors decorated the rooms, their dark wood contrasting lighter colors. Gray light seeped through the small windows. Paintings of men and women wearing Renaissance-style clothing punctuated the spaces with bursts of color. A chill lingered in the air, and it wasn't hard to imagine the castle as the seat of vampire legends.

Lucian had to duck as we walked through a narrow doorway. We made it to a set of stairs leading to a door. When we stepped outside, rain scented the air, and thick clouds gathered overhead.

We walked the length of the castle, past ivy vines growing up the walls. Built into the mountain, the fortress rose over us and blocked out half the sky, so tall I had to crane my neck to see the top.

"The entrance to the dungeons is just ahead," Lucian called to us. "We'll have to cross through the cemetery to get there."

"The cemetery?" Officer Goodman asked.

"Yes. My family is buried there."

We took a path over the lawn and around a low wall made of crumbling stones. Thick rainclouds gathered as we took the steep trail down to the graveyard. Granite markers spotted with lichen rose like living stones from the earth, as if they'd been planted there to grow through the ages.

Thunder rumbled as we hiked to a gazebo with an oxidized copper dome rising above the graves. Raindrops fell by the time we made it under the shelter of the roof. The drumming of the rain drowned out the sounds of the croaking frogs. Humidity made my clothes stick to my skin.

Ropes partitioned a freshly dug pit in the center of the space. The scent of damp earth came from a pile of dark dirt.

"Looks like we're early for a funeral," Dr. Warren said with a chuckle over the rain. "Hopefully not ours!"

"It won't be mine," Lucian answered, shaking his head. "Look over there." He pointed to a cluster of graves beyond the roof of the gazebo. "My parents and brothers."

I followed him to the ancient markers. Dr. Warren and the others stayed under the shelter of the gazebo. Rain darkened the cross-shaped stones.

"Here." Lucian knelt by a marker. He brushed his gloved fingers over the etched name.

Constatin Cristian Vidraru.

With a gentle tug, he removed the leather covering his hand. Blunted claws stretched to the carved letters, and he ran his scaled fingertip over each one. He muttered something in Romanian, so quiet I barely heard his words.

I knelt beside him.

He glanced at me, then pulled his hand away, curling his fingers to form a fist. "Do you think my father meant to make me a monster?" he asked, his tone vulnerable and filled with a deep sadness that I had trouble understanding.

I placed my hand on his shoulder. "We've had this conversation before," I said softly, hoping he heard my sincerity. "You're not a monster."

"Look at me, Amaya." He spoke quietly, though I heard the intensity in his voice. As if to prove his point, he removed his other glove, then his glasses, and placed them on his father's grave.

He clasped his hands, scales rotting and seeping pus. I did my best not to grimace in front of him.

"Lucian." I gasped. "You're getting worse."

He only nodded.

"Can't anything be done?"

He shrugged. "Like what? I can't die. But I can't be fully healed either. I'm in limbo. Cursed to always be hungry and in pain. Never able to be free of it." He nodded toward the grave. "Thanks to him."

With another whispered Romanian word, he stood, then faced the gazebo.

"Do you hate him?" I asked.

He didn't answer immediately, his strange red and black eyes pinned on the tombstone. "He had his reasons. But he also didn't realize the scope of his actions. I cling to the thought that if he did, he never would've experimented on me."

He left his gloves and glasses behind as we crossed back to the castle.

"You're not wearing them?" I questioned.

"No. There's no reason now. Not where we're going."

"What do you mean?" I asked.

He only shook his head. The way he'd said it sounded so final. A shiver went down my spine as we left the graves behind. Khan stayed close at my heels, as if he sensed the same unease as me.

We wandered away from the cemetery and down a sloping path until we reached a wooden door set into the mountainside.

"Is that the entrance to the dungeons?" I asked.

"Yes. That's it." Lucian went to the rusted iron rung and tugged until the door opened on unoiled hinges.

I hesitated before following him inside, the damp, cool air wafting, smelling of mildew.

Lucian stood inside the doorway.

I took a deep breath to steady my nerves before I entered the dungeon.

32

Excerpt from the diary of Constatin Vidraru. January 18, 1873. Bran, Romania

My darling wife Elena was terrified when I showed her the box containing the object I found in the Tinos cave. I told her this was to be our salvation, but she could only fixate on the mythology surrounding the item. She said I was cursing our family as she made the sign of the cross, and she told me to never bring it in the house again, of which I complied. I will keep it in my laboratory beneath Bran Castle where I will begin the experiments forthwith. Lucian has agreed to assist me. His name will carry on throughout the ages, although he cannot be aware of it, nor will I tell him of the grave importance of our experiments.

His protection is my utmost priority.

~

AMAYA

LUCIAN'S FLASHLIGHT BEAM REFLECTED OFF GLASS JARS LINING the dozens of rows of shelves as we walked through the dungeon. Birds floating in formaldehyde stared at us through milky, dead eyes. Snakes coiled in the glass containers, and eggs floated in the liquid solutions.

"So many jars," I said, my voice echoing through the enormous room.

"Father's collection," Lucian answered.

We wandered deeper into the dungeon, past the rows of jars, and down a set of steep steps. I held to a wooden banister. Flecks of paint stuck to my sweaty palms. Khan whined, though I managed to pull him down until we reached the bottom.

The pool of Lucian's light illuminated a small area, but the echo of our footsteps bounced around a room that could've risen ten feet above us.

Lucian pulled a matchbook from his pocket and lit a torch attached to a rusted wall sconce. He did the same for another, then another, as he walked the perimeter of the room, until firelight glowed.

The flicker of flames highlighted the room's center—a long metal table, rows of shelves, and odd metal devices with protruding spikes, clasps, and chains.

"Torture devices?" I asked as we approached them.

"Yes." He ran his hand over the metal table. "From the middle ages. Father used them for his experiments."

Black stains marred the rust, the scent of iron hanging thick in the air. Khan sniffed at the dark spots, and I pulled him toward me. Wandering around the machines, my shoulder brushed the chains, the sound making a loud clinking in the silent dungeon.

"What are we looking for?" I asked.

"A box," Lucian answered.

My eyebrows rose. "A box?"

"Yeah. Like the one I kept this in." He reached into his

duster pocket and pulled out a yellowed envelope. With a deep sigh, he placed it on the table's center, as if it were an offering to the gods of his father's past transgressions.

"Your dad's letter?" I asked, standing across from him, excitement making my heart race. Finally, after so long, I'd get a chance to read it.

"Yes," he answered darkly.

"Will you translate it?"

He arched a hairless eyebrow, dark eyes like deep pools reflecting the flames. A chill went down my spine.

After opening the envelope, he slid a piece of yellowed parchment out and smoothed it on the tabletop before he began reading.

33

A letter written by Constantin Vidraru to his son, Lucian Vidraru.
September 23, 1877.

My dearest Lucian,
It is with greatest sadness that I pen this letter. As
you lie upon the table where I attempted to save your
life, I must assume responsibility for unwittingly
taking it. If there is to be a reversal to this situation,
God willing, it will be because of the miraculous
serum I have derived and injected into your blood.
If you are to survive the process of transformation, I
pray you wake to a world kinder than this. I would be
unwise not to warn you of the disease lying dormant
in your blood. You have unwittingly become a carrier
of a dangerous ailment that can preserve your life but
may do the opposite for others.
The only way to eradicate this disease is to discover
its source in the crypts beneath Bran castle. In a box
hidden in the tomb that will become my grave, I have
hidden the serum's source. I pray you discover its
whereabouts before much damage is done.

I leave you with one final warning: I fear I have discovered something I cannot control. In the cave of the isle of Tinos, I sought out one legend that I believed held the key to eternity. The locals feared the beast in the cavern—and I am forced not to reveal its true nature for fear of such repercussions. This demon now resides within you. It may have the ability to possess you, and for that, I will never forgive myself. My intentions were honorable, but I must admit my ambition has blinded me. I do not know what the future holds for you, my son, but I pray you have one.
Remember, the secret to long life is not found in a serum, but in the connections we make with those who join us on our earthly journey, who I am certain are waiting to greet us after our mortal trials have ended, so that we may spend the eternities together.
Your loving father,
Constantin Cristian Vidraru

～

AMAYA

"What does this mean?" I asked as Lucian stood across from me. Flames sputtered from sconces, making me jump. "What kind of demon did your father find in the Tinos cave?"

Lucian pinched his lips. "I never found out. Father feared the locals, so he kept it a secret. He took precautions to keep the truth from me. In all his field journals and diaries, he never once mentions the name of this supposed demon."

I eyed him. "It could be anything."

"Yes." His gaze didn't meet mine when he answered.

I pressed my hands to the table, to either side of his

father's letter, careful not to let my fingers brush the brittle paper. "What do you think the creature is?"

He held up his clawed hands. "You tell me."

I shook my head. "We've been through this before. I don't know, but your father must've left some kind of clue."

"Yes. He says the cure will be inside his tomb in the crypts, but he died sooner than he realized he would." Lucian's tone turned somber, and I wondered if he were reliving the gory scene that he had witnessed in this very room after his first awakening. What remained of his father had been strewn over the walls and across the floor—and he'd been the one responsible, though he had no memory of it. "He was never buried in the crypts, and when I was last in Romania, I wasn't allowed access inside them."

"But where else could it be?" I asked.

"Nowhere else. I searched the first time I came here, and I found no evidence."

"Then we go to the crypts again," I said matter-of-factly. "Where are they?"

"There." He pointed behind me. I looked over my shoulder, spotting a narrow hallway built into the stone, its metal doorway barely visible in the dim firelight. He picked up the letter, folded it and slid it carefully back in the envelope, then placed it into his duster pocket.

We headed toward the crypt's entrance when Khan stopped. I pulled on the leash, but he whined, refusing to budge.

"Come on, Buddy," I urged him, but he shook his head. "Why are you acting this way?" I looked up at Lucian. "He's never been like this. What do you think's wrong?"

"Well." He spoke with a hint of dark humor in his voice. "We're going into the dark, spooky, possibly haunted crypts," Lucian said drily. "I'd say he's being smart by refusing to come."

"Khan," I said sternly, managing to drag him with me, but his whine turned to a high-pitched yelp.

"Maybe you should tie him up here," Lucian suggested.

"You think he'll be okay?" I asked.

"He should be. I'm not planning to be in there too long."

"Fine," I said with a nervous exhale, then walked him back toward the doorway and tied him to the staircase railing. I knelt to be eye-level with him and ran my hand over his furry head. "You take care out here, all right?"

Khan licked my palm. A pang of worry stabbed at me. Leaving him behind felt like I was abandoning a piece of myself. That negative voice in my head told me he was just a dog, but it was impossible not to think of him as anything other than family. I gave him one final scratch behind the ears, then I stood to face Lucian.

I had to catch my breath at the sight of the man.

The flames dancing around him reflected in the deep pools of his eyes, bringing out the hues of red.

Demon, the word whispered through my head, and I couldn't push down the fear that tingled as if cold fingers trailed along the exposed skin of my arms.

What kind of creature was he? And did I really want to find out?

With a deep breath, I left my dog behind and followed Lucian to the door. Our footsteps echoed, reminding me of the ping of a blacksmith's hammer.

A rusted metal lock barred the crypt door's entrance. Lucian grasped it and inspected the mechanism. He tugged on it, then pushed the door, but it only rattled as it remained sealed.

"Locked," he said.

"What do we do now?"

His eyes shone with a guarded, intelligent glint as he looked at me. "Promise you won't tell anyone about this?"

"About what?" I asked, confused.

"About what I'm about to do." He removed his duster and handed it to me. I took it from him as he rolled up his sleeves.

He cradled the lock in his palms. After closing his eyes, his skin glowed—actually *glowed*—as if he were lit from within by pale silvery moonlight.

I gasped, stunned. "Lucian?"

Flames exploded from his hands. Heat singed my face. I jumped back, the roar of the fire filling my ears. Khan barked. I stumbled to gain my balance. My mouth slacked open as I watched Lucian's hands burn. Complete shock slapped me. The metal lock glowed bright orange, so intense I had to shield my eyes.

Liquid metal dripped to the floor. The pungent scent of scorched iron filled the air. My breath caught in my throat, and I had trouble believing what I was seeing was real.

How had he kept such a secret for so long? He'd always been so terrified of fire.

When the lock was nothing more than a puddle of molten iron on the floor, Lucian stepped back.

His clawed hands glowed for a second longer until returning to their normal state of sluffed scales and broken talons.

"You…" I breathed, trying to process what I saw while my heart pounded with a wild tempo. "Lucian, how?"

He ran a hand over his smooth head, his gaze not meeting mine. "Discovered it a few years ago."

"You're, what, superhuman or something?"

His lips quirked into a half-smile, not a happy expression, but one that held a haunted fear. "Superhuman? Hardly. Call me what I am."

I took a step to him. The way he'd so casually manipulated fire to burn through his body was something I could hardly comprehend. They'd called him a vampire, but he was more than that. "Do you know what you are? Be honest with me."

He shook his head, and I placed my hand on his arm.

When his gaze met mine, I forced my feet to hold their ground.

I shouldn't fear him. I knew he would never hurt me. If he had any say in the matter, he'd never hurt anyone. But his strong, muscle-corded frame loomed over me, nearly a head taller than me. Had he always been so tall? In the shadows of the dancing torchlight, my imagination took over, and it wasn't hard to see dark wings curling around him, like a demon come to life.

My breath stuttered, and I couldn't hold his gaze.

"Amaya, what is it?" he asked.

I shook my head.

"Amaya, please tell me," he pleaded. "Am I scaring you?"

"Of course, you're scaring me." The words came from my mouth before I could consider the consequences.

His face fell, and he released my arm quickly.

"I understand," he said quietly, turning away from me. He pushed the door to the crypts. After centuries of disuse, the rusted hinges squeaked with an ear-splitting wail.

He took his duster and put it on, as if to cover more than his physical form, but to hide his true self.

After grabbing a torch from a sconce, he led me through the doorway and into the blackness of the tunnel. The narrow passageway of ancient bricks and mortar closed in around me. Stale air tasted of the cloying scent of damp earth. The walls didn't allow us to walk side by side, so I stayed behind Lucian, focusing on the torchlight in the otherwise blindingly dark world.

I fisted my empty hands, wishing I had the comfort of Khan's leash to hold. My stomach twisted with unease as I followed the man called Lucian—someone I had to admit I had feelings for, ones that ran deeper than friendship. A man I'd never really known. One who'd kept secrets from me. One who wasn't human, but something I didn't want to ponder.

Demon.

The sight of hands bursting into flames wouldn't stop playing through my head.

Legends of demons surfaced from my memories of reading Daddy's encyclopedia of Greek Myths. The minotaur. Hades. *The typhon.* It was the one that had especially frightened me. Known as the father of all monsters. Birthed from Gaia and Tartarus in the depths of hell. Had Lucian's father come upon such a creature?

No, no, no. I can't be seriously believing these things.

But Lucian's hands had burst into flame!

He was considered a vampire. He'd been infected with a virus. He was nothing but a byproduct of his father's experiments and nothing else. Nothing mythological.

But what had his father found in the cave?

The tunnel widened until we stepped into a circular chamber lined in niches where elaborately carved coffins rested.

A marble carving of an angel rose over us. At least twelve feet tall, its hollow eyes stared at the floor. The angel hefted a cross, its back curved, its wings arching over its body as if for protection.

We circled the crypt's perimeter where coffins ran the length of the walls.

"Which one belonged to your father?" I asked, my voice sounding empty in the tunneled-out cavern.

"I don't know," Lucian answered. "Read the inscriptions."

"You think his name would be inscribed on it?"

"Yes," he answered. "Romanians are superstitious. None of them would've wanted his coffin after he died the way he did. They would've left it here—and hopefully not disturbed whatever my father left inside." Lucian locked his eyes on me. I had to peer up at him. "Amaya, I have to warn you…I don't know what we'll find. When I was last in Romania, I used the excuse of a locked door to keep me from finding the truth. I've been avoiding it for years. Dr. Warren begged me to come here and find out what my father had hidden, but I refused to go through with it."

"Why?" My quiet voice echoed.

Lucian balled his free hand into a tight fist. "Because I fear what I'll find. Amaya, for me, the only cure is death."

The haunted tone of his voice gave me pause. "Are you sure?"

"Yes," he said. His gaze turned wistful and sad as it fell on me. The old Lucian—the one I'd known in the sanitarium, the one I'd come to love—seemed to peer from his eyes.

With a deep, calming breath, I took his hand in mine, threading my fingers through claws.

He flinched at my touch, his shoulders bunched, and the pensive, tight lines in his forehead creased.

"Lucian, whatever we find, we'll find it together. There's so many people who need the cure—more than just you and me."

He nodded, taking a deep breath, as if to steel his resolve. "Yes, you're right."

But the way he said it made it seem as if he kept something from me. I decided not to push him. I'd gotten him this far. I couldn't let him go back.

"We can do this," I assured him.

With hands clasped, we stepped away from the looming statue and crossed to the wall of caskets. The smooth marble carvings of demons and angels decorated the rectangular boxes. Romanian names ran the length of the coffins.

I ran my fingertips over the carved indentations of the letters. Focusing on dates, I stopped at one missing a death date. I stepped to the head of the coffin and read the name.

Constatin Cristian Vidraru.

"I found it."

Lucian stood behind me. "Nice work." He placed the torch in an empty sconce. "We'll have to move the coffin to the floor so we can take a look under the lid." He gave a forced smile. "Shouldn't be too hard, right?"

I eyed the muscles bulging underneath his duster. "Maybe not for you."

Leather creaked as he removed his long jacket, then tossed it aside. "Let's get this over with." He nodded to the foot of the coffin. "Take that end. I'll take this one."

"Okay," I breathed, my words shaky. "We're sure it's empty, right?"

"Of course." He winked. "I'm sure about everything."

I rolled my eyes. "You know, I think this fame thing might be going to your head."

He shrugged. "Side effect of being one-hundred-and-sixty. Makes you think you know everything."

Moving to the head of the stone casket, he grasped the top. I did the same at the foot of the box, the stones cold to the touch, and grabbed the embellished robe of a carved angel.

"Ready?" he asked.

"Yeah." I breathed deeply. "Ready."

"Good." He nodded. "On three?"

I nodded.

Claws grasped the edges as he took a deep breath. "One, two, *three*."

I strained against the box until it shifted an inch, then another, with the sound of scraping stone. A cloud of dust billowed.

"An inch more," Lucian said through clenched teeth.

Muscles burning, I tugged on the coffin until it slid free of the niche and leveraged it to the floor with an echoing thud.

Breathing heavily, I dabbed at the sweat on my forehead. "If there are any vampires in here, I'm pretty sure we've woken them up now."

"Good thing vampires aren't real," Lucian said.

I laughed. "Says the man who can live forever and drinks blood."

Humor shone in his eyes as he raised an eyebrow. "Ready to get the lid off?"

"Sure."

I stood at the foot of the coffin, and he stood at the head. We grasped the lid. Grating stone echoed as we slid it to the side, revealing a red velvet lining, and a single object sitting at the coffin's center.

A single box.

My heart sped as anxiety flooded my blood. Was the cure inside? Had we finally found it?

We moved to stand over the wooden, dark-stained box. Images of cherubs and dragons had been carved to decorate the object's sides, though its lid held an image of Medusa, snakes fanning out around her frozen, screaming face.

I pointed to the box. "Interesting carving."

"Yes. Not surprising though. Father had a fascination with popular Orthodox religion along with other belief systems. Greek and Pagan mythologies. Russian. Eastern beliefs, as well. It's what drove him to seek out creatures of myth. He thought the universal beings that appeared in all mythologies were the ones most likely to be real, since they'd appeared all over the world with nothing linking them. Dragons. Wraiths. Demons."

Demons.

I stood motionless over the box, feeling as if I touched it, it might burst into flames or disappear into a pile of dust.

"Should you take the lid off, or should I?" Lucian asked.

I bit my lip. "Maybe we should take it off together?"

"Sounds like a plan." He pursed his lips, his pensiveness apparent in his dark eyes.

I reached for the box, but he grabbed my arm. "Wait."

"Wait?" I asked.

"I-I'm not sure."

"Lucian, we came all this way. All those people. We have to."

The fear in his eyes spoke of something else haunting him.

"Is there something you aren't telling me?" I asked.

His shoulders rose and fell with his deep breath. "No." He shook his head. "Nothing. Let's do this."

He squeezed my hand, as if to reassure us both, and together, we reached for the box.

34

From the diary of Lucian Vidraru

I didn't get a last meal before I died in prison, but if I had, I would've asked for my mother's ciorba soup. Of course, no one could cook it like she could. I imagine if anyone were to recreate the Romanian stew to perfection, they would've only accomplished it by channeling the spirit of my mother. If that had happened, perhaps I could've convinced her to take me with her to heaven, and I could've had the chance to escape this prison called life.

However vain, a person can dream.

~

AMAYA

LUCIAN AND I STOOD OVER THE OPEN BOX.

A football-shaped object rested inside. Its mirror-like surface danced with pearlescent colors.

"Is it an egg?" I asked quietly.

Lucian reached for it and picked it up. He inspected the smooth, glossy exterior when the two sides split apart. A vial with golden liquid fell silently to the box's padded bottom.

He set aside the two halves, then picked up the vial.

"That's it?" I asked. "The cure?"

His Adam's apple bobbed as he swallowed. "Let's hope so."

"There's not very much."

"No. But I suppose it doesn't take much to reverse the virus's mutation."

I reached for the broken egg, running my fingers over the glassy surface. "I've never seen anything like this. What's it made from?"

He shook his head. "I don't know. It's like nothing I've ever seen before." His eyes—wide, dark and tinged in fear met mine. "You think it's possible Father really found a creature in that cave? Whatever was inside this egg was its offspring? He made me—" he pointed to the broken shell—"from that?"

"Yes, I think it's very likely."

"But—what is it?"

"I don't know. We may never know. But that isn't why we came." I pointed to the vial. "We're here for this."

"Yes." He held it up to the torchlight. The semi-translucent liquid sparkled with colors of gold and mother-of-pearl.

"It's beautiful," I said. "It doesn't look demonic."

"I agree." He placed the vial in his duster pocket. "And the good news is that it's unlikely I'm the byproduct of a vampire."

"Right." I allowed myself to smile. "What are we doing now?"

"Taking this back to Dr. Warren. He'll test it first. See if it's what we think. With any luck, he'll be able to engineer an anti-virus from it."

"Can't we just drink it to find out?" I asked.

"Sure," he answered. "But do you want to be the one to test it?"

The cylindrical shape of the vial stood out in Lucian's duster pocket. With the excitement of finding the cure, I'd ignored my pounding headache and nauseated stomach, but they only served as reminders of the virus slowly killing me. "It's tempting."

"Yes, but it's also extremely risky." He took my hand. "Let's go. Dr. Warren and Officer Goodman are waiting."

I glanced back at the coffin, a trickle of fear tingling along my spine. To come all this way and find it so easily should have given me comfort, yet why I did feel something wasn't right? As if we were meant to find just this and not something else?

"What's the matter?" he asked.

I shook my head, as if to dispel my unease, but the fear stayed with me. "Something about this place—it doesn't feel right."

"Why?"

"I don't know. Hard to describe." I looked up at him. "You're right. We should go."

I kept his hand in mine as we walked out of the crypt, leaving the vault of coffins behind—and the remains of an egg from a creature who would forever remain a mystery.

The thought crossed my mind to go back and take a piece of the shell with me, try to find out what sort of creature it came from. But to remove it from the place it had been housed for so long felt as if I were robbing the grave. Either that, or the *wrongness* I'd sensed while in there stayed with me, and I didn't want to bring any more with me than I had to.

Frantic barking pierced the stillness of the air.

Khan.

The hairs on my arms prickled as fear ran through my veins.

Growls turned to high-pitched yelps.

My feet pounded the stone floor, my lungs heaving for air. I couldn't run fast enough.

When I made it to the main catacomb, four men stood with torches. Their guns glinted in the firelight. My dog lay on the floor at their feet, unmoving.

Panic stopped my heart. I couldn't draw in enough air to breathe.

"Stop," one of the men yelled, pointing his pistol at me. "Both of you." His Romanian accent carried through the harsh timbre of his words.

"Get on the ground. On your knees!"

"What do you want with us?" Lucian asked calmly.

One of the men spat, then said something in Romanian.

"On the ground!" the first man demanded.

Lucian held out his hand, as if to calm them as he stepped in front of me. "There's no need for violence."

He reached for me, his hand grasping for mine, and I took it. Together, we knelt. My mind went into overdrive as I stared at my limp dog lying on the floor. I didn't see blood. At least there was that. More than anything I wanted to go to him, but the four men paced toward us.

Their menacing glares focused on Lucian. They spoke in hissed words to one another. One of them held a coiled rope. He jerked Lucian's arm, then tied Lucian's hands behind his back.

Another man did the same to me. Rough cords bit into my skin as the man tied the rope around my wrists.

Ouch, I muttered.

The man gave me a dark look, then cinched the ropes until I feared he would stop my circulation.

He spat at my feet, uttering a Romanian word, then slapped me—hard. My teeth sliced the inside of my cheek. Warm blood swirled through my mouth, tasting of iron.

"Stop." Lucian's voice cut through the ringing in my ears. "Leave her alone."

"No." The man standing over Lucian jerked him to his feet.

Strong hands clenched my arm and hauled me up. The Romanian dragged me behind Lucian.

We passed by Khan, and I jerked my arm away. The man yelled. The others gathered around. Screaming at me, two men grabbed me while another slammed a fist into my face.

Pain shot through my skull. Stars spun in my vision.

I went to my knees beside my dog.

Under his fur, his chest rose and fell.

He's alive, I thought, right before the world went black.

From "Paint it Black." The Rolling Stones. Aftermath Album. Released May 7, 1966. Produced by Andrew Loog Oldham

I look inside myself and see my heart is black.

~

AMAYA

Cold water drops splashed my face, bringing me back to reality. As I opened my eyes, a steady rain pelted around me. The damp scent of grass filled my lungs. I tried to sit up, but a migraine radiated through my eyes and pounded through my forehead. Bile stuck in my throat. My swollen hands felt three times too big. Through the darkness, I tried to focus on anything I could.

A pale dome stood out against the dark skyline. As I focused, I realized it was the gazebo.

Drizzling rain muffled the voices coming from inside. Firelight glowed under the structure. The sharp scent of smoke carried through the air.

I finally managed to swallow, my tongue swollen and throat so dry it could've been made of sandpaper.

How long had I been here? Where was Lucian?

Sticky blood caked to my hair and pulled at my head as I tried to sit up, but I failed, and remained on the ground. Focusing on the men's voices, I stared toward the gazebo where they surrounded Lucian, his wrists and ankles tied, a gag in his mouth.

I managed to crawl to a sitting position when something sharp scraped my calf. Stinging pain radiated from the cut. Wincing, I pulled my leg to my chest.

Searching the area, a shard of a busted beer bottle glinted on the ground. I grabbed the glass, the sharp edge knifelike. Could I used it to cut my ropes? I stuck it securely between my knees before running the ropes back and forth over the jagged edge.

The fibers snagged and popped open. Blisters formed where the rope tore against my skin, but I didn't stop.

From the corner of my eye, Lucian's silhouette stood over the men surrounding him. Raised voices turned to yelling. The shot of a gun rang out, piercing through the night.

He collapsed.

My heart leapt to my throat.

No!

I sawed glass over ropes, fibers ripping and tearing unevenly. The final strand snapped. My hands broke apart. As my circulation returned, tingles spread through my fingers as if ants crawled under my skin. I shook out my fingers, the wind stinging open sores.

Tears mingled with the rain coursing down my cheeks as I got to my hands and knees. I crept toward the gazebo. The mob of men stood arguing over Lucian.

I could only see his profile and his prone form from my position. Moving quietly, I crawled to the hilltop where the gazebo stood in the light of the men's fires.

Blood spread across Lucian's chest.

A voice in my head reminded me he couldn't die, though fear still gripped me. I welcomed the added adrenaline. It dulled my pain as I crawled. Rain soaked through my clothes. It washed away the clumps of blood in my hair in rivulets down my face that tasted of salt and iron.

The men's raised voices echoed under the domed gazebo. One of them held a gun and pointed it at the rest. His screaming turned frantic. The others yelled back at him. One of the men pushed another out of the gazebo. The others followed, their shouts growing distant in the night.

Crawling to Lucian, I stopped when I reached his side. I cupped the sides of his face, his skin pale and cold. Sweat slicked his bald head. His eyes were closed.

"Lucian," I whispered.

He turned his head toward the sound of my voice. "Amaya?" he asked hoarsely.

"I'm here." I gave him a kiss on the forehead, his skin clammy. "What should we do?"

His eyes cracked open. "Amaya," he repeated, a smile ghosting across his perfect lips.

A shot blasted. My ears rang in the bullet fire's wake. Officer Goodman ran into the gazebo, followed by a group of men carrying guns behind him.

My shoulders slumped, weariness tugging at me as I collapsed by Lucian. More shots fired, and I kept my body over his to protect him.

"It's about…time," Lucian breathed.

"Yeah."

Shuffling and pushing only lasted moments before the four men who'd abducted us knelt on the ground, their hands cuffed behind their backs.

Officer Goodman trotted to us, his bulky frame moving as if he weren't used to physical exertion. His eyebrows raised with concern.

He cursed as he knelt by Lucian. "Am I too late?"

"No," I answered. "He can't die, right?"

"Maybe not, but he still feels pain." He gawked at the sight of Lucian's claws, but his grimace soon turned to fear as he took in the bullet wound to Lucian's chest.

"What kept you?" I asked.

"We got ambushed right after…" he took a deep breath, then wiped the sweat from his brow. "After you went inside. A dozen or more came after us. We managed to stop most of them, but those four got past and made it inside the dungeon. I'm so sorry Amaya, Lucian. I thought I had it under control."

"We're okay," I said, rubbing my wrists. "But my dog. He was still in there. He's hurt." Panic sped my heart as I thought of Khan lying unconscious on the dungeon floor.

Officer Goodman nodded. "Yeah, no worries. I'll go after him." He smiled, though I saw the exhaustion in his eyes.

"Where's…Dr. Warren?" Lucian managed.

"Inside the castle. He went inside right before that group showed up. Said he had to attend to something. Didn't say what."

Uneasiness prickled over my skin, and I couldn't keep my suspicions at bay any longer. "Odd timing."

Officer Goodman nodded once. "Yeah. My thoughts exactly."

"You think he knew they were coming?" I asked.

The officer nodded. "Most likely."

"No." Lucian moaned, grasping his hands over the wound. "He's not." He took a deep breath. "Not like that. You're looking at this all wrong."

"Then how should we look at it, Lucian?" I asked as gently as possible.

"He had nothing to do with those men. I swear he didn't."

"Maybe not, but it is strange he knew to go inside at the exact moment."

"It's just…a coincidence." His pleading tone made me wonder if he was trying to convince himself it were true.

"Whatever the case," Officer Goodman said, "we'll need to regroup and get out of here as soon as possible. You got the cure, I hope?"

"Yes. We got it."

"Good." He rested his hand on my shoulder. "I'll get your dog, Amaya, if you think Lucian will be okay?"

I pulled away Lucian's duster to reveal a shallow gash. Only a little blood seeped out. "He's not bleeding out," I said. "At least, not externally."

"I'm fine," Lucian said. "It grazed me, that's all."

Officer Goodman raised his eyebrows. "You're sure?"

Lucian slowly sat up. He ran his hands over his face, as if trying to remove the cobwebs disorienting him.

"Easy." I grabbed his arm. "You were shot, you know."

He gave me a guarded smile. "But I'm fine."

Men shuffled behind us as they were led away from the gazebo. Red and blue lights flashed from the driveway in front of the castle. None of them glanced at us as they were marched to the police cars.

Unease tugged at me as I watched them go, as if they were only a distraction for something worse to come. But as their forms retreated into the blackness of the night, I finally allowed myself to take a deep breath.

My worries turned to Khan.

"My dog," I said to Officer Goodman.

"On it," he said without hesitation. "Wait here. I'll be back before you know it. We'll make this right. I give you my word. Be eating Romanian crepes and sausages before you know it."

"Thank you," Lucian said, sincerity in his voice.

Before he turned away, he gave us a look fraught with worry. "I know this may not be my place, but I wouldn't trust the doctor if I were you. I've been looking into some of his business dealings. They aren't right. None of this is right."

I stood to face him. "What do you mean?"

He glanced at Lucian still sitting on the ground, who regarded us with narrowed eyes. "I know you might not want to hear this, but I'll say it anyway. It's only right you know the truth."

"The truth about what?"

"About who Dr. Warren really is."

"Who he really is?" Lucian asked, still sitting, hands resting on his knees.

"Yeah, the thing is, that's not his given name. He was born as Walter Francis Hawthorn in San Diego."

"So that's not his name. So what?" Lucian asked, his tone defiant, though I saw the concern in his eyes.

"He was a con-man, Lucian."

Lucian clenched his fists. "No."

"Yes. And that's not all."

"What else is there?" I asked.

"No." Lucian stood slowly, wobbling, and I grabbed his hand—*claw*—to steady him. "No. That's not true."

"Unfortunately, it is. That's the reason I was sent to Crimson Hollow in the first place. Dr. Warren was good at covering his tracks, but no one can completely erase their past. He was married. To Sally Anderson."

"What?" I gasped.

Lucian's forehead wrinkled.

"She conned you, Lucian. But she didn't do it alone."

Lucian's clawed hand squeezed mine. "This can't be true."

"It can't?" Officer Goodman questioned.

"But why do that to me?" Lucian demanded.

"They wanted your virus, Lucian," I said quietly, choosing my words carefully. "They wanted it so they could spread it worldwide, make people suffer until they could dig you up years later and claim they'd cured you, when in truth, they had the cure all along. They created the vaccine from your blood."

"No," he argued. "This doesn't make any sense. Dr. Warren wouldn't do that. He wouldn't intentionally hurt people."

"Hurting people wasn't his purpose," I said. "How much money did he make from the vaccine? He kept all the research to himself for a reason. If he had the knowledge of how the vaccine worked, he made money. He made a *lot* of money—so much that he piqued the curiosity of the CDC."

"Which is why I'm here," Goodman nodded.

"How do you know this?" Lucian asked. His hand was cutting off my fingers' circulation, but I decided not to mention it.

"Because, like Amaya, I've been doing my homework."

"And he may've found where to look." My eyes shifted from Lucian's to the security guard. "A woman named Adelle Gibson was renting an apartment in Manhattan." I hesitated before saying the rest. "She also went by Constance Barrington."

"Warren's ex-wife," Lucian said, his tone quiet and subdued.

"Yes."

"What did she have to do with this?" he asked.

Officer Goodman shook his head. "I'm still working on that one." His sigh spoke volumes.

Something struck me then, a clue I only pieced together now. "The doctor had travel receipts. Some with a code of letters on them. I realize now what those letters stand for. They're airport codes. He must've been sending someone—a nurse, perhaps—all over the world to spread the virus. Then, he'd go to *cure* the ones who got infected. That's how the virus kept popping up everywhere."

"This is ludicrous." Lucian rubbed his forehead, his voice verging on tears.

"Lucian." I squeezed his hand. "It's better to know the truth."

Goodman nodded. "Amaya's right. I couldn't figure out how the virus kept spreading, but he must've been sending someone to spread it. Someone with the pseudonym of Adelle Gibson or Constance Barrington." Goodman's eyes pinched with worry, then shifted to the entrance of the crypts. "I'll go now. I've kept your dog waiting long enough."

He turned away without another word, his bulk fading into the distant night. The rain had stopped, leaving the chirping of crickets and a looming white fog in its wake.

"I can't believe it," Lucian's words carried through the still air. "Why didn't I see who he was?"

"He kept everything hidden from you, that's why. He kept it hidden from everyone."

He rubbed his forehead. "What do I do now?" he asked, his voice hoarse and hopeless. "Without Dr. Warren, I'm nothing. I have no home. No purpose. He gave my life to me, and he'll take it away the second I confront him."

"But you have to confront him," I said calmly, though inside, I burned with rage. "You can't keep living a lie."

"Living a lie?" Dr. Warren's voice came as if from the air itself, as if he were a disembodied ghost. The man walked through the fog to step inside the gazebo, his white suit matching the mist.

Lines creased the skin around his eyes, and his lips—usually plumped with Botox—were shrunken and wrinkled. "Who's living a lie?" he asked.

I swallowed the nervous knot in my throat as we faced the man.

"You lied to me," Lucian barked. "Why?"

The doctor spread his palms in a conciliatory gesture. "Lied? That's a rather harsh word from someone I consider my son."

"I'm not your son," he said, his voice raised, anger in his

words. "I never have been."

"No?" The doctor raised an eyebrow. "Why the sudden change of heart, Lucian?"

"We know," I bit out. "We know who you really are. Walter Hawthorn."

His ice-blue eyes narrowed to slits. "Who told you that?"

"Does it matter who?" I asked. "We know the truth. You were married to Sally Anderson when she met Lucian in college. Was it her idea for him to give her the virus or was it yours?"

He took a step forward, jaw clenched, anger burning in his eyes. "Careful with your accusations. I'm the one who revived Lucian. I took him from that shithole prison and gave him a better life. Everything he has—all his success, power, every cent to his name—is because of me."

"How much is that, exactly?" Lucian questioned. "Don't you take eighty-five percent of my earnings?"

"That's standard rate for someone who does everything I do. You're nothing without me, Lucian."

I glanced at Lucian. "He seriously takes *eighty-five* percent?"

"Yeah."

The doctor stalked toward us. "So, what now, Lucian? You leave the facility?"

"I haven't thought that far yet," Lucian said through clenched teeth.

"Well then, let me help you make your decision." He reached into his breast coat pocket and pulled out a pistol. He casually pointed it at me. "Take her," he hissed to someone behind me.

Fear tingled down my spine as I spun around.

My heart stopped.

Wearing a white dress, bare feet, and the glint of madness in her eyes, the woman I'd once believed to be a ghost loomed before me.

36

*Andrew Shapman was the first explorer to discover dinosaur eggs in the
Mongolian desert in 1923, in a formation known as the Flaming Cliffs.
The type of creature discovered was never confirmed, though from Mr.
Shapman's field journal, "…the beasts had feathers, and talons
containing five distinct claws on each appendage." In recent years, several
of these types of nests have been discovered around the world, including
China, Russia, and Greece.*

~

LUCIAN

I stumbled toward Amaya as she faced the phantom.

"Who are you?" she demanded. I stood beside her and
grasped her cold, trembling fingers.

Dr. Warren's footsteps reverberated over paving stones as
he paced around us. He stood beside the woman in white. She
looked wholly human and of solid form—not a ghost, though
her skin was unusually pale, her eyes dark and ringed in deep
shadows. But her features, by God—those lips held a hint of a

secretive smile, and her dark hair hung in long strands over protruding, bony shoulders.

"Hello, Lucian," she rasped. When she spoke my name, I had no doubt it was her. That seductress's voice could belong to none other than Sally.

Amaya glanced up at me. Her wide eyes must've mirrored my fear. "Sally?"

Dr. Warren stepped slowly to us. "Yes," he said with a chuckle, as if this were all a big joke. "Yes, it's Sally."

"Isn't she dead?" Amaya asked.

"That's what we were led to believe," I answered.

"She's just as dead as you are," Dr. Warren answered.

I rubbed my temples, my head throbbing, my brain felt as if it would explode. I'd always known Dr. Warren had kept his private life to himself. It had never bothered me. He needed his space and I needed mine. But now? I could never trust him again. My anger made it difficult to speak to him without strangling him—and I would've had I not needed explanations.

"What's going on?" I ground out. "Tell me. Now!" My anger threatened to overwhelm me.

Dr. Warren crossed his arms, though kept his pistol in plain view. "Do you think I owe you explanations, Lucian? No, I owe you nothing. You owe me. I'm your savior. I *made* you, and I can unmake you."

Amaya stiffened beside me. "You brought Sally back," she said. "Just like you did to Lucian. She was infected with the primary virus. You allowed her to die, to be buried, then you must've dug her up. Changed her name to Adele Gibson, then Constance Barrington. Whenever anyone got close to learning her true identity, she'd die again and come back as another pseudonym. It was her living in the attic. Did you kill Jayden Black to keep Lucian from learning the truth? Blaming him for the missing food when it was really Sally Anderson stealing it?"

The doctor's knowing frown told me Amaya must've been right. Sally was Dr. Warren's wife. She died of the virus, and then he dug her up and revived her.

I pried my hand from Amaya's, stepping between her and the doctor. "Why?" I demanded, looming over him.

He raised a grizzled, bushy eyebrow. "I owe you no explanations."

"Because," Amaya's voice cut through the fog of my anger —my hatred. "He did it for money," she said quietly, though her words pierced with intensity. "He's hailed as a great doctor and scientist, on the cover of Time Magazine, a Nobel Peace Prize, when he was once nothing. A conman on the run. He met Sally and everything changed. He understood your potential when no one else did. He knew how much you were worth. But he knew they'd have to spread the virus first, let it become an epidemic before they introduced the vaccine. You became a star. A hero. But really, you were a means to an end. A project. An investment. You never meant anything to him."

"So," I said, my voice dripping with hate. "I was your science experiment, just like I was to my father. You never cared for me."

"No. You are so much more. For years I've been sending Sally all over the world to spread the virus—and then I go to *cure* it." He said the word with a chuckle. "She became Constance Barrington for a time, my second wife." He smirked. "Traveling the world with her briefcase full of liquid vials of the vampire virus, but that didn't last. Her mental state wouldn't allow it. So, she became a ghost. Living in the facility during the times she wasn't mentally well or hiding in her apartment in Manhattan when she was. I've taken care of her. Just like you."

"Then why the gun?" I growled.

"What? This?" He inspected the pistol. "This is my safety net. You see, if you've indeed found a cure, then I'll need you to give it to me. Can't allow the entire population to be healed, can we? Or then I'd be out of business. And you would lose everything. Think of it, Lucian. If we eradicate this disease, there's no more funding. No more facility. Our lives end the moment we introduce a cure."

"You're deranged," Amaya spat.

"No. I'm smart. I understand what poverty feels like, and so does Lucian. I'll never go back to that life of scrounging just to find my next meal, not knowing where to sleep at night, being terrified of dying as a no one, a nameless corpse in the street."

He waved the gun at me. "I've asked nicely, haven't I? Where's the cure? What did you find in that crypt?"

"Nothing." I straightened. "We didn't find anything."

"You're lying. I've known you long enough to tell that." His eyes narrowed. "Where is it?"

Sally swayed behind the doctor, as if she were only half-conscious of what was happening. With her white dress hanging over her bony frame and her eyes glazed, it wasn't hard to see why Amaya thought of her as a ghost.

I squared my shoulders. "I won't give it to you."

"Like hell you won't," he bit out.

Gunshots blasted before I had a chance to react. Pain exploded through my shoulder and hip. My body hit the ground. The gazebo's stonework swirled in my vision.

Amaya screamed as she landed beside me. Shocking red blood spread over her abdomen and soaked into her shirt. Her eyes squeezed shut. She gasped, breathing frantically, pressing her palms to cover the wound.

"Amaya!" I whispered through clenched teeth. When I started to crawl to her, a kick in my ribs knocked me back.

Dr. Warren and Sally loomed over me. Bony, skeletal fingers reached for me, running over the length of my clothes.

"Sally," I moaned. How could she be here? This was a nightmare. I was dead and this was hell. Any of those possibilities were better than the truth. "Sally, stop!"

Her hand slipped into my duster's pocket. She pulled out the vial of golden liquid.

Dr. Warren's eyes lit up. "That's it," he said, his smoker's voice rasping as he took it from her.

Sally's pale visage danced in my vision. Her smile—yellow teeth against bone-white skin, eyes that glinted with a madness —made bile churn into my throat.

She patted my chest in a motherly gesture. "Lucian," she said, her voice honey sweet, just as Dr. Warren stood over me with a torch. The flicker of flames danced in her dark irises.

Liquid sloshed as she hefted a can of gasoline. A wicked smile curved around her lips. "Burn," she hissed.

"Fill the grave with the gasoline," he instructed her. "Use it all. We'll have to make sure it's hotter than hellfire. Can't let anything remain. Not even bones. That's the only way to make sure he stays dead."

Her dress rustled as she stood and drifted on bare feet away from me. I stared at the blank slate of the gazebo's dome. Coldness coiled inside me as blood drained from my body.

Burn.

Pouring liquid splashed the ground nearby. The acrid scent of gasoline flooded the air.

Turning to Amaya, I crawled to the sounds of her quiet whimper. When I reached her, I grasped her bloody fingers, shocked at their icy coldness.

"Lucian," she said, eyes wide and dilated with pain.

"Amaya." I kissed her knuckles gently. The taste of her blood lingered on my tongue—a sweetness I wasn't expecting.

Her grip tightened. "We have to…escape them."

"Yes." I kissed her again, on her cheek this time, her skin wet with tears. "Yes. We will." It was a lie and I knew it, but I couldn't stand to face reality.

For so long I'd wished for death. I'd wanted it more than anything. Craved its freedom. Now, I regretted it ten-fold. I would do anything to keep it from happening. Because of Amaya. I would never be able to express how much she meant to me, but I wouldn't get another chance, so I would do my best now and pray she understood.

"I love you, Amaya. I've never loved anyone the way I love you. I'll die with your name on my lips." I kissed her mouth gently.

"Lucian," she whispered. "No. We have to…to escape. We'll live."

"I wish it were true."

She lifted her head, but grimaced as she tried to sit up. She clenched her teeth to keep from screaming.

Rough hands grabbed my arms, dragging me toward the pit. The stench of fumes made me gag.

"Lucian." She reached for me. My fingertips brushed hers, the shock of her life so strong at the touch of our skin.

What would it have felt like to have human skin—to touch her the way people were meant to?

Tears streamed from her eyes. My heart hurt for her. To be so young. To witness something so brutal. I would forever regret not being able to spend another breath with her in my life.

Dr. Warren and Sally tugged me over the cobbled ground, then the world dropped away from me as they tossed me into the pit. I landed in the gasoline-saturated mud. My breath whooshed from my lungs.

Gasping, I rose onto my elbows.

"Toss it in," Dr. Warren's voice carried distantly above me.

Sally's haggard face appeared over the pit. I stared up at the woman who had betrayed me, who I believed was dead, but had risen from the ashes to return to this world for the single purpose of tormenting me.

For her to bring my death was something I couldn't bear, but I doubted I had any choice. Brilliant, orange flames burned my retinas as she tossed a torch.

A giant *whoosh* exploded—fumes transformed to flames.

Intense heat engulfed me.

A primal scream ripped from my throat.

Clothes and skin burned before my eyes, ignited in plumes of orange and blue—so hot it sucked the air from my lungs and scalded my throat. Somewhere beyond the pain, my thoughts screamed for freedom. The only wish I'd ever had would finally be granted, yet now, I had one other.

After my skin burned away completely, the pain lasted only a moment. Consciousness ebbing, a calm, stillness settled over me.

My vision darkened.

The world went blissfully silent.

If only I could have one more moment with Amaya.

37

AMAYA

I couldn't breathe.

An anvil compressed my lungs as I stood over the open pit, a place meant to house someone's coffin, and now it held what remained of Lucian.

Smoke stung my eyes. Noxious, billowing clouds blocked my view of what lay inside.

Finally, I drew in a ragged breath. The air smelled of charred flesh. When the smoke cleared, I remained where I stood. My hands were fisted so tight, my fingernails cut half circles into my skin.

Tears moistened my cheeks. I took a step forward when warm blood gushed from the bullet wound in my abdomen. Pressing my hands to my stomach, I gasped as the pain radiated like a hot poker through my flesh.

I blinked back my tears, standing tall.

I would stop Dr. Warren. He would never get away with this.

Standing at the edge of the pit, I caught a glimpse of ash piles. Maybe it was best if I didn't look any closer.

Barking echoed behind me.

I spun around to face Khan and Officer Goodman racing toward me.

"Amaya," he breathed, huffing. "Sorry it took so long. The knot was stuck on a nail, and I couldn't get the leash free. Had to cut through…" He stopped mid-sentence. "Are you okay?"

I swiped a hand across my cheek. "No," was all I could manage.

His eyes widened as my tear-filled gaze went to the hole in the ground. "Where's Lucian?"

"There." I nodded. "Dr. Warren. He…burned him." I could hardly say the word. *Burn.*

Officer Goodman's mouth fell open. "What?"

I did my best to explain what happened, but everything was too raw, and my words came out mumbled and hardly coherent.

"He had a woman with him?" Officer Goodman questioned.

"Yes. Sally Anderson. She's alive—has been for a long time."

"How on earth did she get in Romania?"

My head spun with his question, and the image of a coffin-like suitcase popped into my head. "His supposed research," I suggested. "It wasn't research at all. He smuggled her in. She must've been inside the suitcase he was so particular about."

He shook his head. "Incredible."

Khan came to me and licked my palm. I collapsed to my knees, hugging my arms around his furry neck, letting him lick the tears from my face.

Lucian.

But this was what he wanted. He'd told me he wished he could die on more than one occasion. Had this been his plan all along? Had he known that getting the cure meant Dr. Warren wouldn't need him anymore? That the doctor would kill him—*really* kill him—after he retrieved the vial in his father's tomb?

He'd seemed so hesitant to get it. Now I knew why.

My gut clenched tight, as if I'd been socked in the stomach. I fell to the ground. Blood oozed from my wound. The world spun around me. Buzzing rang in my ears.

Khan's frantic barking.

Officer Goodman kneeling by me.

"Amaya!"

A click from the walkie-talkie. His words came to me in a muddled haze, and I could hardly concentrate on what he was saying.

"….emergency. Bullet wound. She's losing blood. Carrier of the virus. She won't make it. Unless…" His fingers pressed my neck. I tried to focus on him, but I saw only a blur of blues and gray. "…intercept the doctor and woman…bring them here with the antidote. Only way to save her now…"

A clammy sweat broke out over my skin. Nausea crawled from my stomach and into my throat. I barely managed to turn my head before my stomach contents spewed from my mouth and onto the paving stones.

Officer Goodman's voice cut through the loud buzzing in my ears. I couldn't make out the words.

I realized my body was cradled next to something warm and soft, and the odor of wet dog reminded me I was alive.

A moment of panic seized me. What would it be like to die? Was there anything waiting for me? Would I see Mom and Dad?

Tears burned my eyes and warm trails streamed down my face. I clenched Khan's furry body to me. My pulse throbbed along with the buzzing. Peace settled in my chest, replacing my fear.

Consciousness ebbed.

Calmness consumed me until the sensation of pain

digging into my arm brought me back. A chill seeped from my shoulder to my chest.

Was that a needle pricking me?

My next coherent thought was of a pen light blinding me. I jerked my head.

"She's alive." Officer Goodman's voice gushed.

I blinked against the brightness when it disappeared. Spots danced in my vision as I tried to focus. The gazebo surrounded me, and a steady drumming rain pelted the roof.

People gathered around. Officer Goodman. A handful of emergency workers. Behind them waited a sour-faced Dr. Warren wearing handcuffs. Two police officers stood on either side of him. His eyes narrowed to slits as he stared at me.

I didn't see Sally.

"What…" I choked, trying to sit up. Rubbing my head, the world finally stopped spinning as I focused. "What happened?"

Khan licked my palm. Officer Goodman smiled as he held up an empty syringe. "Congratulations, Amaya. You're proof the anti-virus is a success."

"You injected me with it?"

"I had no choice. You were dying. We managed to apprehend the doctor just in time before he made it to the airport. He had the vial with him. We only used a portion of the serum on you. We'll have enough left to analyze it. See how it works and replicate it. You're a heroine, Amaya. You did it. Everyone will be cured of VS thanks to you." His smile lit up his round face.

I glanced at the pit behind the officer. The joy I might've felt at being alive faded. A stone settled deep in my heart, and I wasn't sure I would ever be the same. Losing Mom and Dad had been a pain too raw to process, but this was a pain sure to break me.

"Can we…" I choked on my words and tried again. "Can we use the vaccine on him?"

"I'm sorry," he said, his voice whispered with compassion. "I know this is difficult to hear, but we searched. We sifted through everything. There's nothing left but ashes." He gently squeezed my fingers, his big, meaty hands reminding me of my father's. "He must've died quickly. The fire was so hot, he only lasted a few moments before…" He shook his head. "But it's what he's wanted for a long time. He's at peace now. He'll never suffer again."

Yeah, I wanted to agree, but a chasm opened my chest. I would live but Lucian wouldn't. Fairness didn't exist. It never had.

Two medical personnel approached. "Hospital," one of them said in a thick accent.

"Yes," Officer Goodman called over his shoulder before turning back to me. "We've got to go. You need to be evaluated."

"Do we have to?" I asked, my voice verging on tears.

"Absolutely," he said with firmness. "You were shot."

I cast my gaze toward the dark hole only feet from where I lay. "I can't leave him."

"Amaya—"

"No," I said, pleading. "Please. Just let me say goodbye."

He nodded once, his lips forming a tight line and eyes wide, as if he knew why I needed this. His warm hands grasped mine. I wobbled as I sat up, then took a moment to breathe. Wind gusted. The air tasted of rain. The scent of smoke lingered in the strands of my hair whipping across my face.

With a steadying exhale, I crawled to the gravesite. Bits of leaves and sticks stuck to my palms. My heart hammered against my rib cage. The edge of the pit loomed closer, an all-encompassing maw that could've been the entrance to hell.

A damp, clammy sweat made my clothes stick to my skin. If my heart beat any faster, I was sure it would break a rib. The air carried the scent of char.

I stopped crawling when I sat over the edge of the open grave, staring into the dark depths. Not much light seeped to the bottom, and I could barely discern lumps of ash standing out in white hills on the pit's floor.

Lucian?

I imagined he must've escaped the pit before he burned. Maybe he'd gotten away and I hadn't noticed.

But the truth stared me in the face, and I had no choice but to accept it.

He was dead.

He wasn't coming back. He'd gotten what he'd always wanted.

A scream tore from my throat. I pressed my fisted hands to my mouth and bit my knuckles. Tears leaked from my eyes.

Accept his death.

No! I screamed at the voice in my head. Not after Mom and Dad. I refused—*refused!*—to do this again.

I would never embrace this new reality. Something nagged me that this was all wrong. Lucian had died so many times before. He'd come back. Why couldn't now be any different?

My muscles protested as I stood and squared my shoulders. I stared daggers at Dr. Warren who waited just underneath the gazebo's roof.

I thrust my finger at him. "How did you know burning would kill him?"

He only smirked, not answering.

"How?" I demanded, my voice carrying, startling even me.

Officer Goodman came to me. His hand rested on my shoulder. "Amaya—"

"No." I shrugged him away, then set my determined gaze on the doctor. "You knew how to kill Lucian. You knew it all along, and you told no one. How did you know?" I yelled.

Goodman took my arm. "Amaya, calm down. He's already going in for questioning."

"I can't calm down. He knew how to kill Lucian. It was supposed to be impossible. How did you know?" My shrill voice pierced my ears.

His calculating eyes narrowed. "I spent half my life studying Lucian." He spoke with an icy tone, one that sent a shiver down my spine. "Didn't you wonder why he was terrified of fire? Why it was the only thing a person who couldn't die would be afraid of? I observed him. Tested him. Took daily blood samples and experimented on him. Can you believe what I found out? Fire was the only thing capable of making him experience true feeling. It doesn't matter what he told you. He couldn't grasp the concepts of pain or pleasure. Hate. Or love." He spoke the last word with venom in his voice. "His DNA made him impervious to diseases or injuries that would kill normal people like you or me. His genetic makeup also took away his ability to feel."

"That's a lie," I shouted. "He cared for people more than you could possibly imagine. He had a bigger heart than anyone I've ever known."

"Did he?" The doctor's smug laugh grated my nerves. "It was an act. He'd trained himself to wear the mask of a man, when inside, he was anything but human."

"Then what was he?" I demanded.

"Haven't you figured it out? Think of it. Why did he fear fire more than anything else? His eyes and hands. Telltale signs of the creature inhabiting his body. You tell me, Amaya. What was Lucian Vidraru?"

Lightning cracked, making me jump. The rain picked up, gusting on the wind. Drops stung my cheeks. A deafening clap of thunder forced me to clamp my hands over my ears.

A brilliant burst of orange light flared behind me.

Spinning around, I faced the grave. Caught on the wind, ash swirled up in eddies and whorls. Another bolt of lightning lit the world in electric blue. When the light faded, the ash took shape over the pit.

My mouth gaped as I stood facing a humanoid shape formed from ash. Golden feathered wings fanned from his back. Crimson eyes glowed from a face hewn from molten copper. Talon-hands covered in glowing bronze scales curled at his sides.

I stumbled back. My breathing stopped.

Lucian?

Massive wings fanned the wind. Embers glowed with orange fire from his wings and hands. The glowing ash particles got caught on the stiff breeze and drifted on the air currents around him.

I was struck with the sudden realization of what he was. It hit me with such clarity, I forgot to breathe.

"A phoenix. Rising from the ashes."

He spread massive wings, the tips touching either side of the gazebo. With a mighty *whoosh*, they fanned the air. His gaze lingered on me, but the primal, golden sheen of an animal's eyes met mine, not recognizing me. Without another glance, he leapt into the sky, his shriek overpowering the storm.

3 8

AMAYA

Heart pounding, I ran out of the shelter of the gazebo.

My feet slipped on wet grass. In the lightning storm above me, the golden form of a bird soared on the wind.

Shielding my eyes against the onslaught of cold raindrops, I watched the creature—Lucian—sail on the air currents. Shouts and raised voices created a cacophony. People jostled as they pointed to the sky, but my gaze stayed on the man-turned-firebird.

It all made sense now.

His father's obsessiveness with birds and creatures of myths, and the legends he studied around the world. The phoenix linked them all. But was he indeed a creature of myth? Or some species we hadn't yet classified?

I didn't have the answers, but I supposed now, I didn't need them.

My heart soared as he did, as if I were up there with him, flying through the thunderheads and bursts of electric light. A trail of fire followed in his wake, and he dipped so low, heat brushed my face.

I reached for him, but he darted into the clouds until he danced with lightning. Wings fanned the air as he circled the area. Cold rain soaked through my clothes and streamed down my face, yet I hardly noticed the chill.

Behind me, raised voices caught my attention. I spun around to see Dr. Warren jerking his arms away from the officers. Panic strained through his desperate screams, his face turned to the sky, his eyes wide with fear.

"He'll kill me," he screamed. "Let me go!"

A burst of fire exploded on the ground inches from the doctor. The officers fell back, rolling away, but the doctor remained standing as the grass sizzled and popped around him.

The beast who had once been Lucian landed on two legs in front of the doctor. Muscles flexed along his arms and rippled over his exposed back. He tightened his clawed fingers into fists. Flames burned along the edges of his feathered wings as he raised them over the doctor.

Opening his hands, he revealed black-tipped claws longer than a falcon's. He snatched the doctor by his neck. Gargled screams choked from the doctor's throat. With his free hand, Lucian struck Dr. Warren across the face with a *pop*.

Lucian tossed the doctor into the gazebo's pillar. Stones smashed apart. A crash echoed. Blood streamed from three claw marks down the doctor's face. Fear filled his eyes as he tried to rise, but he slipped, and fell back.

Flames burst from Lucian's skin as he stalked to the man on the ground. Men ran toward Lucian, but he pushed them back with such force, they flew backward and landed hard.

When he reached the doctor, he slashed his claws across the man's chest. Blood oozed from deep gashes. Its sharp, metallic scent pervaded the air.

Shots rang out. Bullets pummeled Lucian's back, but bounced off. The phoenix spun around and flew to the soldiers with guns. With one swift slash of his arm, he knocked them off their feet. He grabbed their weapons. Flames exploded from his hands until the metal turned molten and dripped in a pool of sludge to the ground.

Chaos reigned.

Goodman loped to me, his chest heaving as he struggled to catch his breath, his wide eyes reflecting the flames. "Amaya," he breathed. "You have to do something."

"Do what?" I yelled back, my voice hoarse, fear and adrenaline flowing through my veins.

"Stop him," he screamed over the crackling flames.

"Stop him how?" I shouted back.

"Talk to him!"

Molten iron dripped from Lucian's fingertips as he stalked back to the doctor. Murder shone in his predator's eyes.

Embers drifted on the air currents as I walked to the man who had once been Lucian. Fear pounded through my veins, but I walked with determination.

If he killed me, so be it.

I'd gone into the facility prepared to die.

"Lucian!" I called. He stood feet from where the doctor lay. His steps faltered. As I crossed to him, blood hammered through my heart, my pulse thumping in my ears.

I balled my fists.

The beast turned to face me. He rose over me. His wings overshadowed a massive, muscle-corded frame. Despite his monster's appearance, I recognized the sloping curve of his forehead, his straight, statuesque nose, and the rounded lips. It was still him, yet how did I find him?

"Lucian, can you hear me?" I asked.

The doctor stirred, spitting curses as he rose onto his elbows. Lucian's head whipped back to the man on the ground. The phoenix took another step toward him.

I steadied my breathing, uttered a silent prayer, and stepped into his path, blocking his view of the doctor.

"Lucian, stop." I held up my hands. "This isn't you. Listen to me."

The beast growled. His eyes shone with madness. Although I'd seen similarities in the features of his face, nothing remained of him in his eyes.

He killed his father. What would keep him from killing me?

A growl resonated deep in his throat. Spots of blood slicked his torso and abs. He took a step to me, and I swallowed my terror. My hands trembled as I reached for him.

"Lucian," I repeated his name, holding his gaze, refusing to flinch under his dark stare. With another step, he loomed inches from my fingertips. The heat of his body radiated. Gold shimmered over his irises.

He opened his wings and curled his lips into a sneer. Pain glistened in his eyes—all the pain he'd held back for so long was being unleashed.

"Lucian," I said his name again, desperation in my voice, hoping something inside him recognized me. But he stood stoically, his presence overbearing, his claws balled into fists.

Talking to him was getting me nowhere. Would he remember me if I touched him?

Without overthinking it, I pressed my fingers to his forearm. He jerked back as if I'd slapped him.

His shriek pierced my eardrums. A massive arm hit me across the chest. I sailed backward. My body hit the ground with such force, my spine felt as if it broke in two. I winced as I rose to my elbows. Rubbing my hip, I felt a tender bruise forming.

The beast crossed to Dr. Warren. He slammed a massive fist to the man's middle. Dr. Warren cried out with a high-pitched, torturous wail.

"No," he pleaded. "Stop. You're killing me."

Lucian rammed him again and again.

More shots rang out. Bullets bounced off the creature's

hide with *pings* before falling to the grass. The whir of helicopter blades spiraled overhead. A spotlight blinded me as it shone on Lucian's form.

Lucian stood and spun around, staring up at the helicopter. I shielded my eyes against the light. The silhouettes of soldiers leaned out of the open chopper. Red laser beams trained on the phoenix, appearing as dozens of dots on his head and chest.

A growl rumbled through the monster's chest.

No...I couldn't let them shoot him. He'd kill them. He'd kill everyone.

I slipped on the wet ground as I struggled to my feet. Lucian held still under the spotlight, as if the brightness blinded him.

The beating of the chopper's blades mirrored my frantically pounding heart.

"Lu-Lucian!" I screamed as I ran to him.

I grabbed his arm. He spun on me, but he didn't push me away like last time. His eyes widened as they trailed to my hand. I followed his line of sight.

My heart stopped.

Flames burst from my fingers, blue and orange fire rippling over my hand and encircling my wrist. I felt nothing.

My other hand ignited, and I held them in front of me. My jaw sagged open.

The phoenix overshadowed me. Dark wings created a dome. He opened his fists. His claws gripped mine.

Flames reflected in his mirror-black irises, dancing as if living things.

Understanding lit his eyes.

"*Amaya.*" He breathed.

"Yes!" Relief flooded my voice. "You know me?"

He nodded once, and I knew he was mine. My Lucian. My phoenix. "I know you," he answered before the flames engulfed us.

LUCIAN

The beeping of the heart rate monitor cut through the fog in my brain.

A hospital? Was I at the facility?

"Mr. Lucian?" a nurse asked as she rushed to me. I tried to sit up, but stiff muscles protested.

Rubbing my forehead, I stared around the space cluttered with all types of machines and monitors that created a cacophony of noises. Sunlight streamed inside through a floor-length window. Golden sash ties held back thick burgundy curtains. A blood bag loomed at the corner of my vision.

Yep, definitely at the facility. I closed my eyes against the sight of it.

I'd dreamed I was dead.

But I'd woken, as had always happened. Yet, why did this time feel different? Fragments of memories haunted me. The vial in my father's tomb. Dr. Warren and Sally. Burning alive…

After that? A blankness stretched. As I blinked, echoes of

memories whispered. Fire and pain. Rage—blinding and all-consuming. Bloodlust.

Amaya.

"What happened?" I asked the nurse.

Fear flashed through her eyes for a half-second, then a forced smile replaced the anxiousness.

"You're safe now," was all she said. Her silver pendant earrings jangled as she nodded. I didn't recognize the nurse. She must've been new. Where was Teesha?

"I need to get up." I pushed my elbows against the bed, but she pinned her hand to my chest and held me down.

"Not now." Her sugary voice turned stern.

"Why?" I questioned.

She only pursed her lips and shook her head.

"I need to see Amaya. Is she here?"

Her gaze darted to the door.

"Is she hurt?" I demanded.

"Look," she said with a frustrated sigh. "A lot of things happened in Romania. How much do you remember?"

"A little. I don't remember anything after I was thrown in a pit." The pit. I'd been burned. I thought for sure I would die. But something had brought me back. Amaya.

"Where is Amaya?" I demanded.

The door to my room swung open. "Mr. Lucian?" Nurse Teesha jogged inside. She shot a dark look at the other nurse. "I told you to get me when he woke up."

"I know," she argued. "I was about to."

Nurse Teesha made a sour face as she looked at the blood bag hanging over me. She yanked it down and pulled the catheter from my stomach tube.

"What are you doing?" the nurse insisted.

"We don't need this anymore." Nurse Teesha shoved the blood bag in the trash. "Doctor's orders. You're excused."

The nurse's eyebrows rose. She bit her lip, as if she wanted to say something but held her tongue, then turned and marched from the room.

"What was that about?" I asked.

Nurse Teesha chuckled as she held my arm and checked my pulse. "There've been a few changes around here. I'm not the best one to tell you, though." She glanced at the door. "You can come in now."

As if conjured by my thoughts, Amaya rushed inside. A healthy pink tint filled her once pale cheeks. Long strands of dark hair fanned out around her face and cascaded down her shoulders.

Fear uncoiled like a tight cord wrapped around my heart. She brushed past Nurse Teesha and threw her arms around me. The rest of the cord loosened, and my heart hammered wildly in my chest, as if for the first time in my life, I was alive.

Resting my hands on her back, I recoiled.

"Wha—?" I lifted my fingers. Amaya sat up and smiled as I looked in awe at my hands covered in unscarred white flesh.

Flexing my hands, I marveled at the way the tendons and veins moved. For once, fingers not swollen and filled with pus moved fluidly.

Amaya pressed her palms to mine. I gasped at her touch.

A warm tingle rippled through me, spreading from her hands and into my chest, filling the void that had been empty for far too long.

"I have skin," I breathed, awestruck.

"More than that." She winked, running her hand over my head. I reached up and touched short prickly hair growing on my scalp.

Amaya kissed my cheek, a playful grin tugging at her lips. "You look cute."

Nurse Teesha cleared her throat. "I'll leave now." She gave a knowing smile before dashing out of the room.

"Amaya," I asked, seriousness in my voice. "What happened?"

She perched on the edge of my bed and took my hands in hers. Squeezing her fingers in mine, her flesh smooth against my own, I never wanted to let go. She bit her lip and glanced at the window as she spoke, recounting the details I felt grateful to have forgotten.

"Dr. Warren?" I asked.

"He lived. But he's being held in Fresno State for fraud, money laundering, and attempted murder to name a few. He's not going anywhere for a very long time."

"And…Sally?" I almost couldn't speak her name.

She shook her head. "She disappeared like she always does. But with her identity exposed, I doubt she'll be around any time soon."

I ran my fingers over the backs of her hands, tracing her tendons. "What now?" I asked.

"Now?" She arched an eyebrow, her eyes sparkling and dark and lovely. She was so beautiful, I had to catch my breath before I could speak again. "What do we do since Dr. Warren is gone?" I asked. "What about everyone in the facility?"

"Nothing," she answered. "The patients have been cured, Lucian. They're going home."

I didn't think I had the heart for another shock, but at least this was a good surprise. "You're serious?"

"Absolutely." She smiled.

"And they're normal?" I questioned.

"Normal?" she chuckled. "Not exactly." She pulled her hand from mine, then snapped. A blue flame sparked from her fingertips. "We've all been injected with the phoenix serum— just like you. Some say we've evolved. I don't know if that's true. But you were right all along. You weren't a vampire. You were never a monster. You were a phoenix waiting to transform."

"But…" I stared at my hands. "What about the transformation? What's to keep me from turning into a mindless monster again?"

"You won't," she answered with certainty in her voice.

I cocked my head. "You make it sound like you know that for sure?"

"Well, that's because while you were resting, I've been doing some research. In fact, I've been chosen by the CDC as one of the liaisons to research VS. Someone had to help fill in the gap left after Dr. Warren was found out." Her rosy smile lit a fire inside me. "It turns out, your strand of VS had been in incubation since you were woken the first time. It's been slowly transforming you, but the virus was a bit like the seeds of a sequoia tree—it only completes transformation under intense, all-consuming heat."

I mulled over her words. "Do you think Dr. Warren knew what he was doing when he burned me?"

"No. He thought it would kill you. He'd done enough research to understand what your father had discovered in the Tinos cave. It was a mislabeled dinosaur-like creature called Ignis Lacertus. Fire lizard. As it turns out, it shared uncanny characteristics to the phoenix, including the ability to create a chemical reaction in its glands to create fire."

"So, that's what my father discovered in the cave?" I asked. "A living dinosaur?"

"Technically, it's not a dinosaur. It's a distant relative. But I think dinosaur sounds cooler. Just for the record, you've got a new nickname."

I groaned. "What now? Fossil?"

"No." She laughed. "They're calling you Phoenix."

"Phoenix." I repeated the name. "I think I can get used to that." I ran a hand over my head, still in shock at the feel of hair under actual fingertips.

Amaya smiled. "Dr. Warren's research suggested that being completely burned and turned to ash was the only way to kill it. He had no idea what would happen after that."

"He didn't know I would rise from the ashes?" I asked.

"Exactly," she answered. "No one knew. Until now."

Until now, her words rang in my head. As I stared out the window, sun streamed over the distant forest. The first snowfall shone a brilliant white, covering the broken tree branches and scars from the storms of the past year. I'd always dreaded winter. Dreaded the ice and the frozen air, but now, it seemed as though I'd been overlooking its beauty, a scene no other season could offer.

"Will you stay here?" I asked.

"At the facility?" Amaya questioned.

"Yes. I realize this is probably the last place you want to be, but…"

"It's your home." She answered for me.

"Yeah."

"Well then, you'll probably be happy to know that Crimson Hollow is being converted to the new VS research facility. But we need more room for victims dealing with the aftermath of the trauma of VS. I'm working with the CDC to purchase some property down the road. It's a ranch."

My questioning gaze snagged on her. "A ranch?"

"Yeah." She nodded. "Horseback riding has been known to work wonders for people with PTSD. We're hoping it'll do the same for VS survivors. Plus, we've discovered you don't need blood to survive. Genetically speaking, your cells mimic those of a bird of prey. Your tongue has the same amount of taste buds as a hawk's. Your eyes have the same traits of a night hunter like a falcon's. Dr. Warren gave you blood feeding transfusions because you were mislabeled as a vampire—when really, you respond better to a carnivore's diet. So, I'm sticking around a while to help everyone transition to a new diet of steak and pork chops." She kissed my cheek. "You're not getting rid of me any time soon." Her dark eyes glittered with a hint of mischief.

"So, You're staying?" I asked.

"That's exactly what I'm doing. There's still research to be done, plus the vaccine needs to be replicated and internationally distributed. And we need you." She rested her hand on my cheek. "You're the face of VS. You're proof that we can survive."

"No." I corrected her, threading my fingers through hers. "We're proof. And everyone else who's had the serum. Chloe and Damian?"

"Yes. They stayed. They're here to help with whatever we need."

"Good." I sat up, pressing a kiss to her perfectly smooth lips. "Then let's start a new day."

"Yeah." She smiled back and gave me a lingering kiss, one that spread straight to my toes. "Let's do it together."

"I like the sound of that word. Together."

With her hand clasped in mine, I reveled the feel of her skin, soaked in the sight of her bright smile and dark, intelligent eyes.

Together.

~

Late Night with Roman West. Air Date November 25

LUCIAN VIDRARU RECENTLY CONFIRMED HE'S IN A relationship with fellow VS survivor, Amaya de le Vega. Despite the age gap of nearly a century and a half, the couple was stunned to find they failed to break the previous record set by Catherine Zeta-Jones and Michael Douglas. Good night, everyone!

THE END

Tamara Grantham is the award-winning author of more than a dozen books and novellas, including the Olive Kennedy: Fairy World MD series, the Shine novellas, and the Twisted Ever After trilogy. *Dreamthief*, the first book of her Fairy World MD series, won first place for fantasy in INDIEFAB'S Book of the Year Awards, a RONE award for best New Adult Romance of 2016, and is a #1 bestseller on Amazon with over 200 five-star reviews.

Tamara has been a featured speaker at numerous writing conferences and has been a panelist at Comic Con Wizard World. Born and raised in Texas, Tamara now lives with her husband and five children in Wichita, Kansas.

ALSO BY TAMARA GRANTHAM

Twisted Ever After

The Witch's Tower

Dragon Swan Princess

Rumpel's Redemption

Fairy World MD

Dreamthief

Spellweaver

Bloodthorn

Silverwitch

Goblinwraith (novella)

Deathbringer

Grayghost

Shine series

Raze

Never Say Reven

Into the Fire

Storms and Spirits

ABOUT THE PUBLISHER

Babylon Books is a division of Bernhardt Books, a family-owned publishing house founded in 1999 that showcases emerging authors and compelling fiction.
    Editor-in-Chief: Alice Bernhardt
    Chief Financial Officer: W. Harrison Bernhardt
    Marketing Director: Ralph Bernhardt